MURDER
at
ST. SAVIOUR'S

BOOKS BY MERRYN ALLINGHAM

MURDER
at
ST. SAVIOUR'S

Merryn Allingham

bookouture

Published by Bookouture in 2022

An imprint of Storyfire Ltd.
Carmelite House
50 Victoria Embankment
London EC4Y 0DZ

www.bookouture.com

ISBN: 978-1-80314-875-5
eBook ISBN: 978-1-80314-874-8

1

ABBEYMEAD, SUSSEX, MID-NOVEMBER 1956

Flora Steele glanced at the Victorian station clock that hung on the opposite wall, and sighed. It was a timepiece her dear Aunt Violet had been thrilled to find at one of the many auctions she enjoyed, and every evening had wound it religiously before she locked the bookshop door. Over the years, Flora had grown to love it as much. But not today. Today, its hands were telling her she was going to be late when she'd promised her friend, crime writer and fellow sleuth, Jack Carrington, she would be ready to leave at five this evening.

The clang of the All's Well's doorbell had her look up expectantly and put to one side the wad of one-pound notes she'd been counting. Jack's lanky frame filled the doorway, behind him the dark of a November night.

'I bring news that will gladden your heart!' Jack announced cheerfully, taking off his fedora and dropping it onto the table that Flora kept for the very latest publications. 'Difficult to believe but Overlay House is actually getting a telephone! Not quite yet, it's true, but I'm assured by the Post Office they'll be calling later this week.'

'That's good,' she said absent-mindedly, closing the till and, when he planted a gentle kiss on her cheek, repeated, 'Yes, very good.'

'It's monumental! So, how are you, my favourite sleuth? How's your week been? You seem... distracted.'

'I am a little.' Flora tugged back the strands of copper hair that had escaped their anchor, then took herself to task. She hadn't seen Jack for several days – he'd been squirrelled away in his study, writing furiously – and, really, she should sound a good deal happier to see him.

'Sorry, Jack. It's excellent news about the phone, though I must say it's about time – how long have you been on the waiting list?'

'Forever, but everything comes... And even better news – incredible as it seems, the new book is almost ready to send.' His smile widened.

'I didn't dare ask, but that's brilliant!'

'It is, but you're looking a trifle hangdog. What's the problem, if there is one? You can tell me as we go. We should be on our way if we're going to make the Dome in time.'

'I know we should. It's that dratted man. I've been waiting for him to collect his book so I could cash up, but he hasn't come.'

'Who are we talking about?'

'The reverend.'

'Reverend Hopkirk?'

'No, his new curate, Beaumont. The book he ordered has been in for days and he promised to collect it this afternoon.'

'Does it matter that much? He can come another time, surely? *Giant*, on the other hand, waits for no man. The *Worthing Echo* judged it a great film in the review I read.'

'I'm sure it is.' Flora tucked away the cash she'd counted and locked the brown foolscap envelope into a small safe that Violet had installed in the pedestal beneath the desk. 'I'm just keen to get the book sold. Our new clergyman promised to come by on

Wednesday and then didn't. It was an expensive buy, and I don't want to be stuck with it. It's not an item I can return and it's not exactly going to fly off the shelves.'

She pointed to the volume sitting amid the clutter on her desk. '*A Minister's Manual for Funerals,*' Jack read aloud.

'I don't even know why he needs a manual. He's only just out of theological college and must own a dozen books already. At least one of them should mention funerals.'

'He's new and eager, that's what. He'll be out to make his mark on Abbeymead – dish up something special for the congregation. The book's been ordered for Miss Lancaster's funeral, I take it?'

She nodded, slipping her feet into thick fur-lined boots and grabbing a bright red woollen coat from the wall peg. November had been particularly cold and, even without the first fall of snow, the temperature had barely risen above freezing for days. The village of Abbeymead lay some miles inland, the encircling Downs helping to protect it from storms along the Sussex coast, but before she'd left the house this morning, Flora had remembered where the Dome cinema was situated – on the Worthing seafront and likely to face a fierce wind blowing from the Channel.

'Actually, Phoebe Tallant came by yesterday,' she said, dashing into the cupboard that Violet had always insisted was a kitchenette. Loving her aunt dearly, Flora had kept up the fiction, even though it was nearly two years ago that she'd inherited the bookshop and made it her own. 'She came to settle Miss Lancaster's bill. I think Phoebe must want to give her godmother the best send-off she can.' Flora collected her handbag from the worktop. 'Perhaps she's had words with Mr Beaumont, asking him to make it special. I can understand her wanting the funeral to be an occasion. She's looked after the old lady so well these last few months.'

'Do you think she'll stay in the village when all is done and dusted?'

'I suppose she might if she inherits the Gothic monster.' Miss Lancaster's gloomy house sitting atop Fern Hill had never appealed to Flora. 'There seems to be no other relatives and it's likely everything will go to Phoebe. And perhaps it should – according to village gossip, she gave up a very good job in London to nurse her godmother.'

Flora tucked her arm in his and gave him a quick squeeze. 'Speaking from an utterly selfish point of view, I hope she stays. Miss Lancaster was one of my best customers and it would be good for the All's Well if Phoebe turned out to be a voracious reader, too.'

'Tut-tut! How mercenary, Miss Steele.'

'Running a bookshop in a small Sussex village and making any kind of profit is an uphill struggle, I'll have you know.'

'A bookshop that should have closed some time ago,' he reminded her. 'Are we going?'

Flora gave another sigh. 'I suppose we'd better. It's pretty clear the curate isn't coming. I'll make sure to call at the vicarage tomorrow, before I open, and deliver his manual personally.'

For a minute she lingered, her gaze sweeping the shop, checking that everything was as it should be, that every one of her beloved books was in its correct place, their spines standing straight and dust free, and the floor swept clear of litter.

'Come on,' Jack urged. 'The All's Well will still be here tomorrow.'

'The All's Well will be here for ever,' she declared. 'OK, ready to go.' She smiled up at him and stood on tiptoes to kiss him on the cheek.

It still felt strange, nicely strange, that in the last few months she and Jack had moved beyond simple friendship. It was something she hadn't expected, hadn't even wanted until she found that, in fact, she did. They'd been friends for some time – very good friends as well as partners in crime – before they'd crossed the line into what Abbeymead's older generation called sweethearts.

After past romantic disasters, both she and Jack had been reluctant to commit themselves, but since their dinner at the Priory – a thank you from Sally Jenner for helping to solve a murder and get her hotel back on its feet – their relationship had changed. In truth, it had changed long before, but neither had been willing to acknowledge it, Flora thought ruefully. That evening at the Priory, though, the barriers had finally tumbled.

Jack had his hand on the polished brass doorknob and had half opened the shop door when a single chime of a church bell shattered the quiet of the empty high street. The ghostly reverberation echoed and re-echoed through the still night air.

Frowning, he came to a stop. 'Are the bell-ringers at St Saviour's tonight?'

'If they are, one of them hasn't quite got the hang of it.' Flora grinned. 'Harry Barnes probably. You're supposed to ring a peal, aren't you?' She fished out a pair of fur-lined gloves from her coat pocket.

'Mr Barnes is bell-ringing now? I didn't know. Not that I hear a lot of what goes on in Abbeymead.'

'I didn't know either. Dilys passed on the news when I took some parcels into the post office yesterday. She's been a bell-ringer for years, of course, and was scathing about Harry's progress – or lack of it. Said he'd be much better going back to the golf course.'

'That sounds a Dilys kind of comment.' Jack locked the door behind them and handed her the keys. He stood listening, looking up and down the empty street. 'No more chimes,' he said thoughtfully.

'They're probably regrouping. Berating Harry for getting it wrong.'

'Maybe, but that bell... it didn't sound like the normal chime.'

'Really? I've spent so many years listening to St Saviour's bells, I don't hear them any more.' She had begun to walk towards the small red Austin parked at the side of the pavement, when Jack detained her with a hand on her arm.

'There's something about this I don't like. I think we should take a look.'

'Jack! Stop being a crime writer! If we call at the church, we'll never make Worthing on time.'

'We'll never make it anyway. Rock Hudson will be well and truly married by the time we get to the cinema. He may even have discovered the oil. Come on, let's trot up to the church and take a look.'

He fumbled in his overcoat for the pocket torch he carried, a winter necessity in a village that lacked street lights. Despite a petition to the council, signed by most of the inhabitants, lights had never come to Abbeymead. They were seen as contrary to rural tradition, apart from costing too much, which the villagers suspected was the real reason. The wartime blackout had meant little to Abbeymead – it was something the village lived with permanently.

'I suppose we might as well,' Flora murmured regretfully. 'I seem to have ruined the evening already.'

Arm in arm, they strode briskly along the high street towards the looming silhouette of St Saviour's, its Norman architecture solid and fearless. They had reached the churchyard wall when a sturdy figure clad in what, beneath a wash of moonlight, appeared a glorious magenta, came bustling into view from the opposite direction. Flora squinted at the vivid splash of colour – Dilys had excelled herself this evening.

'Did you hear that?' the postmistress asked breathily. 'That chime. Soon as I heard it, I ran. Someone messing about, I'll be bound.'

'It's not a practice night then?' Jack asked.

Dilys, still breathing heavily, nodded her head vigorously. 'There's a practice all right, but not till six. Changed from our usual evening, too, though why the verger keeps messing with the rota is beyond me. As it is, I've had to rush my supper to get here. A nice corned beef hash it was, too.'

Flora fidgeted beside him. She was cold and wished they were snug in Jack's car. 'Shall we see what's going on?' she asked, trying to keep the impatience from her voice.

Following Dilys through the lych gate and up the red brick path, they veered right towards the fourteenth-century flint and stone bell tower, its square walls and fortress-like crenellations stark against the bright sky. Ignoring the mighty oak door of the church, they made their way to the entrance that led directly into the tower.

The moon was almost full tonight, swimming across a clear sky, and in its silvery light Flora caught sight of a small group crowded in the open doorway. Straight away, she recognised Mr Preece, the village butcher, and, alongside him, the rounded form of Harry Barnes. On the other side, a man Flora didn't know. He appeared to be holding Harry upright and, beneath the glare of Jack's torch beam, the new recruit to Abbeymead's bell-ringing team looked ashen. Jack had been right – something *was* wrong.

'What's all this then?' Dilys demanded of the butcher.

Mr Preece muttered a barely audible response while Harry Barnes seemed unable to stop the mechanical shaking of his head from side to side.

'I can't believe it,' the butcher mumbled. 'I mean, how could it happen?' He turned to Dilys as though she might have the answer.

'How could what happen?' Jack pushed a path between the group, Flora following close behind, and walked into the tower.

Together, they stood in silence, staring at the scene that confronted them. When Jack reached for her hand and held it tightly, she was glad of its warmth. The tower's stone walls rose vertically on all sides, disappearing into the darkest of shadows, while the dull light of a solitary lamp pooled the floor. Dangling from the rafters many feet above, a solitary bell rope ended inches above the paving and, spread-eagled across the granite flagstones – the body of a man.

Unwillingly, Flora looked down at the waxen face and saw the small trickle of red staining the grey.

'It's Lyle Beaumont, the new curate,' she whispered, feeling slight sick.

Jack stood silent, his face grave, then rousing himself, he said quietly, 'Come outside.'

Taking her by the arm, he led her through the bell tower door to the churchyard beyond.

'You're sure it is Beaumont?' he asked, when they were standing among the gravestones. The curate had only been in Abbeymead a matter of weeks and Jack, she realised, would have had no reason to meet him.

She nodded, convinced her face must be as white as the moon above.

'That's one man then who won't be buying a funeral manual,' he said grimly.

'We'll have to call the police,' the postmistress announced resentfully, as she stomped from the tower entrance and joined them in the churchyard, her figure stiff with annoyance.

Flora was about to agree when the man she hadn't recognised intervened. Pulling up the collar of a thick black overcoat against the creeping frost, he said, 'I already called them, folks. And called for an ambulance. We arrived a bit early' – he gestured towards Harry Barnes who had followed his friend out of the tower and was half lying across a gravestone – 'and as soon as we realised what had happened, I ran to the vicarage and used their phone. Someone called Tring is coming.'

'He's the village constable,' Flora told him, intrigued as to who this man was.

'Fat lot of good he'll be.' Dilys folded her arms in martial pose. 'Tring'll do nothing but dither. He'll keep us here for ever, and I'm getting cold. What do you think, Mr Preece?' she appealed to the substantial figure beside her.

'Search me. Never seen anythin' like it. I dunno what to think. I mean, poor chap, him bein' the curate an'all. Blimey, it's cold tonight.' The butcher fished a peaked cap from his pocket and rammed it on his bald head.

'What's being a curate got to do with anything?' Dilys demanded. 'The man's had an accident, simple as that. The police need to know there's a body and the ambulance needs to take him to the morgue.'

The postmistress hadn't the sweetest of tempers on a good day, and it was clear to Flora that this was not a good day for Dilys. Her supper had been spoiled, her bell-ringing practice summarily abandoned and now, it seemed, she'd been left stranded in a freezing churchyard waiting for the constable she despised.

'Anyways, who are you?' Dilys asked belligerently, turning to the man who had telephoned.

'We haven't been introduced, have we?' he said easily. 'I'm sorry. I'm an old friend of Harry's, though right now he's in no state to perform introductions. My name is Stephen Henshall. I'm staying with Harry up at Pelham Lodge.'

'You're working at the Priory, aren't you?' Flora asked in the silence that followed.

His name had seemed familiar. Sally Jenner had mentioned a Stephen when she'd called at the bookshop earlier that week. Stephen was a businessman, Sally had said, who had offered to work with her co-owner, Dominic, on plans for the hotel.

'Not exactly working,' Henshall said, 'more advising the young chap in charge. He seems a bit at sixes and sevens.'

'He will be,' Flora answered readily. 'Dominic and Miss Jenner haven't had the best start to their new business.'

'So I gathered.' He gave a wide smile, revealing a frighteningly white set of teeth that glinted in the moonlight flooding the churchyard.

'I'm not sure it will be enough to call Tring,' Jack said gravely, joining the conversation for the first time.

'What d'you mean, not enough?' Dilys took a step forward

as though to ram home her question. But before Jack had a chance to answer, the creak of the lych gate sounded in the hushed air and was followed by heavy footsteps on the pathway.

'I was telephoned.' Constable Tring sounded aggrieved. He must have had his supper spoiled, too, Flora thought. 'What's all this about an accident?'

'You'd better come into the tower.' Jack led him and the small party back into the bell tower, Harry Barnes managing to stagger the few steps before sinking onto a convenient bench.

At the sight of the crumpled body, the constable took off his helmet and bowed his head. 'Mr Beaumont, goodness me.' He looked up at the rafters, then down again, and scratched his head. 'Looks like he clung on to the rope to save hisself,' he opined.

'There was a single chime,' Jack offered. 'Just the one. That might have been him clutching hold of the rope as he fell.'

'It didn't work, though,' the butcher said gloomily. 'Still split his head open.'

'It's a long way to fall,' Constable Tring muttered, bending down to look more closely at the dead man. 'I'll need an ambulance and— what's this then?'

He took off his right-hand glove and leaned further forward, his arm outstretched. Flora leaned forward, too, in an attempt to see what he'd found. When the policeman straightened up, there was a sheet of paper in his hand.

'Looks like a note,' Stephen Henshall said, edging so close that Flora thought he would take the piece of paper from the constable's hand.

'It *is* a note,' Tring declared. For some seconds, he fumbled in his uniform pocket before finally bringing forth a pair of rimless spectacles. 'Let's see now,' he said portentously, perching the glasses on his nose. There was an audible groan from Dilys.

Seconds more followed before Tring pronounced, 'Looks like the reverend was meeting someone here.'

There was an uncomfortable silence while the group digested this information and its implications. Flora looked across at Jack and mouthed, '*Not an accident?*'

'Is it signed?' she asked.

The policeman shook his head and looked miserable. He must be thinking of his spoiled supper again, she thought.

'Any of you gents have an appointment with the reverend?' the constable asked, looking hopelessly around the gathering.

Dilys gave a loud snort. 'Gents! You have got a pair of eyes, I presume?'

'Sorry, Miss Fuller, but did you—'

'No, I did not!'

One by one the rest of the group followed suit, denying any knowledge of a meeting with the curate. The constable appeared flummoxed until Jack stepped forward and suggested quietly, 'Perhaps telephone Brighton for help?'

Tring looked grateful. 'Yes, that's what I'll do.' His face brightened. 'Let Brighton sort it out. No need for you folks to hang around. Get home before you freeze to the spot.'

'But we can't leave Mr Beaumont alone, surely?' Flora was shocked. In her mind, the tower had become a likely crime scene.

'I can't stay,' Dilys said hastily. 'I've got Dad to look after. He gets restless as it is when I'm ringing of an evening. I need to be home.'

'And I best get Harry back to Pelham Lodge. You can see the poor chap's all in.' Stephen walked over to the bench and put a hand beneath his friend's arm, pulling the tubby figure to his feet.

'I'll stay until Brighton police get here,' Jack said, addressing the constable.

'We'll stay,' Flora amended.

. . .

Once they were alone, Jack put his arms around her, trying to keep them both warm while blanking out the sight of the dead man. 'It could have been an accident, you know,' he murmured into her ear.

'Could have, but it wasn't, was it?' She slipped out of his embrace but stayed close.

'Still, a clergyman...'

'A clergyman who gets anonymous notes. What was the meeting about? And why ask Lyle Beaumont to meet at the bell tower and at the top of four flights of stairs?' She pointed upwards to the gallery.

'For secrecy, perhaps. It's who Beaumont was meeting that interests me. Whoever it was will know what happened here; if it was an accident or not. They must have realised the curate was dead yet did nothing to sound the alert.'

'He can't have been dead for long, if Tring's assumption is right – that he tried to save himself by clinging to the rope. And I think it is. We heard that chime no more than fifteen minutes before we got here.'

'None of our bell-ringers have owned to an appointment,' Jack said slowly, 'and whoever met Beaumont must have disappeared before Harry and his crew arrived.'

'Unless it *was* a bell-ringer who pushed the curate to his death.'

Jack raised his eyebrows. 'One of your leaps?'

'Maybe, but we should forget any idea of an accident. You don't fall from a gallery with a waist-high barrier by misfortune. It was either a push or the reverend decided to end it all.'

'As a result of the meeting he had?'

Flora stamped her feet to get the blood circulating. Even fur-lined boots weren't enough to keep this cold at bay. 'It's possible Beaumont had suicide in mind, but doesn't the church have something to say about taking one's life? I'm more inclined to believe it was a meeting that didn't go well. A quarrel maybe, a physical assault from either party and bingo, over the barrier goes the curate.'

'Were you serious in suggesting one of the bell-ringers could be involved?'

Flora frowned. 'Not really. Mr Preece, for instance, seemed genuinely confused, and I can't honestly see what business the butcher would have with Beaumont that might lead to such a quarrel.'

'That could be said of every one of them, of course. But no, I agree, Mr Preece is an unlikely villain, and Harry Barnes appeared to be near collapse.'

'Barnes is such a limp kind of person, Jack, he'll always be an unlikely villain. Do you remember him at the golf club after Polly died? I can't see him ever summoning the bravado to attack anyone, least of all a man wearing a dog collar.'

'That only leaves Dilys,' Jack said mischievously. 'It could be her.'

'And how would that work? Dilys wasn't even in the tower when we met her but running towards us along the high street. She would have to have thrown Beaumont over the barrier, rushed down four flights of stairs, galloped up the high street, then galloped back to meet us. And if Preece and Barnes had no reason to harm the curate, she had even less.'

'Perhaps he was rude about her knitting.' There was laughter in Jack's voice. 'Told her he thought her latest cardigan hideous. Which it is – have you seen it? A kind of tangerine blanket with green stripes. It probably gave him a headache.'

'Be serious!' she scolded.

'Yes, be serious, Jack,' a gruff voice said from the doorway.

Inspector Alan Ridley from the Brighton police had arrived.

3

The inspector strode into the tower and took a long look at the body. 'Where's the note you said you found, Tring?' he asked, turning to the constable.

Half-hidden behind Ridley's sergeant, Constable Tring shuffled forward and handed over the slip of paper. For the first time, Jack noticed its edge was tinged a dull red.

The inspector gave the bloodied note a brief glance, then turned back to Tring. 'How many people were here when you arrived?'

The policeman's brow furrowed. 'There was Dilys Fuller, Preece, he's the butcher, Mr Barnes from up the hill and a man I didn't know. And these two,' he added dismissively, nodding towards Jack and Flora.

'And none of them admitted to writing this or knowing anything about the accident?' Ridley flapped the note in the air.

'I did ask them,' the constable said anxiously.

'What about you, Jack? And you, Miss Steele – when did you arrive?'

'I'd say it was around fifteen minutes after the curate fell to his death,' Jack said.

Alan Ridley allowed himself a wry smile. 'That's pretty precise.'

'It's easy enough to be precise,' Flora put in. 'We heard a single bell chime as we were leaving the All's Well. It must have been Mr Beaumont trying to save himself from the fall.'

The inspector nodded. 'We'll get a time of death confirmed very soon – the pathologist is on his way. Were you two the last to arrive on the scene? That is, before our friend Constable Tring here put in an appearance?'

The constable's face twitched. He seemed to have developed a nervous tic.

'We met the postmistress on the street outside,' Jack said, trying to remember the exact order of events. 'But Harry Barnes and Mr Preece were already here, and a friend of Mr Barnes who's staying with him at Pelham Lodge. A Stephen Henshall.'

The inspector glanced around the narrow square that formed the base of the tower, then up at each of its high stone walls. Against the north-facing wall a precarious wooden staircase led to the gallery high above.

'The timing is pretty tight, wouldn't you say? There were three people here before you two arrived with Miss Fuller. If they'd gone ahead and walked into the tower, they'd have been bunched into this small space and certain to see anyone who came down those stairs. And if they were still walking up the churchyard path at the time the bell rang – I'll need to check that with them – they would have seen the intruder slipping out of the tower.'

'There's a possibility they didn't,' Jack prevaricated. 'It's dark and the churchyard is gloomy. And overcrowded – too many gravestones. The perpetrator could easily have hidden.'

'But it's a full moon tonight,' Ridley persisted. 'If there was anyone to see, they'd have been seen.'

It was becoming clear to Jack that the inspector had already narrowed his list of 'persons of interest' down to the bell-ringers themselves.

'OK,' Alan Ridley continued. 'Not much we can do here tonight except wait for the pathologist... if you could both give a brief statement to my sergeant before you leave and let him know the names and addresses of the others who were here. And Jack... I'd like a chat soon. Maybe a beer at the Cross Keys?'

Jack looked across at Flora and knew he'd see a mutinous face. Together they'd been involved with police investigations on a number of occasions – a few months ago they had actually been asked for their help – but he knew Flora would want them to burrow into this mystery alone. The lure of being the first to solve the crime, ahead of the inspector, meant she'd want to keep whatever theories they came up with to themselves until they'd cracked the case. Ridley did nothing to smooth the wheels either, Jack thought. The inspector held a grudging admiration for Flora's detective skills but persisted in seeing her as 'Jack's little girl' and treating her in much the same manner.

'A beer sounds good,' he agreed. At least that way he'd discover just how far the police had progressed.

'Tomorrow OK for you? Say one o'clock?'

When Jack nodded, the inspector clapped him on the shoulder. 'Give your statements, both of you, and you're free to go.'

Flora lay awake that night, shivering slightly. The sitting room fire had remained unlit the whole day and the cottage felt chilly and damp, its old bones creaking from the cold. The several electric fires she possessed had barely made a difference and now she was wriggling uncomfortably in bed, paddling her feet against the tepid hot water bottle.

She was annoyed as well as cold, and that was probably as

much to blame for her sleeplessness. She and Jack were a partnership – friends, sweethearts, lovers, whatever you wanted to call it – but a crime-fighting partnership, too. Tonight, they'd abandoned their trip to the cinema to walk to St Saviour's together. They'd viewed the body together, then stayed with Mr Beaumont, side by side, until the police arrived. And what had happened? As soon as Inspector Ridley came on to the scene, she was dismissed, and Jack given the opportunity to talk to the policeman over lunch.

Jack would share whatever he learned, she knew, but it would come to her second-hand, and she wanted to hear it for herself. She wanted to raise questions, some maybe that Jack wasn't prepared to ask. He was more reticent than she, keen not to jeopardise his relationship with Ridley, who'd been, and was still, a useful contact for Jack's crime writing. Her omission from the lunch party was glaring and she suspected the inspector might have a problem with women, or more particularly with women and pubs. Even now, as the country moved towards the late fifties, there were men who hated the idea of a woman drinking in a public house. Even in the lounge bar. In the saloon bar, alongside the menfolk, never.

To be fair, Flora conceded, she would have found it difficult to take time away from the bookshop, but still... She must start to crack this mystery for herself, she decided. Ridley appeared keen to talk to the bell-ringers. He'd said it was to confirm timings, but it was more likely, she thought, to be a suspicion that one of them was a murderer. Really, she couldn't see Mr Preece or Dilys or Harry Barnes deciding it was time for the new curate to depart this world. Stephen Henshall, though, was another matter.

He was a virtual stranger, had been in Abbeymead a matter of weeks, and Flora had only a vague idea of who he was and why he'd come to the village. At one of the regular Friday evening suppers she shared with her friends – Sally's aunt

Alice, and Kate Mitchell, who owned the village café – Sally had said casually that her business partner, Dominic, was working with a new adviser. Mr Henshall, apparently, ran several successful London hotels and, as a favour, was spending a few hours each day with Dominic to discuss ideas that might improve the Priory's finances. The hotel had begun to recover from the dreadful beginning it had suffered last autumn but had a long way to go before it became profitable.

Stephen Henshall's role had seemed a little odd to Flora, even as Sally mentioned it. Why would a successful hotelier be prepared to mentor a beginner in the trade like Dominic Lister? Henshall would necessarily be an extremely busy man, immersed in the day-to-day running of his own businesses and heavily involved in future plans. Even if he was doing it as a favour for his friend, Harry Barnes, it still made no sense. As far as Flora knew, Mr Barnes and Dominic Lister had only a passing acquaintance.

She huddled further down in the bed, pulling the eiderdown close and swaddling herself like an Egyptian mummy. Her eyelids were feeling increasingly heavy – she might at last be able to sleep. Stephen Henshall would be the focus of her attention, she decided drowsily, whatever Inspector Ridley had in mind. She'd make a plan tomorrow.

4

'So, what exactly were you doing at St Saviour's?'

Alan Ridley leaned back against the wooden settle, nursing a beer in one hand, and tapping out a tattoo on the scored table with the other. He was in his favourite corner of his favourite pub and Jack hoped it might prompt him to divulge whatever the police knew.

Yesterday, he'd written the last word of the most difficult novel he'd ever undertaken, and it had been a wonderful moment. So much effort, so many hours, to produce what in truth was a modest volume. But he'd done it. And done it after he'd doubted that he would ever write again. His only task now was a swift read-through to double-check there were no wild inconsistencies and no unexpected holes in the plot.

Jack could taste freedom. He found himself itching to get out of the house, keen to plunge into life beyond his study – and a new investigation would tick the box. Immersing himself in a real-life crime would allow him to abandon his trusty Remington at just the right time. Not that he'd admit to such enthusiasm to Flora. She was difficult enough to keep in check as it was.

'So why were you there?' the inspector repeated.

'We were on our way to Worthing, to the cinema, but running late – in fact, Flora had been waiting in the shop for Mr Beaumont to collect a book he'd ordered, before she locked up. There was this single chime from the bell tower, and it seemed odd. Odd enough for me to persuade her to walk up to the church and discover what was going on.'

'You and Miss Steele? You're...?'

'We're friends,' Jack said firmly.

He wasn't about to explain whatever it was that Flora and he shared. He found it difficult enough to explain it to himself. Jack knew he cared for her deeply, he would even admit to loving her but, where that was leading, he had no idea.

'Here you are, gentlemen.'

Two large chunks of cheddar cheese, a basket of fresh baked rolls and a small dish of pickle arrived at their table. Jack's eyes widened. Catering at the Cross Keys appeared to have improved one hundred per cent since Daniel Vaisey had moved into the pub a few months ago. The previous landlord had been the village publican for more years than anyone could remember, but his catering skills had not improved with age.

'This looks good,' he said.

Daniel smiled. 'I certainly hope so. We want our customers to come back.'

'You said there was a chap at the church you didn't know,' the inspector pursued, watching the landlord walk back to the bar while chomping down on his first bread roll.

'Yes. A Stephen Henshall. I'd never met him before, but it seems he's a friend of Harry Barnes. Mr Barnes owned a catering firm until he retired and Henshall runs two successful hotels, or so the grapevine has it. They must know each other pretty well through business. I believe Harry recommended him to Dominic Lister – you'll remember Lister, the chap who owns the Priory along with Miss Jenner? Harry invited his mate down to Abbeymead, I think in the hope he could help the Priory recover from the mess it was in last September. The chap is staying with the Barnes family at Pelham Lodge. That's the local palace!' Jack added.

The inspector waved his knife in the air. 'Know all about that place. One of my men went up there this morning and was nearly savaged by their horrible dogs. I could nick them for that.'

'And?' Jack prompted.

'My detective constable took a statement from Barnes and his mate, once the poor bloke had recovered from his fright. But... a stranger in the village could be significant... Abbeymead has more than its fair share of dark deeds, I'm thinking. Sergeant Norris called on Miss Fuller – took him an hour to escape – and my other DC called at the butcher's. The vicar was *my* target for the morning, but he's still in bed feeling poorly. His housekeeper, though – Miss Dunmore? – was very helpful. She'd ferreted around in the deceased's room and found a pile of correspondence which she passed over, thinking it might be useful. As a start, it gave me details of the curate's family. Beaumont came from Dorset, it seems. A village called Whitbury. I phoned what seemed the nearest police station, and asked them to call at the family house – another palace, by all accounts – and deliver the bad news.'

Alan Ridley was proving as helpful as Amy Dunmore, Jack thought. Not that anything the inspector had said was of immediate use, but he'd file away the information on Lyle Beaumont, ready for another day. Dorset wasn't that far from Sussex and Flora might enjoy a weekend trip there.

The inspector cut himself another slice of cheese and pulled a wry face. 'The desk sergeant at Charmouth was thrown into a major panic when I phoned. He realised he'd be the one telling the Beaumont family the worst. They're a wealthy lot, apparently, well known in the district. And highly religious according to this chap. Explains why the son is a curate, I suppose.'

There was a crease in Jack's forehead. 'Lyle Beaumont was starting at the bottom of the tree as a humble curate. You'd think a wealthy family would have done better for him.'

'A younger son? The nobs send their younger sons into the Church, don't they?'

Jack pushed his empty plate to one side. 'I thought that had died out with the war.'

Ridley shook his head. 'Don't you believe it. They're still at it. Oldest son inherits, next one goes into the army, and Johnny-come-lately gets the Church.'

Jack took a last sip of his beer, feeling satisfied. It had been a good meal, the best he'd ever eaten at the Cross Keys. Rationing had finally ended a couple of years ago after fourteen years of privation, but the village pub had never received the message and the food it served had continued to be more or less inedible. The new landlord had certainly turned its fortunes around.

He looked across at the bar where Daniel Vaisey was chatting to his customers in between pulling pints. He was evidently a good host. Narrowing his gaze, Jack saw Phoebe Tallant was among the crowd drinking at the bar. She was a beautiful girl, he thought, smiling and full of fun. Long, dark hair had been tossed over her shoulders and she was wagging a manicured finger at the publican. Jack could see the bright red nail varnish from where he sat. For some reason, the image disturbed him. He supposed you couldn't be sad all the time and Miss Lancaster had been Phoebe's godmother, rather than a blood relation. But still, there was something in the small vignette that sounded a false note.

'I'm sorry,' he said to the inspector, coming out of his haze. 'I've not been much help, have I?'

'It's always useful to talk to the locals,' the inspector said placidly. 'Particularly when they're a writer. They tend to notice things. And if they've got a nose for crime... How's that going, by the way? You were a bit iffy about it last time we spoke.'

Jack relaxed his shoulders and smiled across the table. 'It's going well.'

He still found it incredible that at last he'd have something decent to send to Arthur Bellaby. He was almost there, and the hours spent editing, revising and generally polishing to a shine a manuscript that would be good enough for his agent, now felt worthwhile. It hadn't seemed that way when he'd started to write again back in September, after months of being unable to manage a word, let alone a fully developed crime novel. Arthur had been supportive, trying hard, Jack knew, to suppress a natural impatience. But the terms of the latest contract had been clear – a book by early January – and his protégé had been woefully behind. Contrary to expectations, though, Jack had come through and it felt remarkably good.

'Glad to hear it.' Ridley put down his empty glass and wiped his lips. 'Now you're on a roll, best you leave the detecting to me. You and your... you and Miss Steele.'

'It's always possible, isn't it, that there's nothing to detect?' He was playing devil's advocate, keen to test which way Ridley would jump. 'Couldn't it have been an accident?'

'It could,' the inspector said slowly, 'though I'm thinking not.' His fingers rapped out another tattoo. 'I'd like to keep an open mind, but it's the note that bothers me.' He screwed up his face. 'Did the person who wrote that note actually meet Beaumont? I've no evidence they did, but let's say the meeting happened and someone pushed him over that gallery wall. Why did they leave the note behind? It incriminates. It shouts out that someone else was involved. Without it, there'd be few questions over Beaumont's death. An accident would be the natural assumption.'

Jack took a last sip of his beer, thinking over the inspector's words. 'Perhaps the villain didn't realise that Beaumont was clutching the note,' he said at last. 'Or perhaps there was no time to retrieve it. If the murderer had just pushed the curate to his death when they heard the bell-ringers arrive, they'd be too intent on making their escape to think of taking the note.'

'Maybe.' Ridley stroked his glass. 'I can see that happening. The bell-ringers approaching, the villain in a panic. And yet, according to the statements we've taken, our three bell-ringers – sorry, two bell-ringers and a friend – were making their way to the tower at the time the bell tolled, and none of them saw a thing. I wonder!'

And so would Flora, Jack thought.

5

Alan Ridley's remark about strangers in the village stayed with Jack. Now that he considered it properly, there had been a fair number of new arrivals in the last few months, and that was unusual. He'd lived in Abbeymead for six years, most of them spent tucked away at Overlay House – as a recluse, Flora accused him, or on her better days, a hermit – and the daily rhythms of the village had largely passed him by. But under her tutelage he'd emerged again into the wider world and become conscious of how insular the village could be. Years spent living abroad as a journalist – Rome, Sydney, New York – were bound to colour his perspective. Yet... it was strange there had been such an influx of new blood. The phrase invaded his mind and drew a shudder of distaste.

He sat at his desk, swinging back and forth in his old leather chair – this was always where he thought best – and mentally ticked off a list of Abbeymead's most recent inhabitants. Phoebe Tallant had relinquished what, by all accounts, had been a high-powered job as a personal assistant to the director of a large London retailer. She'd even done some modelling for the business, the rumour went. Abbeymead knew all about modelling and tutted. Look what happened to poor Polly Dakers, they said, shaking their heads. It was soon clear, however, that Miss Tallant had come to the small Sussex village only to care for her godmother and, by general agreement, had done Miss Lancaster proud.

Daniel Vaisey, who'd served Jack his lunch no more than an hour ago, was also a newcomer. He'd moved into the Cross Keys this autumn and taken over as landlord. The change had surprised the pub regulars, but their grumbling had quickly stilled when, under Vaisey's management, the hostelry had become a decent place to eat and drink. The man seemed to have immersed himself seamlessly into village life and, as far as Jack could judge, had been accepted with few quibbles.

And then there was Lyle Beaumont himself, the recently appointed curate, and something of a mystery still. Reverend Hopkirk's health had been failing for some time and employing an assistant was supposed to have made parish work easier for the elderly man, but only six weeks after welcoming Beaumont, his protégé had come to a sticky end.

The very newest arrival was Stephen Henshall, though no more seemed known about him than the curate. Was there any connection between Stephen and Lyle Beaumont? Henshall was a friend of Harry Barnes, a long-term business contact, that was all that Jack knew, and that had come to him via the mysterious network that was the village grapevine. It wasn't much to go on.

Who in Abbeymead might know more and be worth talking to? Alice perhaps? She worked as head cook at the Priory and, if Henshall was advising the hotel, she must have met him on a number of occasions. Alice Jenner, Sally's aunt, wasn't a gossip by any means, but she had her finger on the pulse of the village and what she said could be trusted. And if Jack remembered rightly, she also knew the Barnes family. Hadn't Flora said that

Alice and Kate Mitchell had once catered for them at their palatial abode?

He should check. He'd go to see Flora, share with her what
Ridley had told him, and generally talk things over. If he went now,
he might catch the bookshop on a quiet afternoon. Galvanised into
action, he ran down the stairs, shrugging on his ancient ulster and
grabbing his fedora and a pair of leather gloves. The temperature
had stayed well below zero these last few days and, despite having
braved New York winters in the past, he'd begun to feel very cold.

~

There was only one customer browsing when he walked into
the All's Well half an hour later. It seemed an ideal time for a
private talk. Flora was reshelving a small pile of books, a stripy
woollen scarf around her neck. The All's Well felt particular
chilly.

'I've only one electric heater working,' she said, in answer to
his unspoken question, 'and the engineer can't come for days.
After last night, it feels as though I've been cold for months.'

'A case for wearing more clothes?'

She sighed. 'I'm doing just that. More layers and fewer
customers. Do you have any news to lighten my day?'

'Not much, I'm afraid. I'm hoping to get some from you –
Stephen Henshall and Harry Barnes, what do you know of
them?'

'Hardly more of the Barnes family than you do. Really, only
what we learned when we investigated Polly's death. And only
a little about Stephen Henshall. Until yesterday, I'd never met
the man. I'd heard his name rumbling round the village, but
that's all.'

'A name is more than I had! On the grapevine, he was the
unknown figure who'd come to rescue the Priory!'

'Now I think of it, Alice has mentioned him several times.' He felt a spurt of interest. 'But only because he's made her very cross, barging in and out of her kitchen,' Flora added. 'She thinks he's criticising the way she works, but that could just be Alice being Alice. She's a perfectionist.'

'Is there a possibility, do you think, that Henshall knew Lyle Beaumont?' It sounded outlandish but, in Jack's experience, the outlandish could sometimes be true.

'I can't imagine that he did. They would have moved in very different circles. For one thing, Henshall is in business and owns at least two London hotels.'

'While Beaumont is a churchman and comes from Dorset,' he said thoughtfully.

'Really?'

'That's what I gathered from Alan Ridley.'

Flora folded her arms. 'And how did the boys' lunch go?' She was still peeved at being excluded, Jack could see.

'It went OK, mainly because the ploughman's lunch was edible. Tasty even. A huge improvement on the usual fare.'

'So, other than the cheddar cheese, was it worth it? What did you learn?'

He put his head on one side and thought. 'Actually, not very much, except that the Beaumonts are a wealthy family and a highly religious one, which makes sense, I guess. And that none of the bell-ringing party saw an intruder in or near the bell tower.'

Flora uncrossed her arms and walked over to the window seat, patting it for Jack to join her.

'So, whoever Beaumont was meeting remains a mystery.' She spoke in a low voice, making sure that her single customer was still out of earshot.

'At the moment, at least. Hopefully not for long – once we get our hands on the case! I'm presuming you're interested?'

'If only to find someone willing to buy that wretched book,' she joked.

'How about Reverend Hopkirk? He might need a refresher.'

'Thank you, for your helpful suggestion, Jack, but perhaps I won't bother the vicar on his sick bed.' She swivelled round to look at him directly. 'Why do you think there could be a connection between Henshall and the curate?'

'I've no definite reason,' he admitted. 'Simply that they're both very new to the village and Abbeymead is a small place.'

'Hmm,' was all Flora said but she wore the distant look he knew meant that she was thinking deeply.

For a few minutes they sat in silence until she said slowly, 'Henshall and Harry Barnes were at the tower in advance of Mr Preece, and definitely in advance of Dilys. Henshall said as much when he told us he'd run to the vicarage to phone for help. He made it sound as though he and Harry had walked to the church together. But what if they hadn't? If Henshall wrote that message and went to meet Lyle Beaumont, he would have had to arrive before Mr Barnes.'

'Which would mean he'd be forced to double back to Pelham Lodge to accompany Harry to the village, while pretending he hadn't already been out and about. Is that even possible? Pelham Lodge is at the top of Fern Hill. How did he puff his way to the top after killing Beaumont, then appear to Harry as though he'd just left his bedroom?'

'He couldn't,' Flora said decidedly, 'but it's possible he joined his friend at some point on Harry's walk down Fern Hill and pretended he'd been taking a stroll around the village.'

'If that's the case, it should be in the statement Harry Barnes gave to the police.'

'Unless he suspects something's not right and has chosen to cover for his friend. I wonder how well they know each other?' Flora jumped up from the window seat. 'I think you're right about Henshall being the wild card. That was my conclusion, too. I might pay a visit to the Priory. Talk to Sally maybe, find out what she knows about our mysterious newcomer. Tomorrow is early closing, so I'll be free, and the hotel is usually quiet in the afternoons.'

Jack smiled. 'It's a start,' he said, getting to his feet and drop-ping a kiss on the top of her head. 'Stay out of trouble but let me know what happens.'

~

The following lunchtime, as soon as she'd hung the Closed notice on the bookshop door, Flora unpacked the sandwich she'd brought from home and made a swift cup of tea. She was keen to get to the Priory as soon as she could before Sally began preparing for evening at the hotel. She doubted the girl would know much, but over the last year or so of sleuthing with Jack, Flora had learned that the seemingly unimportant small details could prove vital. It was having the patience to discover those details and then the patience to wait for them to make sense.

Her much-loved bicycle, Betty, was waiting beneath her shelter at the rear of the All's Well, and Flora bestowed a pat on her handlebars before riding smoothly out onto the high street. The bike seemed glad to have her back in the saddle – rather than young Charlie Teague, she thought. Charlie managed the Friday deliveries for the shop and Flora suspected he was just a little too keen on treating Betty as a racing bike.

She was only slightly out of breath by the time she reached the top of Fern Hill – she must be getting fitter – and, turning right, rode on to the Priory entrance. Dismounting at the tall wrought-iron gates, she wheeled the bicycle along its winding driveway towards the front entrance. The grounds were in a state of winter mourning. All vestige of colour had disappeared from the flower beds that ran alongside the drive and the trees that dotted the parkland stretched their bare branches to a sky that was opalescent. At least yesterday's icy wind had dropped and the walk, even though sunless, was pleasant.

Flora had reached the carved pillars that marked the Priory's entrance and was parking Betty against the wall, its stone still golden even in this muted light, when Sally appeared on the threshold, holding back the heavy oak door to allow a man to pass through. It was Stephen Henshall. How fortuitous!

He had on the same long black winter overcoat he'd worn at St Saviour's, although this time a felt trilby covered his close-cropped hair. He hesitated in the doorway, his small, dark eyes holding an uncertain expression, trying, Flora could see, to remember how he knew her. When the realisation came, there was a quick smile, and then his face resumed its sober lines.

'Miss Steele, isn't it? We met—'

'Yes, we did,' she said quickly. 'But perhaps not the time to talk of it right now.'

She wasn't sure why not exactly, a sense that she would rather not have Sally overhear their conversation, but Henshall looked grateful, raised his trilby to her and walked past in the direction of the Priory gates and the village beyond.

'Come on in, Flora. It's lovely to see you.' Her friend beamed. 'I'll get Dottie to bring us tea.'

'I'll skip the tea if you don't mind, Sally. I've just had lunch. But could we have a quick word?'

Sally ruffled a hand through a head of spiky blonde curls and looked concerned. 'Nothing wrong, I hope.'

'You heard about the curate?' Flora asked, thinking how could she not. The whole of Abbeymead would be discussing his death for weeks to come.

'Yes, it's very sad, but why are you interested?' A frown found its way onto Sally's forehead. There was a pause before she said, 'It was an accident, wasn't it?' Where death and Flora were concerned, it was rarely an accident, Flora could see her friend thinking. In the last few years, there had been too many bodies, too many misadventures, for Sally to be unconcerned. 'You don't believe...' The girl trailed off.

'Can we talk in your sitting room?'

Sally nodded, still looking worried, and led the way into the large wood-panelled space, once the baronial hall of the Templeton family, but now functioning as the hotel's foyer, and up the grand sweeping staircase at its far end. Sally's cosy sitting room had been fashioned from one of the first-floor bedrooms, its tall windows and Juliet balcony overlooking a rolling green expanse at the rear of the mansion. Two squashy chintz-covered sofas, cushions and curtains to match, and a delicate maple wood table, added to its homely atmosphere.

'What's this about?' Sally asked, once they'd sunk down onto one of the sofas.

'To be honest, I'm not sure. Not at the moment. I wanted to ask you about Stephen Henshall.'

'Stephen?' The frown increased. 'What has he to do with it?'

'Probably nothing, but he was at the bell tower when we found Lyle Beaumont. He'd come with Harry Barnes.'

Sally nodded. 'That sounds about right. He's staying with Mr Barnes, up at Pelham Lodge.'

'So I gather, but what do you know about Henshall?'

Sally spread her hands. 'Not that much. He's only been here a few weeks. Dominic was speaking to Harry about how difficult it was proving to get the hotel back on its feet, after... well, you know... and Mr Barnes suggested inviting a friend down from London to help.'

'And that's all you know of him? How about Dominic?'

'I don't think Dom knows any more than me. Stephen Henshall was recommended as someone who ran two successful hotels and might help us with the Priory's recovery.'

'How good a friend of Harry's do you think he is?'

'They did business together over a number of years, I

believe, when Mr Barnes was still working. Harry owned a catering firm and Stephen runs hotels, so I imagine there was quite a lot of contact, and they must have known each other reasonably well. I know Mr Barnes was very admiring of him. He told Dominic that Stephen was one of the most astute businessmen he'd ever met, that he knew the hotel business inside out.'

'Quite a recommendation, but what do *you* think of him?' Flora pursued.

'I've seen so little of him, I couldn't give an opinion. He's very much Dominic's province.'

There was a pause before Sally added, 'I don't know if it's at all relevant, but Dom let slip that, though Henshall is this super professional, he might be having a few problems. It made me wonder at the time if that was why he was keen to come to Abbeymead and help us. A kind of escape.'

'What sort of problems?'

'Money. Isn't it always? A few months back, it seems, there was a big upset at one of his hotels. Stephen paid for this huge order that never arrived and, as far as I know, he's not been able to get his money back.'

Flora leaned forward, studying Sally's face keenly. 'You think he's struggling?'

'No...' her friend said slowly, 'not struggling. He must have enough capital to cope with such troubles. I'd say it was more anger at the thought that someone had cheated him and damaged his reputation as an honest businessman. But I'm just guessing,' she added hastily. 'I haven't spoken to him personally and I don't know what really happened. He doesn't exactly confide in Dominic either.'

'How is Dominic these days?' Flora asked. She hadn't seen Sally's co-owner for some weeks and was genuinely interested in how well their partnership had weathered the storms of the autumn.

Sally flushed slightly. 'He's trying to make things work for both our sakes, but to be honest, Flora, I've decided that it's a business relationship I want now, nothing more.'

'The passion has gone?' she asked teasingly, though feeling immense relief. Sally seemed, at last, to have broken the spell binding her to a man of whom Flora still had serious doubts.

'It was all the lies,' Sally said sadly. 'I've forgiven him, but I can't forget how badly he deceived me, and it's affected the way I feel about him. But what about you?' she asked brightly, clearly anxious to move the conversation on. 'You and Jack! I feel personally responsible for that development.'

Flora pulled a face. 'The Priory's splendid dinner sped things along,' she admitted, 'but I think we were always heading that way. Even though neither of us wanted to admit it!'

'And now? Are you still heading that way? Where's this "friendship" going exactly?'

Flora studied her hands. 'We're happy,' she murmured. Then looking up, she smiled across at her friend. 'I think we've both agreed that it's good to let things rest as they are. Anything more serious and we'd be tempting fate.'

6

Friday evening had arrived, a time for Flora to meet up for a meal with Alice and Kate, her two closest friends in the village. Occasionally, Sally would join them, but not this week. It was Flora's turn to issue the invitation to supper and she was hoping to discover if there was anything more that either of them could tell her about Stephen Henshall. Both she and Jack had singled out the man as worth their attention – he was the latest arrival in the village and largely unknown to the inhabitants. Already, she'd learned from Sally what could be crucial information: that Henshall had been cheated and had not taken it lightly. A scam, but was Lyle Beaumont likely to have been involved in such a thing? A curate who was a cheat? It seemed improbable.

The previous evening, Flora had cooked a beef stew, ready to heat in the oven once she returned from work. A dish of mashed potatoes would go alongside. Having eaten her way through Jack's Maris Pipers, she'd almost finished her own modest pickings, but there was still a thriving patch of carrots and a sturdy row of cauliflowers from which to choose.

The night was intensely dark and, torch in hand, she took time to negotiate the mud-spattered path to the bottom of the garden where her aunt had established her vegetable patch. Violet Steele, for all she had been raised in London, had been a dab hand at growing and Flora had never been able to match her aunt's expertise. But she tried, and kept trying, and this year had managed a very respectable haul of onions, carrots and parsnips, along with cauliflower and several rows of cabbage.

Fixing the torch at a strategic angle on the hard ground – it would be freezing in a very short time – she wielded a trowel to loosen the carrots and, with difficulty, tugged a bunch free and stacked them in her trug. It took some time to dig sufficient for the evening's meal and, by the time she got to cutting the cauliflower, she was shivering with cold. It would have been sensible to have done this in daylight, she reflected, but at lunchtime a flurry of customers had kept her chained to the shop. The All's Well naturally had to come first, and it was gratifying that her hard work was finally paying off, with the shop at last creeping back into profit.

She had only just made it back into the kitchen when there was a knock at the front door. Alice stood on the threshold, a crumpled felt hat crammed on her head and the old plaid winter coat wrapped firmly round her plump figure.

'You should have let me cook,' she said, stepping into the hallway and giving Flora a cold kiss on her cheek. 'I've been off all day, but you've been workin' for hours and here you are still workin'.'

'You must be just as tired as me, now the hotel is back in business.'

Alice banged her hands together to get the circulation flowing. 'It's some busy all right, but it's all good after that dreadful start.' She hung her coat and hat on the bentwood coat stand and walked into the kitchen. 'Now, tell me what I can do.'

'Nothing, Alice, really. Everything's under control.'

Her friend nodded and settled herself on a wooden chair.

'Do you have a puddin' made?' she asked, eyeing the still unpeeled potatoes and carrots.

Flora looked guilty. 'I've the rest of the fruit cake I made last weekend. Will that do?'

'Certainly not!' Alice gave a deep laugh. 'I thought as much and took the liberty of bringing a sherry trifle.' She delved into the wicker basket at her feet. 'There,' she said triumphantly, delivering a white china bowl to the table. 'We had a two-day sponge in the kitchen and Mr Houseman delivered far too much fruit t'other day, so what else could I make but a trifle?'

'You're an angel. So much better than fruit cake.'

'Cake has its place,' Alice said judiciously, 'but not after a beef stew. It is beef I can smell?'

'It is. While I do the potatoes, how about a glass of elder-flower? Mrs Teague's best.' Flora pointed to the full bottle on the Formica counter.

'Sounds good, my love. How's that young Teague gettin' on? Haven't seen Charlie for weeks.'

'There's no gardening for him at this time of year, of course, but he's still doing my Friday deliveries for which I'm grateful. Particularly when it's this cold. I saw him off on his round just before I locked up today.'

Alice poured them both an elderflower and, clinking glasses, Flora returned to her vegetable peeling. 'How's work at the Priory, apart from busy?' she asked casually, hoping she might hear some mention of Henshall. She was gratified when, on cue, Alice began an impassioned complaint against the man.

'I dunno what that Henshall's doin' at the hotel, I really don't. Supposed to be helpin' Dominic, or so Sal says, but all he seems to do is interfere.'

'In the kitchen?' she asked sympathetically, half turning to her visitor.

'In *my* kitchen. He's in and out all day. Pickin' and pokin' around. Seems to think you can produce high-class meals on a shoestring. And it doesn't make sense,' she went on, shaking a head of wiry grey curls. 'He's put together some kind of Christmas menu with Master Dominic. A special offerin', you know, for Christmas Eve and Boxing Day and then another one on New Year's Eve. It sounded a good idea to me, especially if Sal gets the advertising right. Not much else like that round here. But then this Henshall looks at my suggestions for the food and starts pullin' my lists apart. Too difficult to get hold of, he says. Too difficult, my foot. Too difficult to cook and he's talkin' to *me*, Flora! Too expensive. That's the real reason, mark my words. He wants the quality, but he doesn't want to pay for it.'

The front door knocker sounded once more, just as Alice reached a crescendo of complaint.

'That will be Kate,' Flora said apologetically, quickly putting the carrots and potatoes on to boil. 'I'd better go. She'll be freezing on the doorstep. But he sounds stupid, I agree,' she called over her shoulder, as she opened the front door.

'Who sounds stupid?' Kate asked, walking speedily into the hall. 'My, it's cold out there. I forgot my hat.' She shrugged off the cape she was wearing and Flora, finding a space for it, marvelled at how fashionable her friend had become. A very different Kate from the one she'd known for years. Meeting Tony Farraday, the new interest in her life, had done her good.

'Stephen Henshall. He's the man we've decided is stupid. He's helping at the Priory. Come to think of it, Tony must know him.'

'Yes,' Kate agreed, 'I suppose he must.' To Flora's ear, her friend sounded unenthusiastic. 'That's a delicious smell coming from the kitchen.'

'Let's hope it tastes as good. Come and sit down. Alice is here already.'

Settled at the table, her glass of elderflower at her elbow, Kate looked around, her pale blue eyes appreciative. 'Your kitchen is so cosy, Flora. I wish mine was half as nice. It's really bright and spacious and I love the curtains you made.'

'My flying bluebirds?'

'They're such a brilliant colour – almost aquamarine – and you've managed to match your seat cushions.'

'Pure luck, honestly. I don't think I'll be featuring in *House Beautiful* any time soon!' She lifted each of the saucepan lids in turn. 'Good! It looks as though the veg is on its way.'

They were halfway through the meal before Flora felt able to mention Stephen Henshall's name again.

'I know Mr Henshall is being difficult, Alice, but are you likely to get your Christmas menu?'

Alice waved a knife in the air. 'Who knows? Sally should see what nonsense he's talkin' and overrule him. It's rubbish, isn't it, Kate,' she appealed to the girl sitting opposite, 'payin' for publicity to entice more people into the hotel, then cuttin' back on what you're offerin' them? And just when the hotel's gettin' into its stride again.'

'It does seem odd,' Kate agreed in her gentle voice, loading her fork with the last of her mashed potato.

'I'm sure you'll win the argument. You'll have Sally on your side, after all.' Flora jumped up to clear the dishes and fetch dessert bowls from the top shelf of the china cupboard.

'This trifle looks luscious,' she said, delving into the larder for the pudding and bringing the dish to the table. She sank a large spoon into its depths and served each of them in turn. 'I may have some cream somewhere – though we probably don't need it.'

'I hope your menu works out, Alice, but you'll need more staff if the hotel gets a mass of Christmas bookings,' Kate said, taking her first mouthful. 'Or you'll be run off your feet.'

'Exactly. It's what I said when that Phoebe came by.'

'Phoebe Tallant?' Flora put her head round the larder door. 'Here it is.' She brought out a small cream jug.

'She's the one.' Alice's curls nodded in time with her head. 'Nice girl, beautiful, too.'

'Wasn't her sister a beauty queen?' Kate put in. 'I think I saw it in a magazine somewhere.'

'I dunno about that. I don't hold with those magazines, all gossip.'

Flora looked across at Kate and both of them were smiling. Gossip was the lifeblood of Abbeymead.

'What I did hear was that she's plannin' some kind of party for Miss Lancaster after the poor soul is burnt to a cinder. And did you hear about that? A crematorium of all places! I don't approve and I don't approve of the party. A funeral's a funeral in my book, parties are for the livin'. Anyways, the girl called in at the Priory looking for a job. But that Henshall was there, in my kitchen as usual, and said an outright no. Though what it's got to do with him, search me.'

Flora's ears pricked. 'She won't be going back to London after Miss Lancaster's funeral?'

'It doesn't seem so. She more or less said as much. She likes livin' in the village and between the three of us, I reckon she'll inherit Miss Lancaster's house, so she's a ready-made home.'

'She wanted to work in the kitchen?' Kate's forehead wore several creases. 'I thought she had a rather grand job. A personal assistant, something like that.'

'I thought that, too. But that's not the kind of job she's after. Said she thought she could help with the waitin'. No experience, mind, but she's a bright lass and she'd learn easy enough.'

Alice returned to her trifle, and it was a while before she continued. 'Thinkin' about it, we probably don't need more people in the kitchen, even if the orders increase. Young Lucy's doin' well as kitchen maid and I've Tony as my deputy, but we *will* need more waitresses for sure when the restaurant really gets goin'.'

'How is Tony?' Flora asked. These days it was unusual for her friend not to have mentioned the man who had become such a large part of her life.

Kate Mitchell's romance with the sous-chef at the Priory had taken them all by surprise. She had been a widow for less than a year and, though her husband had been a thoroughly bad person in Flora's estimation, Kate had loved him deeply, despite the way he'd treated her. The friendship with Tony Farraday had come out of the blue, but both Flora and Alice had rejoiced to see their friend looking so happy. *Fair bloomin'*, Alice had noted.

She wasn't blooming now, though, Flora thought, looking up from her pudding and catching sight of her friend's worried expression.

As though she realised she was under surveillance, Kate pasted on a smile. 'Tony's fine,' she said. 'We're off to the cinema tomorrow evening. *Giant* is on at the Dome.'

'You must tell me about it. Jack and I never got there!'

Kate opened her mouth, then closed it again. 'I heard about that,' she said at last. 'A terrible business. The poor curate.'

Her voice was jerky, but why? Flora asked herself. How strange. Aloud, she asked, 'Has something upset you, Kate? Is everything all right with Tony?'

The girl's eyes filled with tears and she put down her spoon. 'I don't know, and that's the truth. Something's really wrong, but Tony won't tell me much.'

'I've noticed he's been quiet in the kitchen these last few weeks,' Alice put in. 'I thought it was just we've been a lot busier lately and he was findin' it hard goin', this bein' his first important promotion.'

'It may be that,' Kate said a little desperately, 'but I don't think so. Something else is worrying him.'

Flora leant forward and looked fixedly at her friend. 'When did you first notice something might be wrong?'

'A month ago, maybe... It probably is work,' she mumbled hastily, 'like Alice says.'

'Nothing to do with Lyle Beaumont?'

'Why do you ask that?' Kate looked suddenly scared.

'Only that it seemed to upset you when I spoke of the curate dying.'

'Well, the poor chap had just been killed, my love,' Alice reproved.

'It's more than that, though, isn't it, Katie?' she pursued.

Her friend hung her head. 'Tony thinks he knew him before,' she muttered into her lap.

'In Dorset?'

Kate gaped. 'You know?'

'Only that the Beaumont family comes from the county. But why is it such a problem, Tony thinking he knows him from somewhere?'

Kate sat up straight, seeming determined now to tell everything she knew. 'It was when the curate called on Sally. Beaumont came to introduce himself to the Priory staff and Tony saw him from the kitchen stairs. Only very briefly, but he was sure it was him.'

Flora was puzzled. 'Well, yes, but—'

'You don't understand,' Kate said in a burst. 'The man Tony saw, the man who said he was a curate and called himself Lyle Beaumont – well, he wasn't.'

7

Flora took a long time that evening to tidy the cottage before she climbed the stairs to bed. Kate's announcement had been a bombshell falling amid the sherry trifle. It seemed that Tony Farraday knew a secret, one that might offer an explanation for the curate's death. But Tony wasn't talking, other than to confess briefly to Kate that he'd known the man purporting to be Lyle Beaumont years before. Why was Tony being so tight-lipped? And who, in fact, was the man who'd been living among them?

She'd urged Kate to try to persuade Tony to tell her more, or maybe to talk to Jack if, for any reason, he felt more comfortable disclosing to a man what he knew. If he was worrying about going to the police, he could put the visit on hold. Unburden himself to his friends first and let them decide what to do. Flora had a hunch that by now Alan Ridley must already know the identity of the dead man, but that didn't stop her wanting to know as well. And it wouldn't stop Jack either.

Brushing her teeth that night, her mind everywhere but on the toothpaste, Flora decided that if Kate failed in her persuasion, she would seek out Tony herself. Wait until he was off duty – it wouldn't do to beard him in the Priory kitchen – and ask him directly. Alice's reaction to Kate's announcement, after the first open-mouthed *Oh*, was to look worried. Bent on establishing the Priory restaurant as the best place to eat in Sussex, the last thing Alice needed was the possible involvement of her sous-chef in a criminal investigation.

The following morning, after an indifferent night's sleep, Flora was washed and dressed and eating breakfast before the kitchen clock struck seven. Charlie had used her bicycle for the Friday evening deliveries and left Betty in her shelter at the All's Well, but a walk to work in the chill of early morning would be energising. Or so she told herself. Wavering on the doorstep, she began to shiver almost immediately, and was quick to wind the long red and white scarf Alice had knitted her last Christmas tightly around her neck. It *was* very cold. A sharp frost had formed on the front grass and, once she was through her garden gate, Greenway Lane proved too slippery to walk fast. Her breath clouded the silent air as she picked her way along the lane and into the high street.

It was early enough for the village to be deserted but, turning the corner by the doctor's surgery, Flora almost cannoned into a hurrying figure. A thick-set stranger walking swiftly along the high street towards the crossroads that led to Brighton. Taken aback, she dodged to one side at the same time as the stranger took a similar avoiding action. She dodged the other way, and the stranger did the same. It could have gone on for some time if the man, pulling his hat down low over his face, hadn't strode firmly off the pavement and marched on.

Flora turned her head to watch him as he disappeared into the distance, her eyes narrowed against a cold that froze her eyelashes, then stood for a moment, too surprised to walk on. A stranger in Abbeymead was always worth notice, and one intent on escaping the village so early in the morning something of an event. The man's hat, even before he'd tugged at it, had been low on his forehead and she'd been unable to make out much of his features. A pinkish complexion, slightly fleshy cheeks and a mouth surprisingly rosebud-like. But that was all.

Shaking herself from her daydream, she covered the few steps to the All's Well in record time and, as soon as she opened its wide, white-painted door, crossed to the telephone, putting on hold her usual routine: a zigzag in and out of the angled bookshelves, a stop to stroke her favourite volumes and a few minutes to breathe in the woodiness of a shop full of books. Meeting the unknown man had disturbed her.

Strangers in Abbeymead was becoming something of a theme, and an uncomfortable one at that. An unease had begun to take root, but deliberately she forced it from her mind. Right now, there was a more important matter to deal with. She needed to telephone Jack and, by this time, he should be up and about.

He answered after about ten rings, sounding as though he'd only just tumbled out of bed. 'Have you given up banging my front door down?' he asked blearily. 'And it's torture by telephone now. I knew I shouldn't have asked to be connected.'

'Don't exaggerate. You should be awake and dressed. It's a wonderful morning.' Her still half-frozen breath caught in her throat and she couldn't prevent a cough.

'It sounds it,' he said drily. 'So... you've got me up. What is it?'

'Lyle Beaumont isn't Lyle Beaumont.'

'What?'

Flora's explanation of the extraordinary supper party she'd hosted the previous evening had Jack say immediately, 'Kate needs to get him to say more. If she can encourage him to talk, I'd like to hear it. Maybe we could ask to meet him – arrange a meal at Overlay House.'

'And if she can't?'

There was a short silence. 'I'll waylay him somehow and try my own brand of persuasion. At a time he's not working.' There was another small pause, before he said warningly, 'Don't you try.'

'Why not?'

'Subtlety, Flora, subtlety. Not your strongest suit.'

The door of the bookshop crashed open at that moment and she said hurriedly, 'I'll have to go, Jack. Come round when you can, and we'll work something out.'

'Charlie—' She turned to greet her young helper, then stopped what she was about to say. 'Whatever's the matter?'

She'd never seen Charlie Teague look so downbeat, unless it was when he'd been refused a second helping of Alice's treacle tart. The boy's face was pale and his head drooped. He seemed intent on studying the shop's polished floorboards, kicking against them with a dirty shoe.

'I'm sorry, Miss Steele,' he mumbled. 'Really sorry.'

'But why?' she asked, mystified.

'Cos of Betty.'

A small icy claw took hold of Flora's stomach. 'What's happened to my bicycle, Charlie?'

'It wuzn't my fault, honest. This bloke in a big car ran me off the road.'

'Last night?'

He nodded miserably.

'Are you OK?' The boy looked unharmed but Flora herself had experienced being run off the road and it was anything but pleasant.

'Yeah, I'm OK. My knee got cut but Mum plastered it.'

'That's a relief, but where did this happen?'

'Just past Miss Lancaster's place.'

'But you weren't delivering there.' It still upset Flora that with Miss Lancaster's passing, she'd lost one of her best customers.

'I delivered to Miss Pinner on the Green and then to someone at the Priory – the girl on the desk, I think – and I was comin' back down Fern Hill when this car overtook me so close I had to yank the wheel to one side and lost my balance and landed in the ditch.'

Flora had also landed in the ditch along Fern Hill and knew it wasn't difficult to be unseated on what was a very steep incline, particularly if the car driver was careless.

'You said it was a big car? What make?'

'I dunno. I never saw it before. It wuz black, kind of shiny. This bloke was sittin' in the back. He had a funny hat on.'

'Like Mr Carrington's?'

'Nah. Mr C looks like a cowboy. This bloke wuz a toff.' He glanced around the bookshop. 'It was like that one,' he said, pointing to a book jacket with an illustration of a fashionable couple kissing beneath lamplight.

'That's a... a homburg, I think. But this man was in the back, you say? Then who was driving?'

'Another bloke. He wuz in a kinda uniform.'

That didn't sound like anyone she knew. Or, for that matter, anyone Charlie knew. Cars were a passion for her young helper, and she'd stake her money that he knew every car and every registration plate that belonged in the village. Another unknown man, or was it the same man she'd nearly walked into this morning? She had a bad feeling about this. And a very bad feeling about Betty.

'How badly is the bicycle damaged?' she asked nervously.

'The handlebars got a bit twisted. And mebbe one of the mudguards.' He hung his head again. 'I managed to wheel her back, just about, once I'd got outta the ditch.'

'Come on, let's take a look.'

She led the way to the courtyard, feeling cross with herself that she'd been too intent on telephoning Jack this morning to check the shelter, as she usually did on a Saturday.

The bicycle was a sad spectacle, the handlebars fixed at an odd angle and a mudguard so badly dented it was cutting into the tyre. Flora gazed at Betty and Betty gazed back at her – accusingly, she thought. Charlie had loitered at the courtyard entrance and she knew he was feeling guilty. But it wasn't Charlie's fault.

'Mr Worthington can put her to rights,' she said, resigned to paying for repairs.

Michael Worthington was the village's jack-of-all-trades and what would she do without him? What would they all do?

Nearing lunchtime, a lull in customers allowed Flora to close the shop a trifle early and pay a visit to the Nook where Kate was serving the midday meal. The café was busy, nearly every table occupied, the blue gingham cloths and matching napkins an invitation to passers-by to come and eat. Flora nodded an acknowledgement to the several Abbeymead inhabitants she recognised but waited at the counter for Kate to finish delivering plates of sausage, egg and chips to a table of visitors.

Looking into the kitchen beyond, she saw Tony Farraday's face. Her eyebrows rose slightly.

'You've Tony helping you today,' she remarked to Kate when her friend returned with an empty tray.

'He called in earlier and saw I needed a hand. Ivy has caught a bad cold and taken to her bed. It's lucky for me that Tony has the whole weekend off.'

'And?' Flora asked, nodding meaningfully in the sous-chef's direction. 'Did you manage to persuade him?'

Kate gave a tentative smile. 'It's good news, I think. Since that business at the bell tower, Tony seems to have had a change of mind. He says he's happy to talk to you, if you want.'

'How about we meet at Overlay House tomorrow? About midday – you could come for lunch – a snack lunch, if that would work best.'

Kate looked concerned. 'Tomorrow is Sunday. Will Jack be happy with that?'

'Jack will be happy,' Flora said with certainty.

Walking back to the All's Well, a carton of soup in one hand and a slice of rhubarb tart in the other, she felt a stir of excitement. This could be the first step in what promised to be an interesting investigation. At the moment, the picture was blurred, very blurred. Nothing seemed to be what, at first sight, it appeared. Beaumont wasn't Beaumont. Henshall's financial problems hardly made him the guru he was said to be. Even Miss Lancaster's funeral was raising questions. According to Abbeymead gossip, the special send-off Phoebe Tallant was organising for her godmother would be like no funeral the village had ever seen.

Unlocking the cottage door and taking her purchases through to the kitchen, Flora refused to be downhearted. Every investigation started hazy and unclear. Every mystery at first seemed impenetrable. Tony's secret might amount to little, but at the very least it was something solid to cling to.

8

Flora decided on a picnic for the meeting at Overlay House. It seemed the simplest solution at such short notice and, commandeering Jack's kitchen the next morning, she unpacked the basket she'd brought from home – sausage rolls and mince pies she'd baked earlier that morning – and proceeded to make a large plate of cheese and pickle sandwiches. She was emptying the several packets of crisps she'd found in Jack's store cupboard when he walked in from the sitting room where he'd been lurking for the last half hour.

'I have tomatoes,' he announced, retrieving a small basket from his larder.

'Are they from your greenhouse?'

'They are and still very tasty. I picked the last of them only a few days ago. I'll give them a quick splash.'

On the surface, a picnic in mid-November was an odd choice, but Flora reckoned that its very informality – a blanket spread on Jack's sitting room floor with several large cushions as seats – would help the conversation along. It was plain from Tony's earlier reluctance to talk to Kate that it might need helping along.

'Despite the mince pies, it doesn't feel much like Christmas is coming, does it?' Jack piled his washed tomatoes into a glass dish. 'Having a picnic makes it seem even less.'

'I know, and I'm not sure why. The village normally starts buzzing around this time of the year, but there's none of the usual excitement, no real build-up yet to Christmas week. Maybe it's because the church is involved in so many of the celebrations and Reverend Hopkirk has been unwell for a long time.'

Flora surveyed the spread of food with satisfaction. 'That should feed us.'

'I imagine the vicar hoped the new curate would do his bit. Shoulder some of the responsibilities.'

'He should have done,' she agreed. 'He should have been in the thick of festivities.'

Flora had tried to get into the spirit of things, despite the general malaise hanging over Abbeymead. Mr Houseman would be giving her a Christmas tree, she knew, a present for the little girl he'd once given apples, and she had already unearthed from the outhouse cupboard the bag of decorations she had known most of her life. Decorations that Aunt Violet had brought from London all those years ago, many of them hand-made but now sadly worn. From lack of money, they had never been replaced: brightly coloured cloth hearts, balls made from knitting wool, cut out paper trees, several hand-carved small wooden donkeys – she'd always wondered who'd had the skill to carve them – and a collection of shop-bought baubles that definitely looked the worse for wear. She would use them again, she promised herself. The weekend after next, she would decorate the tree and begin pasting paper chains to hang in the cottage.

As for presents, she had been learning to patchwork since she'd got back from Cornwall and had already sewn two new cushion covers for Alice. She was rather proud of them. And for

Kate, she would splash out on a perfume she'd seen in a Brighton pharmacy when she'd visited the town last month. Charlie would almost certainly be happy with a gift of money and Jack? She was still puzzling over what to give Jack.

When she walked into the sitting room, it was to find that he'd already organised the room for the coming picnic.

'You've been busy when I thought you were simply lurking,' she teased, when he joined her.

'How could you think it? I've chosen the best blanket I could find. A Dutch blanket, I think it's called. Will it work, do you think?' He pointed to the large multicoloured square of wool spread across his sitting room floor, surrounded by cushions of various shapes and sizes.

'I'm not entirely sure,' she said honestly. 'But it has to be better than a sit-down roast. Tony will have had enough of those all week. A picnic is sort of...'

'Distinctive?'

'If you like.' She caught hold of his hand, an earnest expression on her face. 'It's important we get him to talk, Jack.'

He smiled down at her, then encircled her in his arms and held her close. 'There you go again, caring too much. I'm pretty sure Ridley will have worked out Beaumont's true identity.'

'I'm sure, too, and if he hasn't, he will very shortly. But he doesn't understand Abbeymead as I do. Knowing a name isn't going to be enough. We need to learn more about this man and the inspector will find questioning the villagers hard going. Lyle Beaumont was our curate, after all, even if only for a short time. And that commands respect and a certain amount of reticence.'

'A false curate, though.'

'OK, but people won't like what happened to him, and they particularly won't like the suggestion that Ridley seems intent on pursuing, that one of the bell-ringers could be responsible. The villagers will close ranks and then where will he be? So... if we can help a little... and remember, he did invite our involvement this autumn when Sally was in trouble.'

Jack nodded. 'We can try. But the false identity is likely to make it more difficult. We'll have to work hard.'

She loosened herself from his hold. 'You're mellowing, Jack! Be careful!'

He grimaced slightly. 'Rather than mellowing, it's more likely boredom. I finished editing the new Carrington thriller this morning – finally, at a minute past midnight! And once I've posted the book to my agent, I'll be an idle pair of hands.'

'That's splendid news. On both counts. Let's hope Arthur comes back to you soon.'

'Right now, I want to forget writing. While I wait for his yea or nay, I'd rather—' he began to say, when the sound of the front door knocker echoed through the hall and floated into the sitting room, '—find a distraction,' he finished, walking towards the front door.

Kate had worn her best blue winter dress and Flora scolded herself that she hadn't had the forethought to warn the girl that a fitted skirt might not be the best for a picnic, but her friend managed to sink onto a cushion with creditable grace, saying, 'What a brilliant idea to eat like this! Don't you think so, Tony?'

Tony merely smiled and, apart from an initial greeting, said little. He was taking his time to unwind, Flora could see, watching as the cheese sandwiches gradually disappeared, followed by most of the sausage rolls and a bottle of elderflower wine. The conversation was irritatingly general but, when she returned from the kitchen with a tray of tea to accompany the mince pies, it appeared that Tony was at last ready to talk. It seemed he'd needed a full stomach to confide what he knew.

'His name isn't Lyle, it's Hugo,' Tony announced. 'Hugo Rafferty. He's Lyle Beaumont's cousin. I worked in the kitchens at Beaumont Park for around five years and got to know them both.' He delved into his trouser pocket and brought out a crumpled picture. 'This is an old photograph I found. It was taken on some saint's day or other – they were big on saints' days, the Beaumonts. We had to cook a special meal for each one. There was one lunch where someone, the butler, I think, took a photograph of the family sitting round the table, getting ready to eat, with us cooking staff standing behind. This is Hugo.' He tapped the image. 'He was two years younger than his cousin but, as you can see, he looks very much like him.'

The photograph was handed around the group and Flora saw immediately the resemblance Tony had referred to. The two boys, as they were then, could almost have been twins.

'They look to be good friends,' she said, gazing again at their interlocking arms. 'Were they?'

'They seemed so. At least, to me. I only knew them as youngsters, of course, and I didn't see much of them growing up – they were at boarding school, the same boarding school – and away a lot of the time. I believe they went on to the same university, too.'

'Rafferty,' Jack said thoughtfully. 'He must be a sister's child.'

Tony nodded. 'Hugo's mother is old Beaumont's younger sister. The rumour at the Park was that she'd married badly, or so the family thought.'

'With that name, an Irishman?'

Tony nodded again. 'And a Catholic.'

'Presumably you didn't know Mr Rafferty senior?' Flora asked. The idea of a Catholic Irishman marrying into a staunchly English Protestant family was an intriguing one.

'He'd died before I took up the job and he was never mentioned by the family. Several of the older staff knew him and seemed to have liked him. Hugo's widowed mother kept a low profile. I hardly ever saw her when I worked there. She still lives on the Beaumont estate – my mother cleans for her.'

Kate turned to him, her pale blue eyes concerned. 'If the family didn't like his father, did they like Hugo?'

Tony pursed his mouth. 'I'd say so. Maybe they had reservations, his father being someone they hadn't approved of, but I never saw any sign that they didn't like him. As I said, he and Lyle were best buddies.'

'Sorry for all these questions, Tony,' Flora said, 'but what was Hugo like as a person? I know you only knew him as a boy but...'

He took some time to answer. 'Different from Lyle, that's for sure,' he said at last. 'He might look like him, but he was a whole different character. They shared some things – they were both clever – but Hugo's cleverness wasn't exactly... scholarly, if you know what I mean. It was a cleverness that helped him use others. A bit of a manipulator, I'd say.'

'In what way?' Flora was intrigued, absent-mindedly pouring everyone a second cup of tea without asking.

Tony's worry lines deepened. 'I got the impression he was careless with people, and his moral sense – well, it was pretty loose, to be honest. Mind you, he was a lot more fun to be with than Lyle. Lyle could be miserably strait-laced while Hugo was a cheery chap. More approachable, just easier to get on with.'

'It's maybe why he was able to deceive someone like Reverend Hopkirk. And be happy to do it.'

'I suppose. He was certainly happy to spend money he didn't have,' Tony said wryly. 'Even as a kid, he was in and out of trouble over money, though none of us were supposed to know.'

Flora wrinkled her nose. 'It's strange then that he and Lyle were such good friends.'

'I guess as children their differences weren't too evident. That kind of thing becomes more obvious when you grow up. But for all his carelessness, Hugo worshipped his cousin and always wanted to be with him. He seems to have made sure he went to the same university as well as the same school.'

'And after that?' Flora pursued.

'I heard, but it's only hearsay, that he decided to keep following in Lyle's footsteps. This time, it was to join a seminary. I imagine the Beaumonts would have been delighted at the news. Two boys from the same family, both in the Church.'

'Hugo seems particularly ill-suited to have become a vicar,' Jack put in.

Tony considered the remark, a serious expression on his face. 'I think that soon became clear. Something else I heard when I went back to visit old friends at the Park. Apparently, Hugo started breaking rules as soon as he arrived at the seminary. The authorities put up with him for a while – trying to lead the straying sheep back to the path of righteousness, I guess. Eventually, though, they must have had enough, and he was asked to leave.'

Tony gave a sudden grin, lightening his whole face and making Flora appreciate why Kate had fallen so thoroughly for the man. 'If he'd asked any of us, we could have told him the Church was definitely not the right choice!'

'Hugo must have known he wasn't suited,' Flora said, when their guests had left and she and Jack were speeding through the washing up. 'He must have known the Church was the last place he'd fit in. So why go back to it as an illegitimate curate? He could never have been ordained.' She paused, her hands dunking the large glass bowl in soapy water. 'Why decide to come to Abbeymead and pretend to be his cousin?'

'That's the question, isn't it? Did he regret being asked to leave the seminary?' Jack stacked the last of the plates neatly in the drying rack. 'Or was he at a loose end and thought he'd give the Church another try without the bother of passing exams?'

'If so, it was a relatively innocent charade. A piece of whimsy. But the fact that Rafferty is dead suggests that innocence is unlikely. Something much darker than whimsy must have driven the man to come here, driven him to assume a false name and a false personality.'

'Perhaps he was trying to escape that dark something.' Jack hung up the kitchen towel and turned to her. 'But what, exactly?'

She spread her hands wide, unable to answer, and was silent for a moment. 'You know what the other question is? One that could be more important.'

'No, but you're about to tell me, aren't you?'

'If Rafferty is dead, what's happened to the real Lyle Beaumont?'

9

Their only hope of discovering the whereabouts of the real Lyle Beaumont, Jack decided, was to start at the beginning and trace the man back to his home. Since the first mention of Dorset, the idea of a trip had been at the back of his mind. It was a county that Flora had never visited, and he knew she would love its rolling downland and stunning seascape.

Now seemed perfect timing, a short holiday for them both before Christmas was on their doorstep and, for once, the opportunity of spending time together, far from Abbeymead's interested eyes and wagging tongues. Thinking it over, he realised how little chance they'd had to be on their own since that meal at the Priory. People seemed always to be close by, popping up unexpectedly, joining their conversation – a customer wanting Flora's advice, Alice bringing news from the village or Kate bearing a plate of pastries. Even Charlie wanting to know what other jobs he could do to earn money.

The Priory dinner had proved a turning point, the moment when they'd stopped pretending to each other that they were 'just' friends, 'just' trustworthy partners in whatever adventure came their way and, for the first time, admitted to feelings that ran a great deal deeper. He'd kissed Flora and she'd kissed him back, then he'd kissed her again, and they'd both decided that they really rather liked it.

Walking from Overlay House to the post office this morning, a precious brown paper parcel tucked beneath his arm, he thought through how best to plan the trip – even how best to get Flora to agree to it. The post office was very busy when he arrived and, plainly, he should have factored a queue into his day. It was Monday and it seemed the inhabitants of Abbeymead must spend most of their weekend writing letters, composing telegrams or, like him, doing up parcels. The brown paper crackled as he clutched the package to his chest.

Murder in Mantova would soon be on its way to Arthur Bellaby and Jack could only cross his fingers very tightly and wish the book a successful journey. Arthur's reaction mattered, and mattered hugely. The novel had been a long time in gestation, gradually coming together after months of despair. Once the book was posted, though, he'd put it out of his mind. That way, he could pretend to himself that his entire future was not dependent on his agent's approval.

Waiting patiently in the line of customers, he only slowly realised that Phoebe Tallant was the villager standing immediately in front of him. He wondered if he should attempt to make conversation – you never could tell what information you might learn by simply talking to people – but, before he could work out how to introduce himself, Phoebe had reached the counter and was talking to a harassed-looking Dilys, who this morning lacked her usual part-time help.

'You asked me to call?' Phoebe began, her tone verging on the peremptory.

Jack was all attention. How many people were ever asked to call at the post office? When she wasn't knitting eccentric jumpers, Dilys spent most of her time dissuading people *from* calling.

The postmistress looked stern. It was evident she hadn't appreciated the girl's abruptness and Jack suspected that, for the moment, she was struggling to recall just why Miss Tallant was at her counter.

'Ah, yes.' Dilys blinked rapidly. 'There was a man trying to get in touch with you – wanted to know where you lived. I wasn't going to say straight off. I didn't know the chap, never seen him in the village before. But I did promise I'd give you this, whenever I saw you.'

She delved beneath the counter and brought out an envelope. Jack craned his neck and saw Phoebe's name on the front in flowing black characters.

'Right, thank you.' Phoebe took the envelope and turned to go. Then half turned back. 'Thank you for not passing on my address.'

'All part of the service,' Dilys said, her lips pursed.

'Honestly,' she muttered to Jack, when the girl had shut the shop door behind her, 'the things I get dragged into.'

'It sounded interesting.' Jack was fishing. 'Did you discover what it was about?' This might take some time and it was lucky he was last in the queue.

Dilys leaned forward, the lime-green bouclé cardigan she'd chosen that day flashing bright before Jack's eyes. 'I didn't say just now – that girl's a little too hoity-toity – but the chap told me, didn't he? No big mystery, though from the way she behaved, you'd think it was a state secret. Right little Mata Hari. Anyways, this chap was offering her a job and it sounded important. He'd lost her details, he said, except he knew she was living somewhere in Abbeymead, so he'd come down – I think he said from London – to find her.'

'He must want to employ her badly,' Jack said. 'To go to all that trouble.'

'That's what I thought.' Dilys sucked in her mouth. 'I did hear as she was a model in London, before she came to the village to look after Miss Lancaster. You'd think the girl would be glad to be asked back. Probably could name her price, too. But it seems like she's not interested. Strange, don't you think? Why would a young girl turn down that kind of chance?'

'Maybe she's still very upset over her godmother's death and doesn't feel ready to take on a new job. It would mean a move back to the city, wouldn't it? Perhaps she doesn't want the stress.'

'Mebbe. But, there again, mebbe it's because she's no need to move away. She's got a cushy number living in that house. It belonged to the old lady, you know, it wasn't rented.'

'Houses still need money to maintain them, more so if they're your own. Miss Tallant will need a job eventually.'

Dilys leaned even further forward. 'I did hear say that she tried to get one at the hotel. As a waitress! Why would you want to be a waitress when you can be someone special?'

Jack knew from Flora that Phoebe Tallant had called at the Priory looking for work, but he made no comment. 'I daresay she'll feel more settled after the funeral,' was all he said.

'And about that!' Dilys drew herself up to her full height, sitting erect on her stool and pulling the bouclé cardigan fiercely into place. 'It's not at St Saviour's. Can you believe that? Not in the village at all. Some outlandish place up-country.' She lowered her voice. 'A crematorium,' she breathed. 'Doesn't want a lot of fuss, that's what she said, but what kind of fuss is there at St Saviour's? It's a strange business, Mr Carrington. And a strange girl, if you ask me.'

She pointed to the parcel Jack was carrying. 'That's going to cost you a fair bit. Give it over and I'll tell you the damage.'

10

Flora, too, had seen a trip to Dorset as the obvious next step in tracking down the real Lyle Beaumont. If he hadn't taken up the post of curate at St Saviour's, what *had* he been doing, and where? Had he retreated to Beaumont Park, either because he'd made some kind of arrangement with Hugo Rafferty, or had felt threatened by him and gone into hiding? Beaumont Park and the village of Whitbury were clearly important, but she'd assumed that Jack would go there alone. Now that he'd finished the book, and she knew what a struggle it had been, he was a free man. *An idle pair of hands*, he'd said, while she had the All's Well to manage. Expecting to wave goodbye to the small red Austin later that week, she'd been taken by surprise when Jack had called at the shop and suggested she travel to Dorset with him.

'I can't come for days,' she prevaricated, unsure how she wanted to answer. 'I've a heap of parcels to pack up and post.' She gestured towards the stairs leading down to the cellar where she kept customers' orders ready for despatch or collection. 'And there's a new delivery arriving Thursday afternoon that will need unpacking and putting on display. Charlie is coming by after school to help me.'

'That's fine,' he said easily, leaning against a neighbouring bookshelf. 'We can leave Friday morning and make it a long weekend – if you're willing to shut up shop for a few days.'

'Friday is days away. You don't think the trip is more urgent?' Did she want to do this? she was asking herself. 'You could always go alone and leave earlier.'

'I could, but I've no wish to.'

He looked at her directly, his grey eyes dark, challenging her, it seemed, to come up with yet another excuse.

'I'll close on Friday then,' she said, uncertainly.

Jack's response was a warm smile, his changeable eyes almost silver in the winter light streaming through the bookshop's latticed windows.

It was Friday afternoon and now that she was approaching Lyme Regis, Flora was glad she'd come. She still wasn't sure why initially she'd dragged her feet. These days, she and Jack were closer than they'd ever been, but something had made her hang back. Abbeymead was a small community and perhaps it was the passionate interest with which the smallest details of everyone's life were picked over that had made her baulk at a journey that felt too close to making a commitment. Far too many people had shown themselves interested in the Jack and Flora show, watching them closely, exchanging gossip no doubt, concocting a romance that fitted their idea of one.

Flora wasn't at all sure it was a romance – they were affectionate together, caring of each other, and she didn't want to think of her life without Jack. But romance? What did that actually signify? They had kissed and meant it, but neither of them seemed certain of the future or of where they were headed.

Jack had telephoned the hotel he'd found in an old tourist

guide buried deep in his office. It dated from the time he'd been roaming the Home Counties and beyond, looking for a permanent home after the debacle of his failed wedding to Helen Milsom. The guide was years old but the inn it had featured was still welcoming guests and he'd immediately booked two single rooms. Since the AA route he'd requested showed Beaumont Park lying just outside the village of Whitbury, a few miles inland, the Pilot Boat at Lyme Regis would serve them well.

Winding down the steep road into the small town, Flora settled to enjoy the magnificent view opening before her. The sea on this still November day was a sheet of cold blue, spread between deep green headlands that stood tall and proud on either side of the bay. A pale, almost luminous sky arched above.

For a moment, as Jack swept around a final bend, the engine strained and she cast a nervous glance at her companion. 'I hope the car will make it to Whitbury tomorrow,' she dared to say.

'Why wouldn't it?' Jack was inordinately defensive of his beloved Austin.

'It doesn't sound too happy right now, does it? And we'll be doing this journey in reverse. Up a very steep hill.'

A worrying image of gears slipping and an engine belching steam, even catching fire, danced in her head.

'Relax. The car won't let us down.'

It hadn't so far, Flora had to concede, but then they'd never actually set it a mountain to climb.

If the car was doubtful, the hotel certainly wasn't. As they rolled to a stop outside, she was enchanted by the sight of whitewashed walls and blue shutters and a building that filled an entire corner plot.

'It's old,' she exclaimed. 'Really old. Regency!'

'It can have been built by the Vikings as long as there's hot water on tap and a decent breakfast.'

Jack might sound a trifle grumpy – she suspected his arm was paining him – but Flora was delighted. And delighted, too, when she was shown to her room on the highest floor and discovered it offered a south-facing view over the unspoilt seafront and, beyond, a sand and pebble beach.

From the corner of her window, she caught a glimpse of the Cobb, a Dorset icon that she'd only ever seen in photographs. Seven hundred years old and still stretching its tilted, uneven stone into the English Channel. Holding her head at an angle, she was able to make out several tiny stick-like figures taking their afternoon constitutional and, for a moment, felt a compulsion to rush down the stairs and drag Jack from his room to join them. But it had been a long drive with only a brief stop for a sandwich and a cup of tea, and he would be tired. Most of the time the wound he'd sustained fighting across France gave him little trouble, but lengthy car journeys were an exception.

When she eventually knocked on his door, he surprised her. 'I've been waiting for you,' he said, a broad smile on his face. 'Did you have a snooze?'

Flora was starting to mount an indignant protest when he cut her short. 'How about a walk? I'm looking forward to exploring Lyme's most famous landmark.'

'Me, too. A sedate saunter, I think. No doing a Louisa Musgrove.'

He looked puzzled.

'Surely, you remember? *Persuasion.* Jane Austen's characters come to Lyme Regis and Louisa is foolish enough to jump from the Cobb, hits her head, and nearly dies.'

'I'll try to restrain myself. I have to admit I can barely remember the book – you must enlighten me as we go.'

Half an hour later they were on the promenade, carving a pathway through pebbles that recent storms had thrown up from the beach.

'I'm sure this was where Captain Benwick lived,' Flora said, stopping to gaze admiringly at the row of white cottages. 'He was one of the minor characters but still a kind of hero. Quiet and soulful,' she added, taking Jack at his word. 'In fact, look!' She pointed to a blue-painted door. 'This one is called Benwick Cottage.'

'Are we doing the whole of *Persuasion*?'

'No, of course not, but I do find it thrilling to be walking in Jane Austen's footsteps.'

'Thrilling and a touch dangerous, as you suggested,' he commented, once they had walked a short way along the Cobb, the tilt on the harbour wall already uncomfortably steep as it leaned towards the sea. 'It's a good job it hasn't rained for days. If it was wet underfoot, this surface would be lethal. Even worse if it froze.'

By dint of hanging tight to each other, particularly when a sharp offshore breeze buffeted them suddenly, they made it safely to the very tip of the wall and stood for some while looking out on the English Channel, its calm now punctuated by the white riff of incoming waves.

It didn't take long for Flora to feel the cold creeping steadily upwards, icing first her feet and then her legs. She squeezed his arm. 'This has been fun, Jack, but I'm perished. Let's go back to the hotel – there's some wonderfully comfortable chairs in the sitting room and a fabulous log fire. Maybe one in the dining room, too.'

When they walked down the stairs a few hours later, however, there was no sign of a fire in the inn's restaurant, yet the room wrapped them in its warmth. In one corner, an early Christmas tree blazed with lights, throwing out sufficient heat, Flora thought, to roast a joint. Gazing around, she experienced a bubble of happiness. A riot of paper chains criss-crossed the ceiling and sprigs of holly and mistletoe decorated every picture rail.

'This feels much more like Christmas,' she said, smiling at him across the window table they'd been given.

Long velvet curtains of deep green had been pulled against the icy weather beyond and the candles burning bright on each table gave the room a celebratory ring. Thank goodness she'd brought her one posh frock with her; the buttery cream crêpe she'd worn for that fateful dinner at the Priory. Jack, she noticed, was wearing the same dark grey suit he'd had on then. Best not to think about that, she scolded herself. They were in Lyme Regis to do a job. They were here to investigate.

'So,' he said, taking a spoonful of vegetable soup, 'how do we play tomorrow?'

Flora spread her napkin carefully over her lap. Soup and cream-coloured crêpe were not happy bedfellows. 'We start by going to Beaumont Park, I guess.'

'Do we knock on the front door?'

'Tut-tut, Jack. We present ourselves at the servants' entrance, naturally!'

'Or... how about we wander round the village first and talk to people? It may be a better option. If this village, hamlet – Whitbury – is anything like Abbeymead, everyone will know Lyle Beaumont and know where he is.'

'If it's anything like Abbeymead, no one will tell us a thing.'

Jack put down his soup spoon. 'I thought it might be helpful to get a feel of the place before we take the plunge and tackle the Beaumonts of Beaumont Park, but you know best how villages work.'

She laughed aloud. 'How grand that sounds. The Steeles of Abbeymead doesn't have half as good a ring.'

'Neither does the Carringtons of Abbeymead, though my mother would love the title.'

Jack rarely mentioned either of his parents and his mother, in particular, had been absent from any conversation Flora had shared with him.

'Why so?' She wanted to know more.

'I guess because she was always the most fearful snob.' There was a sigh in his voice when he said it.

The waiter interrupted their conversation at that moment, removing soup bowls and serving them a whole fried plaice each, along with fried potatoes, peas and green beans.

'Tartare sauce?' Jack passed her the small cut-glass sauce boat.

'Perfect. Mmm. This fish is scrumptious. Is she still, do you think?' she asked, returning to Jack's mother. 'A fearful snob?'

'I have no idea. I haven't spoken to her for at least six years. Not after I was bombarded by recriminations over the wedding that never was. Forced to listen to how she'd warned me that marrying an *American*, emphasised – the fact that Helen was a Canadian completely passed her by – would always end in disaster.'

'Do you even know where she is?'

'My mother?'

'Yes, of course your mother. Who else are we talking about?'

'I don't know why we're talking about her at all and no, I haven't a clue where she is.'

'Do you think your father knows?'

'Why would he? They're divorced. Two separate people going their two separate ways.'

'But still… not that I know anything about divorced people,' she said hastily. 'Until your father came down to Cornwall, I don't think I've ever met anyone who'd been divorced.'

'That I can understand. Just think of the scandal there'd be in Abbeymead!' He pulled a face. 'There was enough of a kick-up when Evelyn Barnes threatened to get rid of poor old Harry.'

'Poor old Harry deserved it.'

'Let's not get into that. It's old history, like my dad is old history. Though, thinking about it, he's someone who probably does know the Beaumonts of Beaumont Park. He tends to collect people who offer him a free stay.'

'You're too harsh, Jack,' she remonstrated. 'Be glad that you have your parents.'

Flora's were lost to her, their lives and deaths shrouded in mystery. They were buried in Highgate Cemetery, her Aunt Violet had told her, at the same time making clear that was all she was going to say, and the subject was closed. Flora had never had the courage to go to the cemetery and look for their graves, to lay flowers as she'd seen other people do. *Was* it lack of courage, or rather sensitivity to her aunt's feelings? Violet had been happy to discuss the most esoteric of subjects, but reluctant to talk about her family.

Flora had asked, of course she had – a child has the need to know – but her aunt inevitably deflected her questions and, in the end, she had given up asking, realising that Violet must feel too upset over her brother's death to speak of him or his wife.

'Back to the Beaumonts,' she said briskly, coming out of her meditation. 'I think, after all, the village church might be the best place to start. The real Lyle *was* a curate, wasn't he, and properly qualified, so he's bound to have had dealings with his local church.'

'No dessert for me, thank you,' she said to the waiter who'd appeared at her elbow and was waving a fresh menu card at her.

'Nor for me,' Jack told him, attempting to stretch his legs beneath the table. 'That was an excellent meal.'

The waiter had disappeared into the kitchens beyond and a satisfied silence ensued, before Jack asked tentatively, 'Would you mind if I had an early night?'

She saw then that, regardless of the room's cosiness, a tell-tale pallor had crept into Jack's cheeks while they'd been eating. It was plain the journey had aggravated the wound in his arm and she was quick to agree.

'I can see you to your room,' he said, half-jokingly, as they stopped outside his door. 'There could be a Regency ghost hiding in the eaves.'

Flora grinned. 'I think it's unlikely, and I don't think I'll meet the mad axe man on the stairs either. Let's say good night here.'

He bent to kiss her on her cheek but instead she put her hand around his neck and pulled him closer, landing a full kiss on his lips. His response was immediate and it was only Flora edging away that disentangled them. Perhaps it was romance after all, she thought, walking up the final flight of stairs to her attic bedroom.

11

At breakfast the next morning, she was glad to see Jack looking a good deal perkier than he had last night, his appetite for a full English breakfast suggesting he was fully recovered from the journey. Flora felt fidgety and ready to leave, a bowl of cereal sufficient, but she sat on her hands and tried to be patient while he munched his way through sausages, bacon and egg, followed by toast and marmalade and a pot of tea.

'I needed that,' he declared, taking a final sip and pushing back his chair. 'I haven't made us late, have I?'

Flora shook her head, trying to look as though she meant it. 'We have all day, and it won't take long to get to this village, will it?' she asked hopefully.

'It shouldn't do. Why don't you fetch your coat while I check the car?'

The mention of the Austin lowered her spirits somewhat – her mind's picture of the brutal incline that lay ahead was vivid. In the event, the small saloon chugged slowly upwards without a problem, emerging at the top of the hill with a breezy spurt of speed. Flora let go of the breath she'd been holding.

'I'll take a chance and follow the road to Dorchester.' Jack squinted at the signpost they were passing. 'I *think* we'll find Whitbury is somewhere along that route. Unfortunately, it's not marked on any of the maps I've seen.'

It might not have been marked but the hamlet they drove into – Jack had guessed correctly – was as beautifully kept as it was small. The cottages lining the village green were immaculate, their gardens, even in winter, studies in neatness. The one shop had been newly painted and a lone pub on the outskirts had washed its forecourt that very morning, the coloured gravel glinting in a feeble sun. But it was the church, situated at the north corner of the green, that dominated the scene.

'Saxon,' Flora decided, absorbing the tower's delicate lineaments.

'Like St Saviour's?'

She shook her head. Jack had little idea of architecture. 'St Saviour's tower is Norman. Square and crenellated, and quite martial.'

'As far as I'm concerned, a church is a church,' he retorted, parking the car close by.

Together they walked diagonally across the green, reaching the church door as the clock above struck eleven. Unusually, the iron-girded church door was locked.

'Don't say they have thieves in this toy settlement.'

'Why toy?' he asked.

'It doesn't seem quite real, does it? Everything seems just a little too perfect.'

Jack stared at the closed door. 'Not that perfect, if they lock the church door. But I get what you mean.' He turned around, his gaze taking in the pristine sweep of cottages. 'I wonder if Beaumont Park boasts the same flawlessness.'

'Bound to. Perhaps we should have gone there first – *their* door might be open.'

She had begun to walk back to the lych gate that led onto

the green, when Jack caught her lightly by the arm. 'Before we go, let's look round the churchyard.'

'Why would we do that?'

'I like churchyards and, you never know, it might give us more of a sense of the village.'

Flora put her head on one side and thought about it. 'I like churchyards, too, and I suppose it's still quite early. At this hour, the Beaumonts of Beaumont Park will hardly have staggered from their beds!'

Following the brick path that circled the church, they branched off here and there, making inroads into the long grass to study the most interesting of the gravestones.

'Lucy Biggs, Rodney Palmer, Thomas Holland – and I like this name, Amelia Bushrod.'

'Are you collecting them?' she asked, half kneeling to scrape away the lichen on Amelia's stone.

'It's good for a writer to have a store of names, particularly those belonging to dead people. They're most unlikely to sue!'

He walked ahead, while Flora lingered over a grave garlanded with a beautiful posy of hellebores.

'There's a fairly recent one here,' he called to her, bending down to read the inscription.

When he straightened up, she saw his expression – wondering, shocked even, as though grappling with a sudden revelation.

'Well, what is it?'

'Well, indeed.' He turned to her. 'I think we've found Lyle.'

Flora hurried towards him. 'He's dead?' She sounded disbelieving.

'If he isn't, that's a very expensive gravestone going to waste.'

Astonished, she bent to read the salutation, its gold lettering carved into shining black marble.

*Lyle Beaumont, beloved younger son of Lilian and
Gervase Beaumont, brother of Gareth and servant of God
Rest in His care
August 1927–July 1956*

'He died this summer,' Flora said thoughtfully. 'Two months before Hugo Rafferty came to Abbeymead. Hugo must have known. He must have gone to his funeral.'

'He knew all right.' The voice coming from close behind was harsh, a note of threat surfacing in the cold, soundless air.

Jack made a grab for her hand and together they turned as one. She gave a gasp. A man stood inches away, glowering at them, and it was a man she knew. Without his hat pulled low, she could see his hair, a kind of muddy blond, and eyes of an unusual brown, but the pinkish complexion, the fleshy cheeks, the rosebud mouth, were familiar. This was the stranger with whom she'd come face-to-face that early morning in Abbeymead.

Tense seconds ensued until the man said, 'I'm Gareth Beaumont. Lyle's elder brother. What precisely is your interest in him?'

'We've no interest in your brother,' Flora said sharply. She'd hated the man's arrogant tone. 'We're investigating the person who took his identity, Hugo Rafferty.'

'That creature!' His small mouth tightened in derision. 'A disgrace to the family and a permanent millstone around my poor brother's neck.'

'In what way?' Jack asked calmly, releasing his tight grip on Flora's hand.

'Rafferty was rotten through and through. Rotten from childhood. Lyle could never see it. Always defended him, no matter what, even when Rafferty landed him in scrape after scrape. That wretch made Lyle's schooldays a misery – a school which, by the way, my father in his stupidity actually funded. What a recompense!'

'Your brother must have seen some good in his cousin.' Jack was encouraging the man to talk, Flora could see. There were some murky relationships here and the more they could learn of them, the better.

'Good! You think Hugo Rafferty had an inch of good in him! Lyle did all he could to save his cousin, to put him on the road to righteousness, and what was his reward? Nothing but ingratitude and pain. From infancy, my brother lived by the Bible. He was a God-fearing child and grew into a God-fearing man. But Rafferty. Well, what do you expect from a man whose father was Irish? *And* a Catholic,' he added bitterly.

'Hugo's father was a problem for your family?'

Gareth Beaumont kicked a stray stone into the long grass. 'No,' he admitted. 'We were lucky. He died prematurely.'

'And your brother, too, it seems.' Flora found it difficult to feel sympathy for a man who so repulsed her. 'He died very young.'

'Twenty-eight.' Gareth Beaumont's teeth bit into his lips. 'Lyle had the makings of a wonderful churchman. He would have brought honour to our family.'

He bent towards his brother's grave, both hands pulling at a tuft of grass. 'We knew him to be frail,' he murmured, straightening up. 'Since childhood, he was rarely well. An endless circle of colds, influenza, bouts of bronchitis. We prayed for him, time and again we prayed for him, but when the pneumonia struck for the second time, it was not to be. We buried him quietly, a family funeral, as he would have wished.'

His thick-set body slumped against an ivy-covered gravestone.

There was a long silence, Flora unsure how best to question a man so ravaged by unhappiness. She glanced sideways at Jack, hoping for inspiration, but, before he could say anything, Beaumont burst out, 'Can you imagine, even after Lyle's death, that man dared to abuse him and refused to grant us peace.'

'That man was *your* cousin, too,' Jack reminded him. 'And *he* died young as well.'

'Not young enough, more's the pity.'

Surely he would know by now the manner of his cousin's death and express some misgiving, Flora thought. But no. Gareth Beaumont was a vessel filled to the top with bitterness, unable to view Hugo with anything but hate. It was unlikely they would learn more of Rafferty from him, but there was one mystery that she might uncover.

'I think I saw you in Abbeymead last weekend,' she said quietly.

At this, Jack took a step back and half turned to her, a look of surprise on his face. Flora had never mentioned meeting a stranger the morning after Kate dropped her bombshell. She had been too intent on reaching the All's Well to telephone Jack with the news – that the curate was not who'd they'd thought him – and, afterwards, the mystery man had fled her mind completely.

'Yes, you probably did,' Gareth Beaumont admitted grudgingly.

'I was the girl you almost cannoned into at the end of the high street.'

'Right.' He nodded. 'I was on my way back to my car.'

'Why were you in our village?' Jack sounded slightly annoyed.

Was it because she hadn't mentioned the incident to him, or because Gareth Beaumont, in Jack's opinion, had no right to be in 'our' village? She smiled inwardly. From being a recluse who wanted nothing much to do with Abbeymead or its inhabitants, Jack Carrington had made the village his true home.

'You couldn't have been there to see your cousin,' he continued. 'By then, you must have known Hugo Rafferty was dead. The police would have informed you.'

'I knew he was dead, all right.' Beaumont's voice was flat. 'And I knew what he'd been up to in that village.'

'Then why come to Abbeymead?'

He shrugged his shoulders. 'I wanted to make sure he was gone. Rafferty was as slippery as an eel. He was quite capable of staging his demise as easily as he staged playing curate in my brother's place.'

'You were checking he was dead?' Jack was incredulous.

'That's right. And hoping, maybe, to meet the man who killed him. I'd liked to have shaken the chap by the hand.'

'When we collided on the high street, was that the first time you'd visited Abbeymead?' Flora asked, aware suddenly that they could be talking to a killer.

Gareth Beaumont frowned. 'Why do you ask?'

'It seems a little odd,' she said evenly, 'to pay a visit to a village you don't know, and so early in the morning.'

'I told you why I was there, though I've no idea why you feel you have a right to know. And as for visiting early, I have immense responsibilities managing Beaumont Park for my father. He is bedridden from a riding accident and my mother is elderly and largely immobile. It means I'm charged with the welfare of two thousand acres of land, together with three large farms and their tenants. I've little spare time and, if I'm to do anything for myself, it has to be very early in the day. Satisfied?'

With that, he turned on his heel and stomped away, omitting to say any word of farewell.

'One very uptight gentleman,' Jack remarked. 'But at least we know where Lyle Beaumont is residing. Six feet under.'

'*And* how Hugo was able to play at being Lyle without his cousin ever challenging him. I did wonder if the two of them had some kind of pact, or if Lyle had suddenly gone walkabout and Hugo took his chance. In fact, it was far simpler.'

'And sadder.'

They'd reached the car and clambered in, both of them assuming without a word that their job in Whitbury was done.

Flora's forehead was ridged in concentration as the car headed back to the coast. 'I need to think this through,' she announced. 'Hugo knows his cousin is dead, in all probability he attended his funeral and then, for some reason, decides to impersonate him. How exactly did he manage to do it without alarm bells ringing, and why did he choose to do something so risky?'

'Alan Ridley might know the how by now, but the why... I reckon Rafferty's motive for such a dangerous ploy will be harder to discover.'

Flora relapsed into silence. What might have led Hugo Rafferty to do what he'd done? Had he seen Abbeymead as some kind of haven? But it was a small village and strangers were more visible in its streets than in a busy town. Was he hoping the clerical garb might protect him? And if so, what did he need protection from?

Jack's voice broke through her thoughts, holding a note of accusation. 'You never told me you'd met Gareth Beaumont.'

'I didn't know I *had* met him. When I almost ran into him last Saturday, he was simply an unknown man. I thought at the time his presence in the village was odd, but then I forgot about it. When we were accosted just now in the churchyard by the same person, I was astonished.'

'Why ask him about his visits to Abbeymead?'

Flora smoothed down the creases in her woollen coat. 'I started wondering just how many times he'd been to the village. Whether he'd been there before his cousin died. If he'd discovered what Rafferty was up to, was it Gareth who sent a message to meet him in the bell tower? He'd want to put an immediate stop to Hugo pretending to be his dead brother, wouldn't he? They could have quarrelled and...'

'But if Gareth Beaumont was the killer, he'd hardly come back to where he killed. If he met Rafferty in the bell tower, pushed him to his death, then managed a getaway without being spotted, he'd surely want to keep it that way. He lives miles distant and, without any link between himself and Abbeymead, he'd be safe from suspicion.'

'All true. It was his bitterness that cut through to me. He's certainly bitter enough to kill.' Her face brightened as they came in sight of the sea once more. 'And don't murderers some-times return to the scene of their crime?'

Jack steered the Austin carefully down the winding road and into the town before he answered. 'It's been known. You think Beaumont came back to the village to gloat?'

'Perhaps. Or simply to make sure, as he said, that Rafferty was dead and feel happy that the job had been done.'

'It's a theory – but that's about all.' Stopping the car a few yards from the hotel entrance, he reached out for her hand. 'How about lunch? I'm starving again.'

12

Settling on a small café in one of the narrow streets leading from the seafront, they ordered ham sandwiches, Jack's number one choice for lunch, and talked over just how far they'd progressed.

They had a new suspect, that was clear. Gareth Beaumont was ravaged by grief for his younger brother and consumed by anger for Hugo Rafferty.

'If we can prove that he visited Abbeymead while Rafferty was still alive, I think we might have our killer.' Flora drained the last drop of tea from her cup.

'He certainly has motive, and he's wealthy enough to have the means to travel easily.'

'And he's his own boss,' she pointed out. 'He may be lord of all he surveys and incredibly busy, but he can take time out whenever he needs it.'

Jack took a last drink of tea. 'I wonder if he's appeared yet on Ridley's radar?'

'If not, we should make sure he does,' she said decidedly. There was a pause before she spoke again. 'So, what next? Is there anything more we can do in Dorset?'

They had literally run Lyle Beaumont to ground and met at least one of his family – probably the only one they needed to, if his mother and father were as frail as Gareth Beaumont claimed. The remainder of the weekend had taken on a different feel. The missing man had been the impetus for their trip to Dorset and, now the search was over, they were left with time on their hands and the necessity to enjoy it as a couple.

Flora felt peculiarly uncomfortable and had to remind herself that it was Jack, a man who over the months had become the best friend she'd ever had, who was walking beside her as they made their way from the café back towards the promenade. Trying hard to lose her discomfort, she suggested they stroll along the beach towards Charmouth, searching for fossils as they went.

'The sun's doing its best to shine,' she said. 'It could be a pleasant walk.'

There was only the faintest beam of light leavening the grey, but the wind that had sprung up yesterday had once more subsided and it was as warm as it would ever be in late November.

Jack seemed happy to fall in with her plan. She could see that he was as anxious as she, wondering how exactly they should spend the rest of their time in Lyme. From the promenade, they walked down onto the beach and set off eastwards. Within a short time, they were clear of the small town and crunching their way across shingle and around huge, oddly shaped rocks.

'It's lucky it's low tide,' he observed. 'It looks as though the beach might get cut off. You could easily be caught out.'

Flora came to a halt and gazed slowly around, at the cliffs to their left and the bulky headland in the distance. 'You're right. I can't see a path leading from the beach. But we've time on our side.' She looked out to sea at the distant line of surf. 'Just about.'

'But not time to walk to Charmouth and back.'

'It doesn't matter if we don't get there. This is fun.' She bounded ahead, jumping onto a particularly large rock, then leaping to another and another, hair flying. For the moment, she lost the self-consciousness that had blighted her since finding Lyle Beaumont's grave.

'Remember Louisa Musgrove,' Jack warned, some distance away.

'I know, but look at this.'

She jumped down and darted towards an oblong slab, the weathered grey rock tilting at an angle as it rose from the pebbles. Like a beached whale, she thought. The imprint of creatures from long ago were clear to see in the deep circles scored into its surface.

Jack caught up with her and peered down.

'It's some kind of snail,' she said.

'A giant snail.' He traced his finger along the grooves in the rock. 'There'll be plenty more of these if we keep our eyes open. This place is a treasure trove.'

And so it proved. Halfway to Charmouth, after stopping every few minutes to examine fossil remains, Jack suggested they sit for a while, and she was glad to agree. It had been an hour of quite strenuous walking, and she'd spied a comfortable perch ahead.

'I could do with a cigarette.' Jack stretched himself horizontally across the boulder's flat surface. 'That could be a lot more fun than clambering over rocks.'

'You don't smoke, remember?'

'Sometimes I do.'

'Only when you don't know what to do next.'

He gave a slight smile. 'I suppose that's true. Well, what do we do next?'

'Now Lyle Beaumont is dead?' she asked, deliberately

choosing to focus on the investigation rather than their friendship.

'If the reason Gareth Beaumont gave for being in Abbeymead is false – and it sounded far-fetched to me – and he is the killer, then we know the reason for Hugo Rafferty's death. What we don't know, though, is why Hugo decided to impersonate his cousin. I've a hunch that's the nub of the case. Hugo's charade is almost certainly why he was killed, whether by Gareth or persons unknown.'

'We might be leaping ahead,' she warned. 'We haven't actually had it confirmed that it *was* murder.'

'It will be,' he said confidently. 'I'm pretty sure I'll find a note from Alan Ridley to that effect when I get back. Hopefully, he'll let me in on the post-mortem results.'

He levered himself into an upright position. 'Come on, I'm getting cold. If you've had enough of being a mountain goat, I think we should head back. That was a delicious meal last night – let's hope for a repeat.'

'It will be a roast.'

'Why are you so sure?'

'I do a lot of these weekend breaks,' she said airily.

He took hold of her hand and pulled her upright. 'No, you don't, and neither do I. Let's make this one count.'

Balancing between two rocks, he hugged her close and kissed her. And kept kissing her until he lost his footing and, together, they tumbled into the gap below.

'That's another bruise,' she said, laughing.

'Sorry. I'm still out of practice.' He helped her to her feet, steadying them both before they turned to walk back the way they'd come.

Outside the hotel, he stopped to reach over and untangle the tousled strands of her hair. 'I must say you wear seaweed well, but I'm thinking it could be just a little too tangy for the Pilot Boat.'

The note from Inspector Ridley that Jack had foretold was on the mat when he unlocked his front door around teatime the following day. It was brief and to the point. The post-mortem confirmed that severe bruising around the dead man's neck could not have been caused by a simple fall from the gallery. Hugo appeared to have been half-strangled, while further bruising on his body suggested a ferocious struggle before his adversary had gained the upper hand and thrust him over the gallery's flimsy barrier.

Now the police had their report, there'd be a funeral fairly soon, and it would be interesting to see who would choose to attend. Members of the Beaumont family? Hugo's mother, Ellen Rafferty? Another stranger or two? In this investigation, that wouldn't be a surprise, but it would be Alice Jenner, he was sure, who'd be the first to know any names being bandied around the village.

Two days later when he walked to the high street, intending to call at Katie's Nook for a cheese and potato pasty, it was Alice he saw first when he walked into the café. She was divesting herself of a coat that had seen rather too many winters and looking unusually ruffled.

'Only just arrived?' he said. 'You're late.' Then flinched at his words. It was definitely the wrong way to begin a conversation.

'Some of us have duties elsewhere, but I try to help Katie when I can,' the cook muttered, bending down to change her boots for indoor shoes, her face turning redder with every second. She straightened up. 'We can't all go on fancy weekends.'

'Sorry, Alice. That was a stupid thing to say, but you seem a little upset?'

'I am that. Riled me, it has.'

'What has?'

'Nearly knocked down, I was. Crossin' the road, mindin' my own business, then this big car sweeps past as though it owns the village. Missed me by a whisker.'

Jack frowned. What had he been saying to himself about strangers? 'Did you notice what kind of car?'

'No, I didn't. I was jumpin' for my life.' She thought for a moment. 'Big black thing, it was. Shiny and smooth, but... there was a man sitting in the back.' A silence fell while she thought some more. 'He had this hat on – dark grey. No one in the village has anythin' like it. I think... it's what's called a homburg? Kate's dad had one tucked away in his wardrobe. Cyril never wore it, mind, mebbe it was given him some time past. Anyways, this man,' she said, returning to her story, 'he was in the seat at the back, like I said, and there was another wearin' some kind of uniform who was drivin'. I saw the uniform when the car put its brakes on.'

'A chauffeur?'

'I reckon so. I watched after 'em when they took off again – had to squint hard to make sure I'd seen it for real. But it was a chauffeur in the drivin' seat, I'm sure. Very posh. Who on earth would be travellin' like that?' Alice looked at him hopefully.

'I've no idea but thank goodness you're safe.'

Alice's expression softened. 'Well, and how was your trip? I haven't seen Flora to ask.'

'It was good. We went to find Lyle Beaumont and we did – dead and buried.'

Alice cocked her head to one side. 'When Katie told me the curate was pretendin' to be this Lyle, it made me wonder if the poor chap might be dead. But Flora?'

'Flora's fine. Lyme Regis was cold but beautiful and we made sure we walked a lot.'

Jack knew the village would be thinking the worst, Alice included. Two unmarried people, spending the weekend together unchaperoned. It hadn't been that kind of trip, he thought regretfully, and maybe never would – both of them too nervous to make that final commitment – but no one would believe them.

Hoping to avoid talking more of Flora, he asked, 'Does everyone in the village know the curate was an imposter?'

'Pretty much.' Alice began laying up trays for lunchtime, while noises from the kitchen beyond suggested Kate was already at work. 'One of the coppers on the case let it slip when he was in the baker's. One minute he was buying a bread roll, the next the whole of Abbeymead was talkin' about it. Poor Amy Dunmore has been in a right dither. Vicar is still poorly, and she doesn't know whether or not to tell him he's been hosting a cuckoo in his nest.'

'She must be upset on her own account,' he said mildly. 'She's been lied to, as well. And wasn't she the one who persuaded Reverend Hopkirk he needed a curate?'

Alice paused, a stack of napkins in her hand. 'She was, and she was right. The poor man needed help, and it's Vicar that Amy's most worried about. She did everything right, checked with the seminary on the curate's credentials – but it was Lyle Beaumont the seminary was checking, not Rafferty.'

'No wonder she's in a dither.'

'I feel for her, I really do. Amy is one of those women who never see evil and spend their lives doin' good. Never ask much for themselves either. Now, she has to arrange the funeral. Apparently, this Rafferty's family doesn't want to know, and it's all down to her.'

'It will be at St Saviour's, I suppose?'

Alice nodded, her wiry grey curls bouncing in time. 'It's what you might call...'

'Ironic?'

'That's the word. A cheese and potato pasty, was it?'

13

The funeral took place a few days later, a hurried affair, Flora thought. It was almost as if in some way Abbeymead felt ashamed and wanted to bury the evidence as soon as possible. Everyone, down to the smallest inhabitant, knew now that Hugo Rafferty had been a fake and the village didn't appreciate being taken for a collective fool. There was the fact, too, that his death had not been an accident. A murder investigation was taking place under everyone's nose and Abbeymead did not enjoy playing host to so many police – Constable Tring was quite sufficient for the village's taste. A funeral, hastily arranged, seemed the general unspoken wish.

Flora arrived a little early for the service and, rather than wait for Jack at the lych gate on what was another bitterly cold day, she made for the church door. She had walked only a few paces up the red brick path when, out of the corner of her eye, she caught sight of a figure lingering beside the church notice-board. As she watched, the girl, head down, walked quickly on, making, it seemed, for Fern Hill. Phoebe Tallant, Flora thought, presumably on her way back to Miss Lancaster's house.

It was a rare sighting. As far as Flora knew, Phoebe had

barely been seen in the village since her godmother's death. She appeared very alone, with no family other than the late departed Miss Lancaster, and, as someone of much the same age who had lost a loved relative herself, Flora was sympathetic. She should at least enquire how Phoebe was coping with the many problems that death brought with it.

Turning back along the path and out of the lych gate, Flora had to run to catch up with the girl and was breathless by the time she was within hailing distance.

'Miss Tallant?' she called out.

The girl half turned, her face set and her body sending unmistakable signals of annoyance.

Flora tumbled to a stop. 'I'm sorry,' she said, 'you seem to be in a hurry.'

'A little.' Phoebe's reply was crisp.

'I won't keep you then. I just wanted to say hello and that I hope things are beginning to settle down for you.'

The girl gave a small, tight smile. 'I'm sure they will.'

'I saw you outside the church. Were you thinking you might attend the service?'

Phoebe looked at her blankly.

'It's Mr Rafferty's funeral this afternoon,' Flora hurried on, flustered by the girl's lack of response. 'The curate. Did you ever meet him?'

'No, I don't think I did. I'm not a churchgoer. But everything is fine with me, thank you.' She went to walk on.

Flora put out a detaining hand, a hardly understood impulse prompting her to continue the conversation. 'I know you have a funeral to arrange yourself, which can't be easy. It's taking some time, isn't it? And it won't be at St Saviour's, I understand.'

'Is there a problem with that?' The girl bristled with the question.

'No, except the village—'

'—the village can mind its own business.'

'It's obviously a very personal choice.' Flora was foundering, finding it difficult to understand the clear hostility with which she was being met.

'It is.'

Despite the girl's anger, Flora felt compelled to speak. 'If you intend to make your home in Abbeymead, Miss Tallant, it's always best to have the village on your side.'

When Phoebe's lips remained firmly shut, she jettisoned any caution and asked baldly, 'Will you be staying?'

The girl's face softened a little. 'I'm not sure,' she said, trying, it seemed, to sound more conciliatory. 'I could stay. I have a home here. Miss Lancaster has been generous.'

'Let's hope you do then.' Flora injected as much warmth as she could into her voice. 'You worked for a big company – in London – I believe. But I'm sure you'll find work locally that you'll enjoy as much.'

Phoebe gave another of her tight little smiles. 'I really must go,' she said, ignoring the invitation to talk more.

Before Flora could reply, the girl had turned and walked away at the same hectic pace she'd maintained earlier.

Jack was waiting for her in the church porch. 'I thought you said half past two,' he complained. 'And what have you got on your head?'

'It's called a hat. It's to show respect in church.'

'That's no hat. It's a... a frill.'

'It's disappearing once the service is over. And I was here at half past two, but I've been on a mission.'

'Not finding another body to bury, I hope.'

'No, but a very odd conversation with Phoebe Tallant. That was what held me up,' she said, taking his arm and walking into the church.

'Intriguing! Tell me later.'

Together they slipped into a pew at the rear of the church. Alice, Kate and Tony Farraday were sitting several rows ahead, but the church seemed half-empty. Only the most devout of Hugo's erstwhile parishioners had made a point of attending his funeral. The vicar, Flora saw, looking pale and thin, had risen from his sick bed to do his duty; Amy Dunmore had done hers, Flora knew, providing tea and sandwiches at the vicarage after what was likely to be a brief service.

She had met the housekeeper earlier that week and learned of Amy's concern that the church would be largely empty, the Beaumonts having refused an invitation to attend and Ellen Rafferty, Hugo's mother, too distraught to come. Miss Dunmore had been right, it seemed. Apart from themselves and the few village stalwarts, there were no other mourners.

Flora gave a quick glance around. Harry Barnes had come and settled himself in a pew on the other side of the aisle, with Stephen Henshall beside him. It was generous of Harry to make the long walk down from Pelham Lodge, particularly when, as far as Flora knew, he rarely went to church and might never have met the dead man. But he *had* been there the night of Hugo's death and so had Henshall. Another glance sideways and there was Daniel Vaisey of all people. She hadn't put the landlord down as a churchgoer. Perhaps Rafferty had been a good customer, despite the dog collar.

The coffin had arrived at the church entrance and what congregation there was had risen to its feet, when heavy footsteps sounded at the rear of the church. Craning her neck round to look, Flora saw the disturbance had been caused by a late-comer who was even now slipping into an adjacent pew. Jack had followed her gaze, raising his eyebrows but saying nothing.

Beneath her lashes, Flora stole a look at the man who had just arrived. He wore an expensive dark grey suit, his heavy overcoat bundled onto the pew beside him. As she watched, he hastily removed his hat and placed it on top of the overcoat. Something in the gesture, in the shape of the hat, caught at her memory, and for the rest of the short service her mind was busy trying to decide why exactly the image might be meaningful.

It was with a start she realised that the prayers were over and the last note of the last hymn had sounded. The pall-bearers were lifting their burden to carry the coffin back along the aisle and into the churchyard – would there even be a grave-stone? she wondered – while the congregation had once more got to its feet in a traditional show of respect.

As parishioners began to shuffle their belongings together, the stranger jumped up quickly, in an attempt, Flora thought, to be first through the church door. He failed and remained trapped in his pew, forced to watch the rest of the congregation walk past. Flora, waiting her turn to leave, was astonished to see Harry Barnes wave the hat he carried at the stranger – another hat! – as he passed the man's pew. And astonished to see the stranger nod back. Jack's altered expression told her that he'd noted it, too.

Suddenly, the moment Flora had been chasing came to her. Charlie had said the car that ran him off the road had a male passenger in the back, a man who was wearing what he termed a funny hat. A homburg, it had turned out. Was this the same man?

'Jack,' she whispered urgently, as they made slow progress up the aisle. 'I'm sure there'll be a very expensive car parked outside the church, with a chauffeur at the wheel. Can you go ahead, get him to talk and find out who they are, while I waylay his boss?'

'I'll try,' he said, and without questioning her further, sidled a path in and out of the villagers waiting in front of him. Reaching the church door, he was dutifully thanked for his attendance, his hand grasped by the vicar who was looking white and unsteady.

Flora watched from a distance as Jack walked quickly up the red brick path to the lych gate, while trying not to look too obviously in haste.

A uniformed man was smoking a cigarette, leaning against the bonnet of the car, but when he saw Jack approach, he threw away the cigarette butt and ground it with the heel of a polished boot.

'Afternoon, squire,' he said, as Jack approached.

'Good afternoon. I'm sorry for interrupting your rest time, but I had to come over.' Jack found his warmest smile. 'Had to come and admire your car – it's a beauty.'

'Pretty good, eh?' The man flicked some imaginary dust from a deep blue sleeve.

'A Daimler, by the look of it.'

'A new Daimler,' the man corrected.

'That would be my dream.' Jack gave a realistic sigh. 'But it's never going to happen.'

'Nor for me, mate. Some have got it, but most of us haven't.'

'Your boss certainly has.'

'He should do. Owns Mason's. One of the biggest department stores in Kensington.'

'Phew, that's impressive. I bet there's a big house that goes with it, too.'

'Not half. You don't live in Knightsbridge without plenty of cash. Bloody great villa – only the best for Mr Mason! Here, I better look sharp. The old geezer's comin'. Gotta drive him to the local pub. Makes a nice change, I s'pose.'

'I'll make myself scarce then,' Jack said, with another smile, and walked casually away as though he'd only stopped to say a brief hello.

Flora, watching the scene unfold, hurried to catch him up. 'That man has been here before,' she said excitedly.

'Abbeymead seems to have become unusually popular of late.'

'Hasn't it just? Like you said, far too many strangers for comfort.'

'I reckon that's the car Alice was complaining about.' Jack straightened the brim of his fedora. 'The man who nearly knocked her down. How do *you* know him?'

'I don't, but Charlie does. Or did. That chauffeur is a danger. It's the same car that ran Charlie off the road. I had to get Michael to work his magic on Betty and make her whole again.'

'Was it deliberate? He was aiming for the boy?'

'I don't think so. Driving too fast would be my guess. But who's the man? Did you find out?'

Jack looked smug. 'Meet your intrepid interrogator. He's the owner of a store called Mason's and lives in some luxury in Knightsbridge. Though what a wealthy man wants with the Cross Keys, I can't imagine.'

'Never mind the Cross Keys. What's his name?'

Jack tapped his forehead theatrically. 'Mmm,' he mused. 'Strangely enough, it's Mason.'

He deserved a poke in the ribs for that, Flora decided.

14

'Are we going to the vicarage for tea and buns?' Jack asked a few minutes later, having escaped the poke in the ribs.

Flora pulled a face. 'I suppose we should, if only to support Miss Dunmore. There was such a poor turnout for the funeral and the vicar looks anything but well.'

Taking her arm, Jack steered a path along the front of the church and past the infamous bell tower to the vicarage front door which had been left ajar.

'Before we go in, I really must ditch the hat. It's itching so much it feels as though I've a hive of bees in my hair.'

'That's much better,' he said approvingly, standing back to view the copper-coloured waves he loved. 'You're Flora again. But what's that you're holding? It looks lethal.'

'This is a hat pin, Jack – actually it's Aunt Violet's favourite hat pin. I don't own one, thank the Lord. Come on, we'd better go in,' she said, tucking the pin away in her pocket.

Amy Dunmore was hovering in the hallway, a nervous smile on her face.

'Come in, do.' She sounded a trifle breathless. 'Refreshments are in the dining room. You'll know the way, Flora.'

Flora only vaguely remembered the layout of the vicarage, but she walked along the long hall and turned into the last door on the left, hoping she'd guessed right. It was the official dining room of the vicarage, a cold space at the rear of the building, and barely used, she guessed. Reverend Hopkirk, when he wasn't on his sick bed, no doubt preferred to eat in the kitchen along with his housekeeper.

Amy had followed in their wake, her smile still nervous. 'I wasn't sure how many people would come, what with all the trouble there's been. Mr Beau— Mr Rafferty... wasn't exactly popular, but I hope there'll be sufficient to feed everyone.'

When Flora looked at the platters of sandwiches and the several plates of small, iced cakes filling the width of the crisp linen tablecloth, her first thought was that St Luke's hospital was likely to receive a teatime donation by the end of the day.

'Can I get you a cup of tea?' Miss Dunmore pointed to the stack of cups and saucers and a giant teapot. 'Or maybe we could run to a beer.' She looked hopelessly up at Jack.

'Tea would be fine,' he said in a rallying tone. 'These sandwiches look very good, Miss Dunmore.'

'Thank you, Mr Carrington. I wasn't sure, you see...' She tailed off, looking distractedly towards the stairs. There had been a noise from the floor above. 'Vicar isn't eating with us, I'm afraid. The service has taxed him rather. And then all the people calling here when we're usually so quiet. The vicarage has been besieged. Yes, that's the word. First Miss Tallant, then Sergeant Norris, then his inspector. It hasn't been easy.' She scrabbled to rearrange her pinafore which had become untied, the ends now in a fearful tangle.

'Mr Carrington is right,' Flora said brightly. 'The sandwiches look delicious.' She took a plate from the waiting pile and purposefully filled it to the rim.

'Do bring your food into the sitting room. It's a bit warmer there.' The housekeeper was apologetic. 'We can only manage one fire downstairs. Coal is so very expensive.'

In the interim, several more parishioners had drifted through the front door and Miss Dunmore scurried off to welcome them and introduce them to the refreshments.

'Rafferty doesn't deserve such consideration,' Jack said, balancing a plate in one hand and a cup of tea in the other.

He chose a seat by the window, a safe distance from the fire blazing in the grate, and Flora plumped down beside him. 'I hope for Miss Dunmore's sake a few more of the congregation decide to walk over. Alice and Kate have gone back to work, and I saw Harry Barnes making his way towards Fern Hill. He had Henshall with him, so they won't be coming. We need to speak to Harry,' she added thoughtfully. 'I was hoping to nab him after the service, but he was out of the church door before I could.'

'Well, you nabbed Phoebe Tallant beforehand. What did she have to say? I never got to hear.'

'There wasn't the time. The mystery man arrived out of the blue and then the service started.'

'A man who's no longer a mystery. So, the beautiful Miss Tallant?'

'She is beautiful, isn't she?' Flora took a bite of egg sandwich. 'I can imagine the stories going around the village are true for once – the stories about her modelling.' She took another bite. 'Phoebe may be lovely to look at, but she's certainly not happy. And she didn't like my stopping her to talk, not one little bit.'

'Why were you so keen to speak to her anyway?'

Flora gave a tiny shrug. 'She seems very much alone, and I thought she might welcome a friendly hello.'

'You evidently didn't fit the bill.'

'To be honest, I don't think anyone would. She was... defensive. Although why she should be, I've no idea.'

'*Were* you being friendly or just nosy?'

'I was perfectly nice! I did try to give her a little advice, but in the gentlest of ways.'

When Jack shook his head at her, she protested. 'What? All I did was hint that if she was intending to make her home in Abbeymead, she'd be best not to upset the village. And she's done that already. The funeral she's arranged for her godmother – it's horrified most of the older villagers. Miss Lancaster lived in Abbeymead all her life and she should be buried at St Saviour's, her gravestone in the churchyard, is what they feel. And I think they're right.'

'If Phoebe isn't intending to stay, she may have decided she's no need to take account of village sensitivities.'

'That was the odd thing. It's plain she expects to inherit the house and she seemed to be happy with the idea of living there, but when I mentioned the job she'd left in London – I was wondering if she intended to go back to it, it's just about possible to travel from the village – she simply walked away.'

'Only if you've lived in a small village for ever would you think it odd that she didn't answer. Not everyone wants to share their life history or their future plans. If Phoebe Tallant prefers to keep her intentions to herself, I can understand that.'

Flora had picked up an iced fancy and had it halfway to her mouth when she stopped and stared at the opposite wall, then put it carefully back on her plate.

'Tell me the worst!' he joked.

'Miss Tallant worked for a large retailer, that's what I heard.'

'So?'

'Department stores are large retailers, aren't they? And this morning, the owner of a department store turned up out of nowhere for Rafferty's funeral.'

Jack was wearing his pained look, and she waited for him to demolish her idea.

'She could have worked for any shop or any chain of shops,'

he said. 'It doesn't have to have been a department store. Even if it was, there are plenty of those in London. It wasn't necessarily Mason's.'

'But what if it was?' She swivelled round in the window seat to face him. 'What if Phoebe Tallant knows this man, Mason? What if he was her employer? Don't look like that – it's not such a great leap. When I first caught sight of her, Phoebe was lingering outside the church without any obvious intention of going in. Why was she there?'

'There could be any number of reasons.'

'Give me one.'

'A mild interest in the proceedings?'

'How can you be mildly interested in a funeral? It's not like a wedding. There are no pretty dresses or bouquets of flowers. Just a coffin and a few wreaths.'

'OK. She was taking a walk around the village and happened to stop outside the church when she noticed the activity.'

'Phoebe Tallant doesn't take walks around the village. She doesn't walk anywhere – she's rarely emerged from Miss Lancaster's house since she arrived in Abbeymead, except to do a small amount of shopping and visit Miss Dunmore.' Flora gripped his hand, almost tipping his last iced fancy onto the swirls of the vicar's broadloom carpet. 'It's too much of a coincidence.'

Jack put down his plate and ran a hand through the flop of hair that never lay flat. 'There was something the postmistress told me,' he said slowly. 'I didn't think it relevant at the time and since then, to be honest, it's gone to the back of my mind.'

'Yes?' she said eagerly.

'Dilys mentioned there had been someone looking for Phoebe. Apparently, he'd been in contact with the girl but didn't know her precise address – just that she was living in Abbeymead. He called at the post office for help. Dilys refused to tell him directly but promised to pass on a letter he'd written to her. Whether he ever found Phoebe, I've no idea.'

'Did Dilys know who the man was?'

'He couldn't have given a name. If he had, Dilys would have been keen to tell me, and she didn't. The chap told her he'd come with a job offer for Miss Tallant. A very good job, it seemed, though don't ask me what exactly.'

'Whatever it is, the situation is interesting. Very interesting. An unknown man is so keen that Phoebe Tallant works for him that he travels to Abbeymead in search of her. It must be some job. Yet, as far as we know, she hasn't responded. She's stayed in the village.'

'You don't know for sure that she's uninterested. She might still go. And, if she doesn't, it could be that she's fallen in love with the village and doesn't want to leave.'

'And would rather take a menial job here?' Flora gave a small snort. 'I don't believe it. I wonder what the real reason is, and I wonder if Mason was the man Dilys spoke to. She wasn't at the funeral, unfortunately, or we could have asked her. If Mason was that man, did he come today to repeat his offer?'

'While popping into St Saviour's to take part in a funeral? That doesn't wash. And if he was the man Dilys saw, he must have left the limo behind when he called at the post office. She wouldn't have been able to contain herself if she'd had a uniformed chauffeur to report.'

Flora gathered their empty plates together. 'We need to talk to Harry Barnes,' she said firmly, as Miss Dunmore ushered several more parishioners into the room bearing food and drink. 'More than ever, now we know he's acquainted with Mason. We mustn't forget that Henshall is a good friend of his and Henshall is still our number one suspect.'

~

The following day, Jack had a call from Alan Ridley. Returning from a walk, he heard the insistent ring of the telephone as he opened his garden gate. Thinking it might be Flora, he ran the rest of the way and was through the front door in seconds.

'I'm in Steyning this afternoon, old chap,' Ridley said cheerfully. 'Nothing to do with the bell tower case but thought I might drop in on my way back. How about a pint in the Cross Keys around six?'

Jack wasn't in the mood to socialise, having that morning received a detailed report from Arthur Bellaby on the book that held his hopes for a return to writing form. His agent had liked the book, in fact enjoyed it immensely, but there were points that needed more work, areas where Jack had 'rather slid over the surface'. Points where I had nothing much to say, Jack thought wryly. Would he have anything more to say now, three weeks later?

He'd read and reread the three pages of amendments for most of the day and, with each reading, had felt a little more depressed. Confidence had begun to crumble and he'd been on the point of ringing Arthur – was it such a good idea that Overlay House had a telephone at last? – to tell him that he couldn't do it, that he couldn't write any more, but had resisted the urge. Ignoring the telephone, he'd taken himself for a long walk. If he chickened out now, Flora would think him a quitter. She'd never say it, but she'd think it. And she'd be right. He couldn't give up. He had to try.

A drink at the Cross Keys might offer temporary distraction, he supposed, from the foolscap sheets of notes that lay waiting, and heard himself agreeing to meet.

Alan Ridley was already in his favourite corner when Jack arrived, with two glasses of Watneys Red Barrel, the inspector's preferred tipple, on the table.

'Thought we should catch up,' he said in greeting. He raised his beer in a salute as Jack took a seat. 'See if you've come up with anything on the Rafferty business.'

'Thanks for the drink.' Jack raised his glass in response and took a sip. The beer had improved as well as the food and, feeling more relaxed, he settled himself on the cushioned bench, glad that the Rafferty case wasn't his responsibility. He and Flora might be able to help, they appeared to be edging their way forward, but it wasn't up to them to find the killer and, in truth, they'd made little real progress.

'There's not a lot to report,' he said, putting his glass down. 'Abbeymead has seen several strangers lately, which is unusual, but whether there's a connection to Rafferty, I'm not sure.'

'Tell me about these strangers. Do you know who they were?'

'One was Gareth Beaumont, Rafferty's cousin.'

'Oh, him,' the inspector said offhandedly. 'Can of worms there, old chap. Never seen a man so eaten up by resentment.'

'I'd call it a rank bitterness. He's been to the village at least once. Flora saw him. She literally ran into him.'

Ridley lifted an eyebrow. 'I didn't know that. But was it before Hugo Rafferty was murdered? Casing the joint, as I believe you crime writers call it?'

'Not this crime writer,' he said a trifle sharply. 'Flora bumped into Beaumont after the man died, but it's possible he visited earlier, and no one saw him. He could have been the one meeting Rafferty that evening. Rafferty would have responded to a note sent by his cousin – he would have recognised the handwriting – and the bell tower would be a quiet place to meet.'

'But if Beaumont had killed and gone unnoticed, why revisit the scene of his crime?'

That was the question, Jack thought. 'When we asked him why he'd come to Abbeymead, he said it was to make sure his cousin was actually dead.'

Ridley chuckled. 'I can believe that. Like I say, never known a man so chewed up. Still, I take your point that he could have paid a visit before Rafferty died. In time, it might be worth circulating his photograph around the village in case anyone saw him.' He studied his glass of beer thoughtfully. 'If we reach a dead end, I'll get one of my men on to it.'

'There was someone else,' Jack said. 'Another unknown. He turned up at the funeral.'

'Ah, funerals. Good place to spot a likely villain. I couldn't get to the service myself and asked Norris to go in my stead. But then the stupid fellow did his back in emptying a sack into his coal bunker. Who was this chap?'

'A man called Mason. He owns a department store in Kensington.'

'Mason's? That's a big shop. A man with serious money.'

'As I understand. The question is why he came to the funeral.'

'Perhaps he was another Gareth Beaumont? He came to make sure Rafferty was dead?'

Jack fidgeted on the settle, trying to get comfortable. He'd been sitting in one place too long. 'Beaumont blames Rafferty for his brother's short life, but what did Mason have against him?'

'Probably nothing. It's likely he knew Rafferty in an earlier guise – before the bloke pretended to be a curate – heard he was dead and wanted to pay his respects.'

'If Mason was close enough to Rafferty to attend the man's funeral, wouldn't he have known about the charade he was playing and blown the whistle? Mason is evidently an important man. If he knew what Rafferty was up to, he wouldn't have stayed silent, surely.'

'Why would he know, though? He's in London, Rafferty is down here, and probably fed Mason some story or other. He seems to have been good at those. There are probably a whole lot more stories for us to uncover.'

Ridley swallowed the last of his beer. 'Another one?' When Jack shook his head, he said, 'Your strangers are interesting, I'll give you that, but they don't make me change my mind. It's Stephen Henshall I'm interested in. He was at the bell tower that night with no good reason to be there. There are rumours about his business, too – nothing concrete, mind, but they're getting louder. When I interviewed him, he was an angry man. Almost as angry as Beaumont. Henshall has been taken for a ride, it seems, and it might well have been by our friend, Rafferty.'

Ridley looked up and beamed. The landlord was approaching with a laden tray.

'Just the job,' the inspector said. 'You should have ordered as well, Jack. Ham omelette and chips with treacle pud and custard for afters. What could be better?'

'Can I get you anything, sir?' Vaisey asked Jack, laying out china and cutlery.

'Not for me, thanks, but the beer is very good!'

'That's what we like to hear.' The landlord delivered the inspector's supper with a flourish.

'You might be right about Henshall,' Jack agreed. He was conscious that both he and Flora had plumped for Henshall as their main suspect. 'Even so, I think I might take a trip to London. This man, Mason – I'd like to know more about him.'

15

'I think I should go to London,' Jack said, when he called at Flora's cottage on Sunday morning. 'Find out more about this Mason chap. He interests me.'

'Is it going to help?' She was doubtful. It seemed to her an unnecessary journey. 'You said the inspector is gunning for Henshall, and we have him in our sights, too.'

'I still reckon Mason is worth investigating,' he said stubbornly.

'Are you sure it's not escape that you're after? Something to excuse you from writing.'

Jack had mentioned Arthur Bellaby's notes when he'd first walked through the door but passed over their arrival with suspicious brevity.

His grey eyes darkened. 'The notes will still be on my desk when I get back,' he said airily. 'I'll go tomorrow, catch the early train and be home by teatime.'

'If you're determined... but maybe leave it until Tuesday, after I've bearded Harry Barnes. I'll walk to the golf club after work tomorrow, or maybe ride Betty there at lunchtime. Even if

Harry isn't at the Lexington, I can find out when he's likely to be.'

'You could always try him at Pelham Lodge,' Jack teased. Washing up his glass, he picked up his hat from the kitchen table and started towards the front door.

The Barnes family kept guard dogs on their property and Jack knew she'd not want to risk another encounter. The last time Flora had ventured to Pelham Lodge, she'd come off relatively lightly, a blood-stained gash on her hand but little more. Betty, on the other hand, had looked a sorry sight after Badger and Rocco had taken an aversion to the bicycle.

'If I'm out of luck, you can be the one to call at the Lodge,' she called after him, as he strode down the path to the garden gate. 'The dogs might even like you!'

There had been a light fall of snow on Sunday evening, casting doubts on Flora's ability to ride up Fern Hill and from there to the golf club, but it was impossible to walk to the Lexington and back in the hour she closed for lunch, and she was fairly sure that Harry would have made his way home to the dreaded dogs by the time the All's Well finally closed.

In the event, a faint sun had melted most of the thin covering by midday, only leaving icy patches beneath the trees that lined either side of the hill. By dint of keeping to the middle of the road and praying there would be little traffic, she puffed her way safely to the top. Taking a right turn, she rode past the Priory's iron gates and onto the golf club where she left the newly mended Betty in the cycle rack.

Walking through the club's glass doors, she made for the bar, judging it the most likely place to find Harry, and was rewarded by a loud laugh coming from the row of velvet-cushioned stools which lined the bar counter. Harry Barnes was entertaining his friends, his tubby figure suggesting he did more eating and drinking than actually swinging a golf club.

Flora didn't hesitate. It meant interrupting the fun with his cronies, the few hours when he could forget Evelyn, the wife who kept him under strict control, but on the other hand it also meant that Harry would be relaxed and possibly in a good enough mood to answer her questions.

She tapped him on the shoulder. 'Mr Barnes?'

He swung round, the smile slowly sliding from his face. 'Oh, it's you, Miss Steele,' he said uncertainly.

'I wonder if I could have a word.'

'What now? I'm with my friends,' he protested.

'I won't keep you long, I promise.' She tried her most winsome smile.

One of his friends had begun a long and tortuous story, the beginning of which had passed Harry by, and he shrugged his shoulders as though to say, why not? Flora led the way to a small table some yards away and, picking up his exotic-looking cocktail, he followed her.

'Did Evelyn send you?' he asked gloomily, as he slumped into the seat.

'No, of course not. I haven't spoken to your wife for months. It was you I wanted to see. I wanted to ask you about Stephen Henshall. He's not with you, I see.'

'He's at the Priory,' he said briefly, seeming to brighten at the thought that his wife would not after all be dominating the conversation.

'He's still helping out at the hotel?' she asked innocently.

'He's a good chap, Stephen. Wants to be useful, you know.'

'I'm sure he does,' she said sweetly. 'It must help him, too. A distraction, I suppose, from his own troubles.' Jack had confirmed from his conversation with Inspector Ridley that Henshall was in definite financial difficulty and knowing that had given her confidence to broach the subject.

'Steve will sort it out soon enough. He's a good business-man. Honest, too, which is more than you can say for some people,' he added darkly.

'Are you thinking of Hugo Rafferty?'

'That's the bloke. Now I know what he was up to...' Harry took a very large sip of his cocktail, dislodging the paper umbrella and causing a coughing fit.

'But you went to his funeral.'

'Stephen wanted to go, not me. Wanted to see the man buried for good.' It was remarkably similar to the sentiment Gareth Beaumont had expressed.

'Mr Henshall was at the bell tower when Rafferty's body was discovered,' she pushed gently.

Harry sat suddenly erect in his chair. 'What are you suggesting, Miss Steele?'

'*I'm* not suggesting anything, but I think you should know that it's a line of enquiry the police are working on. Stephen had the opportunity and a motive. It seems he's been badly affected by Rafferty's actions. What did that man do, by the way? There are rumours travelling round the village, but you must know the truth.'

Harry sat back, his chest expanding. 'I should do. I'm one of Steve's closest friends.' He lowered his voice. 'Rafferty persuaded him to order some product or other for his business and sell the surplus to other hotels. Caviar, I think it was. The most expen-sive kind, but he said he could get it cheaply and Stephen took a ton of the stuff, to be delivered at intervals, but paid for upfront. Rafferty insisted on that, it was the only way Steve would get the knockdown price, he said. But then he took the money and ran. There was no caviar, and the people Steve had promised it to and who'd paid *him* upfront started issuing threats.'

'What kind of threats? Did they intend to sue Mr Henshall?'

'That and worse,' he said tersely. 'Word gets around in the business, and pretty soon there were people pulling out of contracts with Steve, loans being called in. That kind of thing can ruin you. The hotel trade is pretty cut-throat, it exists on a thin profit margin, so...'

'Mr Henshall is in trouble?'

'At the moment but, like I said, he'll come right, you'll see. And as for the police, what's the matter with them? Totty-headed, I reckon. He might be glad Rafferty is dead, but Stephen Henshall is no killer.'

Flora was silent for a moment, then realised she should be offering some kind of reward for the information. 'Can I get you another drink, Mr Barnes?'

She was relieved when he turned the offer down – the cocktail had looked expensive. 'Thank you for telling me about Stephen. I can understand why he was keen to be at the funeral. Mr Mason, though, is a different matter, isn't he? You're acquainted with him, I saw. Why do you think he came all the way from London?'

'That's easy enough.' Harry scratched lazily at his thinning hair. 'The bloke used to work for him.'

'Hugo Rafferty worked for Mr Mason?'

'In Len's department store until he got the boot.'

'He was sacked? Did it have anything to do with the caviar?' The muddle in Flora's mind was taking on a shape of some kind.

'I reckon so. Rafferty worked in the food department. Bloody great food hall at the Kensington store, excuse my French. Have you been there?' Flora shook her head. 'Rafferty was in charge of ordering for the store, but he had this little side-line, apparently, which earned him plenty.'

'And Mr Mason found out about the sideline?'

'I dunno. All I know is that one day Rafferty was working at

Mason's, and the next day he wasn't. Len Mason isn't a bloke you cross, if you've got any sense.'

'You know Mr Mason because your firm supplied his store?'

'That's right, for years we did. I dunno if the bloke who bought my business still does, but probably. Mason's was a good customer. I never knew Leonard Mason well, just to tip my hat to him in passing, you know.' He picked up his empty glass and twiddled with its narrow stem. 'Is that it then, little Miss Curious?' Harry smiled at her. He'd relaxed considerably since they'd begun talking.

'Just one more thing. Why do you think Rafferty came to Abbeymead?'

'Obvious, isn't it? He was escaping. Hiding away. Pretending to be a curate is pretty good cover.'

'Escaping from what, though?'

'Maybe the heavy mob was after him.'

'The heavy mob?' Flora was confused again. 'Would Stephen Henshall employ a mob?'

'Lordy, no. Not Stephen.'

'Then who?'

'Len Mason, of course. Rafferty must have trashed Mason's reputation with what he did, just as much as he trashed Steve's. But the old boy? He'd not sit back and let him off scot-free.'

16

Flora telephoned Jack that evening to pass on what she'd learned from Harry Barnes. It didn't cause him to change his mind about Stephen Henshall – Alan Ridley seemed pretty convinced he was the prime suspect – but it did deepen his suspicions about the mysterious Mason. At the very least, it suggested his trip to London would not be a waste of time. Rafferty had worked for Mason and been dismissed for what was, in effect, theft.

And, according to Harry, instant dismissal might not be the end of it. Mason would seek revenge for the reputational damage inflicted on his business and Rafferty was likely to have been pursued and threatened by Mason's henchmen. He had always wondered what could have caused the man to embark on the highly risky pretence of taking his cousin's name and job. If Rafferty were being hunted by a violent gang, it made sense. Jack allowed himself a satisfied smile: this case was beginning to hang together.

Early the following morning, he took the first bus out of the village to Worthing station – the Austin had been misbehaving and he didn't want to risk the drive – and was in time to catch the half past eight train to Victoria. From the London terminal, a bus took him the few miles to Kensington High Street. The Old Vestry Hall was his destination which, from his time living in London, Jack knew to have a reference library.

The only information he had on Mason was that he lived in Knightsbridge, which meant the man should be on the electoral roll for Kensington and Chelsea. If Jack were lucky, the reference library would hold that register, though he'd need even more luck to track down Mason's actual address. Electoral registers were generally arranged by polling district or ward, and then by street or road. Useless for the task Jack had set himself, but he was aware, too, that even before the Second World War some London boroughs had begun to compile indexes of the surnames of electors in their areas. He could only cross his fingers that Kensington and Chelsea, which must include Knightsbridge, was a forward-thinking borough.

Traffic was light and within twenty minutes he'd alighted at a bus stop yards from the hall's magnificent frontage – a beautiful façade of red brick and white stone. A symmetrical pair of Dutch gables enclosed a central section boasting a grand cupola and a baronial door that would not have been out of place at the Priory.

The reference section was easy enough to find and a request to view the register of electors was met with a guarded agreement, once he'd spun a tale of wanting to find his old employer.

'All I know is that he moved to Knightsbridge,' he said winningly, 'but unfortunately I lost touch with him after that. Our old firm have organised a celebratory lunch – fifty years, you see – and we want him to be there, if at all possible. Our guest of honour!'

The assistant listened and, nodding, heaved a huge ledger onto a nearby desk. She continued to hover nearby, however, watching Jack closely.

At first sight of the ledger, Jack knew he was in luck. The electoral roll had been compiled in both forms, and immediately he focused his attention on the register that listed electors by surname. Turning the pages rapidly, he reached the letter M, only to find another problem waiting for him. Mason was not an uncommon name in Knightsbridge, it appeared, and there were a fair number residing in the borough. By dint of reading carefully through each entry and using the sparse knowledge he possessed, he chose three names living at what he judged were the most expensive addresses. Making a quick note of each, he retrieved his fedora and briefcase, thanked the assistant and bolted for the door before she could ask more questions.

The day was chilly but reasonably bright and he decided to walk into Knightsbridge from Kensington High Street, using the London A to Z he'd brought with him to find the first of the addresses he'd noted down. It took him only a short time, but the house turned out to be disappointingly small and, when he enquired at a local corner shop for information, all the shop knew was that the owner was a retired lady who had a copy of the *Daily Telegraph* delivered every morning.

Jack walked on again, this time covering a good distance until he found the next address on his list. The register's entry had boasted a house name which, he hoped, indicated an expensive property – the chauffeur, he remembered, had talked about a large villa. Lynton Street was wide and tree-lined, white stucco mansions lying behind large, leafy front gardens. It looked a definite possibility and halfway along the road, he spotted what he imagined must be Albert House.

Outside a pillared gate, two large men stood one on either side, drinking from china mugs. They were dressed in dark coats, trilby hats pulled low on their heads, occasionally exchanging a word but in the main, as Jack watched, simply drinking and watching. Always watching. As soon as they saw him approach, their posture changed, their figures tensing and their faces alert. Flora's mention of a heavy mob came to mind. These were security men and Jack knew then that he'd get nowhere near the house. He walked past, offering them a smile and a 'Good morning' and received a curt nod in response.

He'd found the house, but now what? Find another corner shop? They were treasure troves of information, but this area seemed too wealthy to have need of one. As he reached the end of Lynton Street, though, a woman carrying a wicker basket came towards him. She'd obviously shopped from somewhere and he was about to ask her for directions when her foot slipped, and she let out a loud curse.

'Sorry,' she said, seeing him hesitate. 'This damn heel has broken.' She hobbled over to a garden wall nearby and sank down. Taking off her shoe, she studied it crossly.

'I hope you don't have far to go,' Jack commiserated.

'Not far.' She grinned. 'Just as well. My hubby is always lecturing me on wearing sensible shoes – I'm glad he's not around to see me limp home.'

'He's at work?' Jack wondered if 'hubby' might be Mr Mason.

'Away on business,' she said, sounding happy at the thought.

'Well, it's a lovely road to limp along.'

She laughed. 'It is, isn't it. We've lived here a while now and I still love it.'

'I can imagine. I know someone who has a house in the street.'

'Really?'

'A Mr Mason. He lives back there.' He waved a hand in the vague direction of Albert House. 'He owns a department store in Kensington.'

'I've met him – at the Coronation party the street threw – though I can't say I know him well.' Her face fell. 'But poor man!'

'Yes,' Jack said uncertainly, hoping he'd pick up a clue.

'She was so young.'

'She was,' he agreed.

'And to do that!'

'A terrible accident,' he hazarded.

She leaned towards him. 'That's the official version, but people round here reckon it was deliberate.'

'Surely not.'

'I don't, of course,' she said hastily. 'I mean, who would drive a car into a brick wall on purpose?'

Jack flinched at the thought and she saw it. 'I know. It doesn't bear thinking of, does it?'

'And so young,' he repeated.

She sighed. 'I did wonder... about the marriage.' She lowered her voice. 'Those kind of marriages... well, they're not usually a good idea.'

He had been congratulating himself on following the surreal conversation, but this had him bewildered.

'May and December, you know,' she said, seeing his puzzlement. 'It doesn't do to marry with that large an age gap, does it?'

He shook his head. 'Not at all. But I best not keep you.' He offered his hand to help her to her feet. 'It might take you a while to make it home.'

'I'm taking the damn things off and walking in my stockinged feet, though I'll probably get frostbite.' She gave a small giggle. 'It's been nice to meet you.'

'And to meet you,' he said, with a wave of his hand.

It seemed then that Mason had been married to a much younger woman who had died in a car crash, the cause of which was not entirely clear. Enough mystery to make the tongues wag, certainly. It had been an interesting encounter, but was this new information worth following up? There might be a newspaper report on the incident, he thought, particularly as it concerned the wife of a prominent business-man. Could he do what he'd done in the autumn and ring the local paper? Ask them what they had on the crash that had killed Mrs Mason?

There was a problem with that. Unlike Oxford and its local paper, London newspapers covered an enormous area. The *Evening News*, for instance, wouldn't necessarily have been interested enough in a Knightsbridge resident to have written up the crash. There might be more local papers, but Jack didn't know of them. To discover their names, it would mean a tramp to North London and the newspaper library, and there simply wasn't time today.

A plan began to formulate as he walked back to the High Street. His father lived close by and might just be at home. Ralph Carrington tended to travel in better weather and most often hunkered down in his London flat for the winter. It was worth a chance, Jack thought. If he could beg a bed for the night, he'd take the underground to Colindale tomorrow and explore the newspaper library.

Meanwhile... there was a department store in Kensington, wasn't there, with staff who might just be willing to talk?

It was no more than a ten-minute walk back to Kensington High Street and Mason's grand frontage was among the first shops he came to. Christmas might have suffered a slow start in Abbeymead, but at Mason's it was in full swing. Pushing through one of the many revolving glass doors, he was hit by a blast of hot air and a loud rendition of 'Jingle Bells'. Coloured chains looped their way from ceiling to ceiling and every wall sprouted swathes of artificial holly and mistletoe. Jack wove a path around an obedient line of young children, not yet old enough for school, holding hands with their mothers as they waited to see Father Christmas. He couldn't remember any Christmases when he'd even seen a Father Christmas, let alone visited him in his grotto.

The perfume department was one of the first he came to. It seemed a good choice, staffed in the main by young women who were likely to know whatever gossip was circulating the store. Jack waited a while, watching the ebb and flow of customers and, when he spied a space at the counter, walked over and began his hastily constructed story.

'I'm looking for a Christmas present,' he said. 'For my wife.'

He saw the girl glance down at his hand. No ring, but then few men wore a wedding band. Its absence wasn't about to trip him up.

'Do you know the perfume your wife wears, sir?'

'I don't.' He adopted what he thought might be the look of a harassed husband out of his depth, which wasn't too far from the truth. 'It's kind of jasmine,' he said vaguely. Jasmine was Flora's scent and he could buy her a bottle while he was here. Christmas presents had so far not been on his to-do list, but it was a neat ploy.

'Perhaps this one then?' The assistant reached down and sprayed perfume on a small stick, waving it under his nose.

'Quite strong, isn't it?' It had smelt fine, but he needed to extend this purchase as long as he could.

'Maybe this one?' Obligingly, she chose another bottle, repeating the same action.

'That's a little more like the one she uses, I think. You must have a host of clueless husbands to deal with at this time of the year.'

The assistant gave a weak smile. It wouldn't do to agree. 'We could try one more if you want to be completely certain,' she suggested.

'Thank you, you're very patient. Mason's is a brilliant store. I make sure I shop here whenever I'm in London,' he lied. 'Actually... it's an odd coincidence, now I think of it. Only the other day, quite by chance, I met someone who used to work here.'

'Oh yes.' She was mildly interested.

'Rafferty. His name was Hugo Rafferty.'

Her eyebrows rose steeply.

'You know him?'

'I should think all the girls did!' she said, unguardedly.

'A lady's man, was he?'

'You could call it that, though most of us didn't. He doesn't work here now.'

'No, I understood that, though we had only a brief conversation. At the time, I didn't like to pry but I got the impression that he left under a bit of a cloud.'

The assistant nodded, while the perfume sat neglected on the counter. 'No one knew why, exactly, but one day Rafferty was here and the next Mr Mason had given him his cards.'

'My hunch was right then. I'm glad I didn't say too much. But poor Mr Mason. It must have been unpleasant having to sack a trusted colleague – and after he'd lost his wife, too.'

'It was a bad time, all right.' The girl seemed to have forgotten entirely why Jack was standing in front of her counter.

'Such a young woman.' He shook his head. 'I suppose it was the car – probably too powerful for her to handle.'

Th girl looked sceptical. 'It was a Morris. An ordinary family car. I remember seeing Mrs Mason drive into the car park here. And it was broad daylight when it happened.'

'Really? She must have suffered some kind of illness then. A stroke maybe?'

The girl looked to either side of her before leaning forward and saying in a whisper, 'Some of us thought differently.'

'You don't mean... it was deliberate?'

The assistant nodded solemnly.

'But she was young,' he protested. 'And wealthy – look at all this.' His hand traced an arc around the surrounding space. 'She had everything to live for.'

'Except what she wanted.'

He fixed an expectant look to his face.

'We reckoned it was a love affair gone wrong,' the girl began, only to be interrupted by a customer who had been loitering in the background for some time and decided she'd had enough of waiting.

The woman thumped her purchase down onto the glass counter. 'When you're ready, love,' she said.

'Yes, of course.' The girl was flustered. 'And for you, sir?'

'The second bottle, I think, thank you.'

It was more expensive than Jack thought possible. But what did he know about perfume? Thinking back, he'd never bought scent for Helen in all the years they'd been together – another black mark against his name – and now he was glad he hadn't. Flora was worth it. Nevertheless, he found himself crossing his fingers that his agent would enjoy the finished book, that Arthur would easily find a publisher, and very soon he'd bank a satisfying advance.

17

Jack tossed up whether or not to take a taxi to Elystan Avenue. It had grown colder as the day progressed and, though the fedora was keeping his head warm, a biting wind had turned his neck to ice. In the end, he decided to economise – the mythical advance had not yet been agreed and funds were running low. He would walk the short distance to the neighbouring borough and his father's Chelsea flat as briskly as possible.

He strode southwards through the maze of small streets, remembering the way from when he'd come to live with his father as a teenage boy, the surplus adolescent Ralph hadn't wanted. Looking back, Jack wasn't sure how he'd coped with the years he'd spent in Elystan Avenue. From the outset, he'd felt wholly out of place among Ralph's 'smart set', at sea with the poker playing, the constant womanising, the sheer loucheness of the life his father led.

He was deep in his memories, crossing the final road, when the guttural roar of a car engine startled him back into the present. He turned quickly. A large black saloon was powering towards him, straddling the road, and almost on top of him. There was no time to take avoiding action. No time to reach the far pavement and safety. He heard the thud as metal hit bone, tossing him to one side as though he were nothing more than a figure of rags. Landing in the gutter, he fell into a heap of tangled limbs. Blood splashed from a cut on his forehead and his wounded arm throbbed sickeningly.

As he lay prone, he was aware of lights at the end of the street. Screwing up his eyes to see better, a bolt of pain shot through his head. They were reversing lights! The vehicle had stopped and was about to backtrack. His assailant was coming to finish him off. From somewhere above, he heard the bang of a front door. Then the roar of the car once more. He closed his eyes, waiting for the end, but the growl of its engine faded, and there was the figure of a woman bending over him.

'What on earth happened?' she asked. 'I heard the noise and ran out of the house to see. You need an ambulance – I must go back indoors and telephone. First, though, I'd better get you onto the pavement, if I can.'

'There's no need of an ambulance.' Jack's words were stuttered. He was finding it difficult to talk. 'I'm not badly hurt. If... if you could help me up? Maybe walk me around the corner. My father lives a few yards away.'

'But you were hit by a car. You might have injuries you can't see. And the police should be told as well.'

'I'm fine,' he insisted. 'Just a cut to my head. Don't worry about the police. My father will be sure to report the accident. But if you could take the other arm, please?' He'd winced as she'd taken hold of his damaged limb.

It may have been only a few yards to his father's front door, but they were some of the most painful yards Jack had ever trod. All the while, his Good Samaritan posed a constant stream of questions. Was he still all right? How much further did they have to go? Would his father be in at this time of day?

Jack had no speech left and allowed her to talk on while he

doggedly shuffled a few paces at a time until the deep green door of number three, Elystan Avenue, came into view.

'I'll be OK from here,' he assured her, without any real idea if Ralph was at home.

'I'm delivering you to your father,' she said firmly. 'I want to know there's someone to look after you.'

Jack prayed very hard and, amazingly, his prayer was answered. Ralph Carrington's astonished face greeted him at the door. Barely able to speak, Jack turned to thank his rescuer, then stumbled over the threshold into the small hall. Somehow, he managed to reach the sitting room sofa before he collapsed.

'What on earth's happened to you, old chap?' his father asked, echoing Jack's Samaritan.

'A car – in the next road – knocked me down. But I'm still here.'

'So I see, but not in any fit shape. You need to go to hospital,' and when Jack shook his head, slowly because it was so very painful, his father added, 'or see a doctor. I can get a friend to come round.'

'No, Dad, no fuss please.'

'Come off it, Jack. Some so-and-so hits you amidships and then drives off. He needs reporting, at the very least.'

'I don't have the number plate and really, I'm OK. A plaster for my forehead would be good, though.' He was careful not to mention the throbbing arm or the ribs that hurt every time he took a breath.

'Right-o. I'll fetch my first aid kit. Been with me since 1943 but it should still work.'

In a minute, his father was back and, in an unusually gentle fashion, bathed his forehead with warm water, then applied a stinging swab of iodine and attached a large sticking plaster to the cut.

'It's bled a lot, but I don't think it needs stitches.' Ralph peered at the wound. 'Now, let me take that coat off you. It looks a shambles. Mind you, it wasn't exactly high fashion beforehand.'

He fetched the clothes brush he kept on the hall's mahogany console table and proceeded to brush the garment vigorously. 'That's enough, Dad,' Jack said after about ten minutes. 'I'd like some coat left.'

Ralph walked back into the sitting room and over to the parquet and gold cocktail cabinet that sat in one corner of the room. 'Here, this is what you need.' He poured an amber liquid into the balloon-shaped goblet. 'Brandy. Should work wonders.'

'At four in the afternoon?'

'At any time, Jack.' He ran his eyes over his son's lanky figure. 'Bet you haven't eaten today.'

'I had breakfast.'

'Tssh. That was hours ago. I'll phone the Italian – nice little trattoria a few streets down. Pasta, that's what you need. First, though, tell me why you're here, why you're walking around Chelsea? I can't imagine it was to see me.'

Jack took a long sip of brandy. 'I came up to town to see my agent,' he said smoothly, remembering the story he'd told himself earlier.

Ralph sat down, his legs crossed, and took his own leisurely sip. 'I didn't know you had one. You must be doing pretty well with those books.'

His son sighed. 'I've had an agent for years, but you know nothing of my life. You never have. You've never been sufficiently interested to find out.'

'Different worlds, old chap. Difficult for me to get into yours.'

'It means making an effort. You've never made the attempt. At least I've tried to understand yours.'

'Stuck in my ways, I guess. Can't help it – that's my little problem. Unlike your mother, it seems. She's busy kicking over the traces.'

Jack was surprised. 'You've heard from her?'

'Just a postcard. The old girl's moved to Paris. I suppose she thought she should let me know. Got a new boyfriend apparently – that's probably why she wrote – likes to annoy me, or so she thinks. Some Italian count. She'll enjoy talking about him. Plenty of snob value in a count.'

There was a long silence, Jack drowsy from pain and the brandy almost falling asleep on the soft sofa.

'You should try it,' his father suddenly pronounced. 'Romance, I mean. Keeps you young.' His brows knitted together, the lines on his face deepening. 'There was that girl in Cornwall. The sparky one. Do you see much of her?'

Jack opened his eyes. He had no intention of speaking of Flora to his father or anyone else. 'Not much,' he lied.

'Pity. Well, better make that call to the restaurant. Give them plenty of notice. They'll need to deliver a feast, fatten you up. You're all skin and bone, lad.'

That night Jack slept in his old bedroom for the first time in twenty years and whether it was the strangeness of the experience or the pain that radiated from every inch of his body, he spent most of the night wide awake, staring at the same crack in the ceiling that he'd stared at all those years ago.

Once the hall clock struck six, he felt no obligation to stay in bed. His father wouldn't be up and about for several hours and by that time Jack intended to be on his way back to Abbeymead. Yesterday, he'd fixed on going to the newspaper library before he left London, but he had to recognise that he was in no shape to get himself to Colindale and back. He'd be lucky if he managed to arrive safely in Sussex.

They had eaten a large meal last evening – his father had insisted on three courses – and Jack wasn't particularly hungry. A cup of coffee would be sufficient. He padded into the kitchen and looked through the cupboards. The coffee was exactly where it had always been and still the same brand his father preferred. Lavazza, imported from Italy and expensive. *You can't skimp on decent coffee, Jack.*

He'd downed two large cups and was about to commandeer the bathroom when his father appeared in the kitchen doorway. It was barely seven. No wonder Ralph's eyes were only half-open.

'You're an early bird,' he said, fumbling to tie the cord of his tartan wool dressing gown.

'You, too.'

His father shuffled to the counter and poured himself what coffee was left in the percolator. 'So, what are your plans for the day?'

'I'll be on my way home, back to Abbeymead. I can take a cab to Victoria.'

Ralph Carrington peered at him through still half-opened eyes. 'You look perfectly ghastly,' he said with uncomfortable honesty. 'You can't travel all the way to Sussex on your own, you'll have collapsed before you get anywhere near a train. I'm busy today, but why don't I ring this agent chappie of yours? He can sort you out. Earn his crust.'

'I've no intention of bothering Arthur. I'll get a taxi to the station, like I said, and if I feel that lousy, the cabbie can take me all the way to Abbeymead.'

His father gave a low whistle. 'You'll need a bank loan for that!' He slurped down the rest of his coffee and began preparing a fresh percolator. 'Look, you don't want to be paying out for a taxi when I've a perfectly good Bentley in the mews round the corner.'

Jack looked disgruntled. 'I thought you were going to be busy.'

'I'm flexible, old chap. Always good to be flexible.'

18

Flora had thought it strange when there'd be no word from Jack. She'd expected a call last night, once he was back at Overlay House, and wondered if his silence signified that he'd drawn a blank in London. It was always going to be difficult to find Mason's house and perhaps he hadn't had the forethought to go on to the department store. She kicked herself that she hadn't mentioned it, but surely Jack was a good enough investigator to think of it himself. So why no news? He must still be in London, she reasoned, but hadn't thought it worth telephoning. Having been on tenterhooks all day, she'd gone to bed feeling deflated, and just a little cross.

She was locking the All's Well's door at lunchtime – it was Wednesday and early closing – when Charlie Teague crashed his bike into the kerb, scrambled upright and arrived at her elbow.

'What are you doing here, Charlie? Shouldn't you be in school?'

'School don't start again fer half an hour. I've been home fer my dinner – Mum said I could this week. Them school dinners. Argh!' He put a finger down his throat to mimic a vomit.

'It's good to know you enjoyed your lunch,' she said, bemused by his sudden appearance, 'and I'll see you after school on Friday? I'll have a fair number of deliveries for you by then.'

Charlie gave what looked an impatient nod. 'It's Mr C. That's why I came.'

'What do you mean, Mr C?'

'Mr Carrington.'

'Yes, I know Mr Carrington,' she said, beginning to feel alarm. 'But why are you here?'

'He's had an accident.'

'This isn't a tease, is it?'

'I wouldn't joke about that, Miss Steele. Though some boys at school would, now it's gettin' near Christmas. They're puttin' firecrackers in people's shoes and throwin' their gym kit into the dustbin. Some of 'em actually pretended the janitor's cat had been kidnapped.'

'Mr Carrington?' she said, desperate to know the worst. 'What kind of accident?'

'I dunno but he looks pretty bad. I saw this big green car – a Bentley it was – drivin' up the lane to Overlay and I followed it. Cor, it was some car!'

'Charlie, where is Mr Carrington?'

'At home, o' course'. It was his dad drivin'. I found that out.'

'Is his father still with him?'

'Nah. He helped him up the path into the house, then went back to the car and drove off.'

'I must go,' she said, already half running towards the cobbled courtyard where Betty had her shelter. 'You best get off to school,' she shouted over her shoulder, as she sailed into the high street and turned a sharp right.

Pedalling fiercely along Greenway Lane, Flora felt her stomach hollow. Charlie had said that Jack had looked bad. For a boy of that age to notice a grown-up looking ill meant that Jack must be in a bad state, even though his father appeared to have abandoned him. How was it that Ralph Carrington had driven him down from London? Had Jack been staying with him and, if he had, what had happened there? Head whirling, Flora's mind bounced from question to question.

She pushed open the front gate to Overlay House and let Betty drop onto the square of grass. Running across to the sitting room window, she made a telescope with her hands and squinted through the glass. Jack was sitting in the new chair he'd bought several months ago, his eyes closed, and looking horribly white. Gently, she tapped on the window. Most usually, she banged loudly on his door to get him to hear – it had become a joke between them – but this wasn't a joke and Flora was unsure if he would even make it to the front door.

There had been no response to her tap, and she tried again, this time a little louder. He opened his eyes and she saw he was trying hard to focus on the window. Giving her a weak smile – he'd seen her! – he heaved himself out of the chair. She should have gone home first, she realised, and fetched the spare key Jack had given her, but she'd been in too much of a panic, too desperate to get to Overlay House and see for herself how bad he was.

Several minutes passed before the front door opened. Jack stood on the threshold, holding on to the door and swaying very slightly. She'd seen him injured before, once or twice quite badly, but it was something about the sheer weakness with which he propped himself against the doorframe that caught in her throat. He stood back to let her pass but, instead, she flung her arms around him and burst into tears.

'Hey. None of that! I'm alive.'

'I was so scared,' she said tearfully. 'Charlie told me you'd had an accident and I had no idea how bad you were.'

'I'm amazed he managed to remember that much. He was

far more interested in the Bentley. Come on in. You're hurting my ribs and I need to sit down again.'

She took his arm and supported him back into the sitting room, taking a seat on the sofa once he'd regained his chair.

'How badly *are* you hurt?' was her first question.

'As you see, a cut head.' He pointed to his forehead. 'It's stopped bleeding now which is good, but the cut is pretty deep.'

'And...'

'Bruised ribs – I don't think they're broken – and a painful arm. The same arm the sniper chose.'

'You can't do much about the arm, but shouldn't you get the ribs strapped?'

'If they don't ease in the next day or so, I'll take myself to a doctor. I think I'll be OK, though.'

'I hardly dare ask, but how did you end up in this state?'

'Simple. I was run over.'

Flora's mouth fell open. 'Deliberately?'

'Quite deliberately. Whoever it was. He, I'm assuming it was a he, didn't polish me off the first time and was about to reverse and finish the job when a woman from one of the houses nearby came out to investigate the noise. That was when my assailant scarpered. Yesterday was my lucky day.'

Flora's expression was bewildered. 'I simply don't understand.' She felt frustrated as well as deeply upset for Jack. 'I've been asking questions in Abbeymead, stirring up trouble for days, if you like, and nothing has happened to me. You go to London for a few hours to do the same and someone tries to kill you. Who would do that and why? Who even knew you were in London?'

'That's what I've been asking myself. As far as I'm aware only you and Alan Ridley knew I was going to town.'

'Then the driver has to be someone who saw you in London.'

He nodded, looking more tired than ever. 'The only person

I can think it might be is one of the security guards at Albert House – I found Mason on the electoral roll, by the way, which was an amazing piece of luck.'

'You are clever, Jack. Really well done! But why would a security guard be pursuing you?'

'I've thought about that. The two chaps weren't exactly friendly when I walked by, but on the other hand, they were hardly threatening. I suppose if Mason was at home in Lynton Street and saw me stop outside his house, he might have recognised me from the funeral. His chauffeur certainly would, after our conversation. Perhaps I was too noticeable, in a place where I shouldn't be. Worse, I talked to one of his neighbours for some time, and then I went on to the department store and asked more questions.'

'Killing you to stop you from asking questions seems extreme. But then if Mason surrounds himself with security guards and pays thugs to do his dirty work, he is extreme.'

Jack gave a small shrug and winced as he did. He was so pale and in such obvious pain that she held back from asking whether or not he felt the trip had been worth his suffering. If he'd gained little or nothing, it would be the sourest of outcomes.

'Before you tell me any more, I'll make some tea.' She put on her most cheerful voice. 'You look as if you could do with a cup.'

Within minutes, she was back, having loaded the tray with a plate of shortbread biscuits as well as two mugs of hot tea. 'No extra sugar,' she said, shuffling papers aside on the crowded coffee table. 'I reckon you must be over the shock by now, but the shortbreads are really sweet. I found them at the top of the far cupboard.'

He peered at the plate of biscuits. 'I had a mad moment,' he said vaguely. 'I bought a tin for Christmas.'

'Then I'll have to buy you another. But have a biscuit now.'

She managed to persuade him to eat two and drink most of his tea. Only then did she feel it right to ask what she was longing to know. 'Did you get to speak to Mr Mason?'

'I didn't. I found his house but only got as far as the garden gate.'

Flora put her empty cup back on the tray. 'It's interesting that Mason feels the need to have a guard on his house. Do you think the security men are part of the heavy mob Harry Barnes talked about?'

'They could be – they were fearsome-looking gentlemen. But the mob may be even worse. Too brutal for Lynton Street and have to be kept out of sight.'

'Did you speak to the men?'

'No chance, and no chance of speaking to anyone in the house either.'

Flora was disappointed and it must have shown on her face, because he carried on, 'However...'

'Yes?'

'The neighbour I spoke to turned out to be just the chatty woman I needed. Apparently, until a few months ago, there was a Mrs Mason.'

'OK.' That didn't sound too exciting.

'Mrs Mason was a great deal younger than her husband, a rich man's prize, I think you'd say, and she died in a horrendous car crash.'

Flora frowned. 'There has to be something more than that, doesn't there?'

Jack shifted in his chair. She could see he was trying to get comfortable. 'There *is* something else. The car hit a brick wall and the rumour going the rounds is that the woman drove into it deliberately.'

'Suicide?'

'It's only a rumour,' he warned, 'but there was no apparent reason for such a dreadful accident. The car she was driving was a basic model, nothing too powerful, and it was broad daylight at the time.'

Flora thought for a while. 'Could the marriage have been so unhappy that she'd take her own life? There is such a thing as divorce, despite the stigma.'

'We can't know, can we? As my informant was quick to say, May and December are not a great pairing. But I've a hunch there was something else in play. After I left Lynton Street, I went to the department store and talked to one of the shop assistants.'

'That *was* clever. Did she gossip? Did she think the crash was deliberate?'

'It's rumour again, but she reckoned there was a lover in the background. Obviously, a younger man.'

'Who let her down? Ran out on her?'

'I imagine that's the story, but it's pure speculation. I wanted to check the newspapers. There's bound to have been a report of the accident in a local rag, but it's a fair journey to the news library in Colindale and I ran out of time. I was planning to go today, but...' He pulled himself upright, trying, it seemed, to relieve the pressure on his chest.

'Perhaps I can go,' Flora said quickly, keen that he did nothing to make himself feel worse.

Jack shook his head. 'I really don't want you trekking all the way to north London. I thought about it on the way down in the car and came up with an idea which might possibly work. Dad brought me home, by the way – I imagine Charlie told you who was driving the car of his dreams.' He grinned and, for a second, the pain creases vanished. 'I was on my way to his flat yesterday to beg a bed for the night when I almost joined the dear departed.'

'Why didn't your father stay in Abbeymead? You've plenty of room here.'

'After a night and a two-hour car journey, he'd obviously

had enough of me!' When she looked severe, he said, 'Only kidding. He had a poker game to get to this afternoon, one where he was hopeful of making a killing.'

Flora pursed her lips, her opinion of Ralph Carrington lowered. 'So, what was your idea?'

'I thought I'd telephone an old colleague. Someone at the *Daily Mercury*, the national I worked on for years. In the past, I did him a few favours and maybe he'd be willing to take on the research. He'll probably know the name of the local paper that's likely to have carried the accident report and can ring them directly, rather than making the trip up to Colindale. This car crash seems important, and I reckon there's more to know about it.'

Flora collected their empty cups and stacked them on the tray. 'It's looking that way.' She paused, the tray in her hands. 'When you were talking to the assistant at Mason's, did you mention Hugo Rafferty? Ask about him working there?'

'I did. The girl didn't know why he was dismissed. Just that he was there one day and gone the next.'

'That's one thing we *do* know.'

'Also, it seems, he had an eye for the ladies, and that wasn't popular among the assistants. The girl I spoke to didn't seem to like him much.'

'Mmm,' Flora murmured, for the moment storing the information away. 'And Phoebe Tallant?'

Jack looked blank.

'Did they know her at Mason's? Was it Mr Mason who came to Abbeymead looking for her?'

'If Phoebe had worked at Mason's department store, he wouldn't be asking Dilys for her address, would he?'

'True.' Flora couldn't prevent a sigh. 'Still, it's a pity you didn't ask. My hunch that she might have had some kind of connection to the shop is probably rubbish, but it would be good to know for sure.'

Jack pulled a face. 'And just when I thought I'd done so well.'

'You did.' She put down the tray and went over to him. 'I'm sorry. You did extremely well and you've suffered for it.' She gave him a gentle kiss on the lips, and he pulled her down towards him and was giving her a much longer one when the door knocker sounded.

'Is that likely to be your father back?' Flora slipped from his embrace.

'Having lost everything in the poker game?' He gave a faint smile. 'I don't think so.'

When she opened the front door, it was Alice standing on the doorstep. 'I heard as how Jack was poorly,' her friend said, bustling into the kitchen with a large straw basket.

'How...' Flora began to ask. 'No, don't bother answering. The whole village will know by now.'

Alice settled her basket on the kitchen table. 'How is the poor love?'

'Not great, but he'll survive.'

'No one seems to know what happened exactly, but I expect you'll tell me in time. That boy's a worry, for sure.'

Flora blinked at the idea of Jack as a boy but, for a motherly woman like Alice, they must all seem children. As if to prove the point, Alice began unpacking the goods she'd brought. 'I've made him some supper – and you, too.'

'Oh, Alice, thank you. I was just wondering what I should do. You are so kind.'

Her friend tutted. 'No bother at all. My favourite chicken casserole was on the menu for lunch – that poke-nose Henshall hasn't been around the last few days to tell me what not to cook, up at the Lexington, playing golf with Harry Barnes – but everyone went for the fish. Goodness knows why. Anyways, there was so much spare that I thought I'd have it for my supper and you could make it yours.'

Flora gave her a warm hug. 'I'll get the oven going when I can. I do wish Jack would replace his wretched stove. it's so tricky.'

'You'll manage,' Alice said, picking up her basket and giving Flora a kiss on the cheek. 'I'll be off now. I won't bother Jack.'

She peered into the sitting room on her way to the front door. 'Looks proper peaky, doesn't he?' she said in a whisper loud enough to carry to Jack. 'Let me know if there's anything I can do before Friday. Our usual supper then?'

'That will be good.'

'I reckon it will. Kate's trying out a new recipe.'

When her friend had left, Flora walked back into the sitting room. 'I hope you're up for chicken casserole. Alice has brought the most enormous dish – unless you're still "proper peaky" by this evening and don't fancy eating.'

'I'm never too peaky to enjoy Alice's cooking.'

When she'd settled herself back on the sofa, he looked across at her. 'What now? Where do we go from here?'

'You don't go anywhere,' Flora said decidedly. 'I'll be the one to do the adventuring. After the conversation I had with Harry, I'm keen to speak to Stephen Henshall. I'll go up to the Priory tomorrow. Alice says Henshall is always at the hotel towards the end of the week.'

'What are you going to ask him?' Jack had shifted position again. He was very uncomfortable, Flora could see. An early supper and an early bedtime, she thought.

'I want to talk to him about Rafferty. Find out just what his relationship was with the man.'

'Henshall will tell you the same as Harry Barnes has. I don't see you getting any further with that line of questioning.'

'I may not learn anything new,' she agreed, 'but I think it's worth a try. I might just be able to squeeze something more from him.'

Jack managed a grin. 'You do squeeze well, I have to admit.'

19

Flora went to bed that evening feeling depressed. She hated to see Jack hurt and suspected he'd broken ribs from which it would take weeks to recover fully. There was a nagging sense that he was hurting far too much for far too little. What he'd discovered in London was interesting, but it hardly took them much further.

At first sight, Mason's need for security guards at his house was unusual, but he was a wealthy man and it was possible that his safety, or his family's, had been threatened. As for the information on Rafferty, it added to their picture of the man, but little more. They already knew he'd been summarily dismissed for theft – or embezzlement, she wasn't sure which – but how important was it that he hadn't been well-liked, that the store's female staff had been extremely wary of him? And Mrs Mason's car accident? If Jack's colleague agreed to help, it might prove worth pursuing, but then again it might not. All in all, it felt to Flora that time, effort and a good deal of distress had been spent on moving barely an inch forward. She would have to do better tomorrow.

· · ·

It wasn't the best morning to be riding Betty. The temperature was still below zero but now, instead of a light covering of snow, sleet had arrived, driving horizontally at Flora's bent figure as she laboured up Fern Hill on her way to the Priory. Wheeling her bike through its tall gates, she was most conscious of emptiness, as though the estate had fallen into a permanent sleep. There was little, of course, that the gardeners could do at this time of the year, but the general sense of desertion lowered her spirits further. She needed to shake herself free of this mood, she thought crossly. Find the energy to solve this case.

Flora had no particular interest in discovering who had killed the curate – from the various accounts she'd heard, he seemed a man she would not have liked – but Inspector Ridley had asked them for help and her pride baulked at the prospect of failing. More than that, there was a fascination in the puzzle such mysteries set her. And Jack, she knew, was delighted when he could leave behind fictional crime for real-life murder. Neither of them would be happy to give up their 'adventures', but if they were unable to unearth even one significant clue, shouldn't they forget the whole business?

She had reached the final bend in the long winding drive, the Priory's golden mass just coming into view, when a figure appeared walking towards her. At last, some life! It was Stephen Henshall. What could be more opportune?

'Good morning,' she called out as he approached. 'You're just the person I was hoping to see, Mr Henshall.'

He looked up as she spoke, his face, she noticed, tinged a dull red. 'Why's that then?' he asked, his tone sullen.

'I was hoping you could help me. I've some questions I think you can answer.'

He shook his head and went to push past her.

'Please don't go.' She caught hold of the sleeve of his tweed overcoat. 'I wanted to speak to you about Hugo Rafferty. I was wondering how you knew him.' It was a question to which Flora already held the answer, but it might just be a starting point for the conversation she really wanted to have.

'I can't see why it's any interest of yours, but I met him through business.' He pulled himself free of her grasp.

'I see.' She let a beat pass before she said, 'And he was the one who defrauded you?'

'How d'you know that?' he asked angrily, his thick eyebrows seeming to bush even thicker. 'What the hell has it to do with you?'

'Quite a lot, in fact. You've gone to a good deal of trouble to advise Dominic and Sally on how best to recover from the mess they were in. Given your time freely to help one of my best friends – and I don't like to think you've been treated so badly.'

For a moment, he looked mollified, and Flora pushed on. 'I'm worried for you, Mr Henshall. The police consider your relationship with Rafferty crucial to their investigation, and I'm very much afraid it will implicate you in a way you wouldn't want.' She hoped that might rattle him a little. 'Inspector Ridley doesn't seem to understand why you were at the bell tower the night that Rafferty died.'

'What nonsense!' he blustered, pulling up the collar of his overcoat against a fresh torrent of ice. 'There's no mystery. I'm staying with Harry Barnes. Harry's my friend and I thought it right to show some interest in what he enjoys.' There was a pause before he added, 'I've never seen church bells rung, I thought it might be fun. Particularly with Harry involved.' A small crack of humour appeared in a face that was otherwise wooden. 'Kind of an odd thing for the bloke to take up.'

'I hear he's not too good at it.'

'That makes sense.' The smile widened a little.

'And the funeral?' she pursued. 'Did you go to Hugo Rafferty's funeral to support Harry?'

'Naturally. The bloke was shaken up by what happened that night. Thought it his duty to go to Rafferty's do, though I couldn't see it myself. Harry needed company that day and I was glad to oblige.'

'Oh,' she said, casually. 'It was Mr Barnes's idea then? That's strange. He mentioned to me that it was you who wanted to attend. That he went with you, rather than the other way round.'

Henshall's face, which had been gradually losing its tension, froze, and the tide of red, recently subsided, began its creep back.

'What if I did want to go?' he rasped out. 'I made sure the little bastard got his deserts. Made sure he was gone for good.'

It was going to be difficult to find anyone who had actually liked Hugo Rafferty, Flora reflected. She was ready with her next question when Stephen Henshall took a step forward, so close he was almost touching, and glared down at her.

'What is it with this questioning? You've no right – you're not the police. And you shouldn't be throwing accusations around.'

'I'm sorry to have upset you,' she said, not feeling at all sorry. 'That wasn't my intention. I came to find you because I wanted to help. I know the inspector well and know how he works. Once the police began asking questions, I thought I should try to warn you of their interest. Where, for instance, were you yesterday?'

The tufty eyebrows twitched. Flora watched, mesmerised. It seemed as though they had a life of their own and, at the moment, they were feeling extremely annoyed.

'I was here, of course. Working with Dom on publicity for their Christmas events. Something wrong with that?'

There was. Alice had told her that Henshall had been nowhere near the Priory for several days but playing golf at the Lexington. What if he hadn't been on the golf course either? What if he'd taken the train to London and followed Jack? Could he have jumped into a taxi and trailed Jack's bus? It sounded fantastic, but it could have been done. Just. But how would he have got hold of a car, hoping to kill? Stolen one, maybe. That was possible. But then how would he have known the day Jack was travelling? No one, apart from herself and the inspector, had known.

'Nothing wrong at all,' she said hurriedly.

'Good.' His manner had veered to the belligerent. 'You get on with your life and I'll get on with mine. I don't need your interest or your sympathy.' With that, he stormed past her, marching towards the wrought-iron gates and the village beyond.

She found Sally in the office that led off from the wood-panelled foyer. Her friend had her head bent over papers, a pencil in her hand as though waiting to strike.

'Sally?'

The girl swung round on her swivel chair. 'Flora! You've come to rescue me. How wonderful!'

'I can see you're very busy. I can come back another day.'

'Don't you dare!' Sally leapt to her feet. 'These' – she waved her hand at the cluttered desk – 'are invoices. I can't bring myself to total them up. It will be too horrendous. Somehow, I have to cut down on future expenditure which means going through every one of these sheets, line by line. Can you imagine?'

'Is this part of Stephen Henshall's plan to get the hotel back on its feet?'

'It is, but don't talk to me about Mr Henshall. I've just had the most monumental row with him.'

'I actually met him on the driveway,' Flora confessed. 'He looked a little pink.'

'That makes two of us. Come on, let's have a tray of tea sent up to the sitting room. I like our little get-togethers amid the chintz.'

Once they were settled on the soft sofas that Sally favoured, and Dottie, her best maid, had delivered the tea, Flora thought it time to ask the obvious question.

'What was the row about?'

Sally's lips tightened. 'It appears that Henshall is in trouble. Deep financial trouble. I had an inkling there might be problems, but I didn't know until now how bad it was. He looks likely to be sued by I don't know how many people. I've told Dominic we should have nothing more to do with him in case we get dragged into whatever he's about to face. I know it sounds ungrateful, but we can't afford to get involved in more upset, and really Stephen hasn't done much more than we could have done on our own, given time. *And* he's upset Alice – loads. She may be my aunt but she's also the hotel's chief cook and I need her to be happy. And leading a happy team in the kitchen.'

'You told Stephen he had to leave?' Flora guessed, taking the cup of tea Sally handed her.

'I should have asked Dottie to bring the almond slices,' Sally murmured. 'Auntie made a new batch this morning and the smell was glorious. Yes, to answer your question. Dominic should have been the one to tell him – they've been working closely together – but, as always, Dom shied away from anything likely to make him uncomfortable.'

'You were left to do the nasty stuff?' Flora was unsurprised. She thought it a pity Sally had ever become involved with Dominic Lister. As a business partner, he left much to be desired.

'Just about. I tried to do it as decently as I could, but he saw the newspaper column I'd been reading – I'd forgotten to hide it – and started a rant about rats and sinking ships.'

'A newspaper article?'

'Here. This one.' Sally went over to the dainty walnut bureau beneath the window and from one of its narrow compartments withdrew a newspaper cutting which she handed to Flora.

It was a lengthy piece, but Flora read through the whole thing while her tea cooled beside her.

When she'd finished, she folded the cutting and gave it back to Sally. 'I can see why you're so concerned.'

The article had made clear just how badly Henshall's two hotels had been hit by the scam that Rafferty had perpetrated. The criminality had been going on for months, Rafferty taking money for orders that never appeared, Henshall's customers not receiving the goods they'd paid for, all the time no doubt being fed with excuse after excuse. Henshall and his business were now facing a series of legal actions for his unwitting part in the fraud.

'Has Dominic read this?' she asked Sally.

Her friend nodded. 'Initially, he wouldn't hear a word against Henshall, but I expected that. I knew it was something we wouldn't see eye to eye on. It was only when I showed him the article that he agreed Stephen would have to go. What really spooked me was the final paragraph. Did you read it? The writer mentions a man called Mason who owns that big department store in Kensington. He was one of Stephen's customers and he seems to blame him as much as Rafferty. There's a suggestion in the article that he isn't going to stop at legal action. I'm not sure what that means, it sounded quite threatening, but I told Dominic we must cut free. We simply can't have anything to do with this mess, particularly after what happened at the Priory only a few months ago.'

'How was Henshall when he left you?' Flora asked, remembering the tell-tale redness in the man's face.

'Very angry.' Sally was quiet for a moment, finishing her cup of tea. At length, she said, 'You don't believe Stephen had anything to do with the curate's death, do you? Thinking about it, he'd have a pretty strong motive. It looks as though Rafferty has single-handedly ruined a successful business. It wouldn't be an exaggeration to say he might have ruined Henshall's life.'

'Stephen Henshall is an angry man, all right, and he certainly didn't like my questions. But I did my best to warn him the police have an interest in him, and I was telling the truth. To be honest – and please don't repeat this, Sally – Stephen appears to be their number one suspect at the moment.'

Sally's expression was grave. 'You must be careful, Flora. I know you have this thirst to discover whatever bad things are going on and I'm so grateful for your help last autumn, but I've a horrible feeling about this. We might all be at risk again and I would hate for you to come to harm. Or Jack, for that matter.'

In an instant decision, Flora decided to say nothing of the attack on Jack. It would worry Sally unnecessarily to know he had already come to harm. In any case, her friend would learn the news from Alice soon enough.

'I will be careful,' she promised, 'but really all I'm doing is asking questions. Inspector Ridley never seems to have enough staff and Jack and I are "extras", trying to help where we can.'

Sally frowned. 'It shouldn't be your job. Murder is for the police to solve.'

'Of course, but sometimes we get to hear things they don't,' Flora said placidly.

The two conversations had given Flora a good deal to mull over and, once through the Priory's gates, she rode sedately towards Fern Hill, allowing her mind to wrestle with all that had been said. Applying Betty's brakes, she forfeited her usual carefree swoop down the long, snaking road, grassy banks rushing past, trees a hazy blur. It was quiet, thinking time she needed.

It was as she was passing the post office at the top of the high street that she saw Stephen Henshall again. She would have imagined, if she'd given it much thought, that he would return to Pelham Lodge to share his woes with Harry who must be one of his best friends. But here he was in the middle of the village, talking earnestly to Daniel Vaisey, of all people. And not just talking, but deep in conversation.

Now, why would that be?

20

It took Jack several minutes to shuffle to the telephone and he quite expected the caller to have gone by the time he picked up the receiver.

It was Flora and he was glad he'd made the effort, trying hard to sound as though he was well on the mend when in truth every inch of his body hurt.

'I got hold of my colleague,' he said, sinking into the hall chair for support. 'Luckily, he's between assignments and is happy to help. He's a fairly good idea which paper would have carried a report on Mrs Mason's accident, if any did. He'll contact me tomorrow and let me know.'

There was no response but instead a long silence. 'Are you still there, Flora? Did you hear what I said?'

'Sorry, I did, but my mind was miles away from the accident. It's good news, though.'

'So where was your mind?'

'On Stephen Henshall. It's beginning to look as though the inspector is right about him.'

'Go on.'

When Flora had finished relating her encounter with

Henshall and summarised the article Sally had shown her, he had to agree. 'But,' he added, 'I've still questions on Mason's role in all of this. His name appears in the cutting Sally showed you with a suggestion that he might go for more than legal redress. To my mind, that means personal revenge, physical punishment. It accords with what Harry Barnes told you about the mob the man employs. If Rafferty was a louse, Mason seems worse.'

'He might well be. In fact, he probably is, but I'm not sure he had as much reason to kill Rafferty. OK, his employee defrauded him and dragged his business into the mud, but his department store will survive. Did the shop look as if it was dying when you were there?'

Jack had to concede that it hadn't. 'On the contrary, Christmas cheer was in full swing,' he admitted.

'So, for Mason, Rafferty's wrongdoing is bad, very bad, but it's a temporary setback. Mason will get over the problem, the store will go on making a profit, and Rafferty is now conveniently dead. Things can only get better. But Henshall, according to that newspaper report, is facing the loss of everything he's worked for. His hotels are in debt and the legal suits are piling up. By the time he's settled every customer's dispute with him, he'll be bankrupt.'

'All true.' He gave a long sigh. 'I just have this hunch that Mason, or maybe Mason's wife, is the key.'

'A hunch? Jack, you're beginning to sound like me!' she teased.

Early on Saturday, Flora rode Betty to the post office. It meant opening the All's Well late – Aunt Violet would definitely not have approved. She had always insisted they were in the shop and ready to serve by ten minutes to nine every day, no matter that their first customer invariably walked through the door at least an hour later. But there was a stack of books in the cellar waiting to be despatched and if she didn't brave Dilys first thing this morning, Flora wasn't sure when they would get sent.

'These dratted television licences,' Dilys greeted her. 'Why can't people stick to the wireless?'

'What's wrong with television licences?'

'They're too expensive and there's too many of 'em, that's what's wrong. It gets complicated, people wanting to know whether they need a licence for the wireless, now they've got this box thing. How much is the different licence, they ask? Why have I got to pay an extra charge?'

'After all the hardship, isn't it good that people are becoming better off? Able to afford a new cooker now or rent a refrigerator or a television maybe. Television will probably be the future.'

'I doubt it,' Dilys said firmly. 'I doubt it very much. I saw the Coronation on one of those – at my friend's house in Worthing. Lily has to have the latest thing, always has done. But I tell you, Flora, I wouldn't give you tuppence for it. Nice piece of furniture, mind you. Walnut, I think she said the cabinet was. But the screen! No bigger than my hand! Smudgy black and white figures. You could hardly make out Queenie on her throne. I was not impressed. The film was ever so much better when it came to the Dome. Beautiful colour. Did you see it? No, I guess not. You'd have been too busy nursing Violet at the time.'

The postmistress took a breath, readying herself for another monologue, while Flora waited in silence, her heart sharpened by pain. After all these years, she should be inured to Dilys's insensitivity, but the abrupt mention of Violet's name, the memory of the cruel illness her aunt had suffered, still had the power to hurt. It was five years ago, almost to the day, that she'd returned from library school for the Christmas holidays to discover her aunt was hiding a serious problem.

At least today, Dilys offered visual calm, eschewing her penchant for violent colour in favour of an innocuous beige. Flora looked more closely. Dilys's jumper was sporting a felt brooch that was unusually tasteful: a deep red rose nestled within a spray of green leaves.

'That's a beautiful piece of jewellery you're wearing,' she said, hoping to stem the woman's renewed tide of complaints against televisions, licences, and people who wasted money on such fripperies.

Dilys patted her chest, hitting the brooch full on. 'It is, isn't it? To tell you the truth' – she leaned forward – 'it was a present from a customer. I'm not allowed to accept gifts, it can lead to all kinds of bribery,' she said severely, 'but in this case, I thought, why not? He was a decent enough chap.'

'Really? Who was that?'

'The man who came here, you remember? No, it wasn't you.' Dilys rammed a pencil in and out of her tight perm, seemingly to help her think. 'It was Mr C that I told,' she said finally. 'Anyway, it was the chap who came looking for Phoebe Tallant.'

'Jack told me about him,' Flora admitted. 'He came back then?'

'He did, bless him. Well, not exactly came back, but contacted me again. I don't think he got anywhere with that stupid girl, but he remembered I'd tried to help and sent me this. That's what I call a real gent.'

'Old school?' Flora hazarded, now on the scent of something more interesting.

Dilys sucked in her cheeks. 'I s'pose you'd say that, though he was quite a young man. Fortyish with nice clothes. Substantial kind of chap. That girl missed her chance there.'

Her hunch had been wrong, then. Flora was chastened. It hadn't been Mason looking for Phoebe.

'Right.' The postmistress leaned across the counter. 'Let's have those parcels. I haven't got all day to chat.'

. . .

Jack was waiting for her when she rode Betty into the courtyard at the All's Well.

'You shouldn't be here,' she scolded. 'It's far too early and far too cold. Let me park Betty and I'll unlock.'

Pushing back the wide front door, she breathed in the wonderful aroma of books, Jack following in her footsteps.

'I'm going straight home,' he promised, 'but I needed to see you. I wouldn't be happy telling you on the phone.'

Carefully, Flora hung her red woollen coat on a spare peg in the kitchenette, brushing away the flakes of snow she'd collected on her ride. The coat would have to last her a few more years to come.

'Why no phone call? You're not on a party line,' she said, rejoining Jack in the shop.

'I know I'm not, but I can never be quite sure the call is private. I reckon Dilys listens in when she's got a spare moment.'

'No spare moments this morning. She has a stack of parcels to deal with, not to mention television licences. Sit down now! You're still not a healthy colour.'

'Thanks,' he said wryly, walking slowly across to the window seat and glancing through the latticed windows at the high street beyond.

'It's too early for customers. We won't be disturbed, so tell me what Dilys mustn't hear!'

'I've had word from my colleague.'

'Already? That was quick.'

'Only briefly – just a telegram at the moment. He's sending details later.'

'But the telegram is important?' she prompted, coming to sit beside him.

'A bit of a bombshell, I'd say. My friend found several accounts of the accident – a number of papers reported it, and it was evidently big news for the area – and they all made the same point, that Mrs Mason had led a charmed life and it was terribly sad she'd departed it so abruptly and so young. Part of the charmed life was her marriage to a wealthy man, and before that, which explains the marriage to some extent, was her success as a beauty queen.'

'A rich man's prize, as you said.' Flora frowned. Where was Jack going with this? The news hardly constituted a bombshell.

'What I didn't say, though, because I didn't know, was that this particular beauty queen was called Cicely Tallant.'

She stared at him and, in the silence that followed, Jack spelt out the name's significance.

'The deceased Mrs Mason is likely to have been Phoebe Tallant's sister, which paints a rather different picture to the one we've been looking at.'

'That's unbelievable!' Flora's eyes were wide, her expression incredulous.

'We'll know more when we get copies of the various articles my colleague combed through. In his telegram, he promised to mail them today.'

Flora jumped up from her seat and walked to the nearest bookcase, then back again. 'That's why Phoebe wanted to stay in Abbeymead! It's why she didn't want to take whatever magnificent job was being offered her.'

He looked mystified. 'I don't see the connection.'

'It's simple. When Phoebe came here to care for Miss Lancaster, she must have been grieving for her sister, but living in a small village has helped her regain her peace of mind. She wouldn't want to go back to London, would she? Not to all the bad memories it must hold.' Flora walked back to the bookcase, then turned again. 'I feel really bad.'

'But why?' His puzzlement had increased.

'I thought she was being difficult when she said she didn't

know whether she would stay in the village or not, but she was simply trying to decide what was best for her. She must be heartbroken still and trying to find a way through. I know what that feels like.'

'She didn't look that heartbroken when I saw her in the pub a week or so ago,' he said a trifle sharply. 'She looked like she was having fun.'

'People have different ways of coping.' Flora knew from experience how true that was. 'What it means – and what's really interesting – is that Phoebe Tallant is Mason's sister-in-law.'

'So?'

'His interests are likely to be hers.'

'Not necessarily. She might not even have liked him. She might have blamed him for her sister's unhappiness. For her death, even.'

Flora considered the point. 'Do you think that's why she was lingering outside the church before the funeral? To see Mason and confront him?'

'She could have done that in London before she ever arrived in Abbeymead. It's more likely she was at the church to see Rafferty was safely on his way. The same as her brother-in-law, and Stephen Henshall.'

'Gareth Beaumont, too. We mustn't forget him.'

'But...'

Flora sighed loudly. 'There's always a "but".'

'But,' he continued, ignoring the interruption, 'it's a great theory – all these people making sure the man was gone for good – but we can't be sure that Phoebe even knew Rafferty.'

'She must have done. Even if she didn't work there, she must have visited the store at some point – her sister was married to its owner – and if she did, she would have met Rafferty. He was one of the management team.'

'Then why didn't she recognise him when he turned up in Abbeymead pretending to be a curate?'

'That's a good point.' She gave an irritated flick to her hair, brushing several strands back from her forehead. 'It's possible she didn't know he was in Abbeymead. She might never have seen him here. She's not a churchgoer and she's hardly ever walked into the village.'

'Yet she was hanging around the church before the funeral, wasn't she, and didn't Miss Dunmore say something about her calling at the vicarage?'

'I was surprised at that. It didn't seem in character. I think we should speak to Amy Dunmore and find out what Phoebe wanted with her.'

Flora walked back to the window seat and sat in silence for a long time until Jack, shifting his position to get more comfortable, hauled himself to his feet. 'I'd best be off,' he said.

'Jack... you mentioned how Rafferty was seen as a ladies' man. One for the women. I'm wondering...'

'Wondering what?' He stretched his arms high above his head and gave a gasp of pain, then coughed to pretend it hadn't happened.

Flora knew better than to comment. 'Is it possible,' she began slowly, 'is it possible that Cicely Mason was having an affair with Rafferty?'

'That's something I hadn't thought of but, yes, it's a definite possibility. Even if Phoebe never met Rafferty, Cicely is likely to have. She was a beautiful woman, bored perhaps with her marriage to an older man and with too much time on her hands.'

'And Rafferty had charm,' Flora added. 'Even Gareth Beaumont admitted that. If Cicely had an affair with Rafferty and he abandoned her, or her husband found out, or both, she might have been desperate enough to do something as terrible as driving her car into a brick wall.'

'If she did, it gives Mason another reason to kill Rafferty.

And a more powerful reason than fraud. Or order one of his mob to do it,' he added.

Flora pulled a face. 'Think how badly Rafferty sinned against him! He thieved from Mason's store, damaged its reputation, cuckolded its owner, then drove the man's wife to suicide.'

'That's quite a list.'

21

After some thought, Flora decided that rather than bothering Amy Dunmore for information – the housekeeper had enough to worry her with the vicar still unwell and police regularly calling at the vicarage – she would go straight to Phoebe Tallant. By lunchtime on Monday the weather had cleared slightly, the sky no longer snow-laden and the bitter easterly wind that had been blowing for days finally abated.

Wrapped in woollen coat, scarf and hat, she once more pedalled Betty up Fern Hill, this time turning left at the top to arrive at the gates of Miss Lancaster's house, little of which was visible from the road. Dark pines grew tall on either side of the short driveway, masking most of the building, except for the very top of a tower, its sharply angled roof a vertical lunge at the sky. A few paces took Flora to the pointed arch of the front door.

Leaning her bicycle against the coloured brickwork, she glanced up at heavily scrolled Gothic windows. They frowned down on her, their gaze seemingly emptied of all life, and it was only when she took a step back that she saw a faint light shining from the rear of the house. She walked up the shallow flight of stairs to the front entrance and took hold of the serpent-shaped knocker. The sharp crack as iron hit iron echoed through the empty hall beyond, reverberating through the entire house until the sound was finally lost beneath the pointed roof.

Flora was about to give another knock when she heard the soft pad of footsteps on the other side of the door. Then the scraping back of bolts, the turn of a key in a lock that had not been oiled for some time, and Phoebe Tallant stood in the open doorway, her face impassive.

'Yes?' she said without any attempt at courtesy.

'I had a delivery locally.' The lie tripped off her tongue. 'And as I was passing the house, I thought I'd check the details for Miss Lancaster's funeral. And ask how you're feeling.'

'I'm fine. The funeral is at Oakleaves Crematorium. Ten o'clock next Monday.'

At last, Flora thought. Poor Miss Lancaster, waiting all these weeks to be buried, and then not even buried. 'I don't know the place. I wonder, would you have directions?'

The girl stood staring at her for a moment, then nodded and walked away.

'Would you mind if I wait inside?' Flora called after her. 'It's very cold out.'

She interpreted the silence that followed as agreement and walked into the hall, catching sight through an open door of what must have been Miss Lancaster's sitting room.

Flora allowed herself a swift glance. The room was a Victorian's dream, but then Miss Lancaster would have been Victorian. Every surface was covered in some form of ornament: porcelain boxes, small wood carvings, glass and china vases, and in each of the far corners two large display cases held a collection of stuffed exotic birds, their flight arrested, and their colourful plumage now sadly faded.

In between the ornaments, there was frame after frame of photographs. Quickly, she darted into the room, hurrying from one to another, stooping almost double at times to study them. It was as Phoebe appeared in the doorway, a stony expression on her face, that Flora saw the photograph she'd been hoping for. A studio portrait of two young girls posing in their best organdie party frocks. One child had to be Phoebe, already devastatingly pretty, and the other almost certainly an older version, her sister Cicely. Cicely, if anything, was even prettier.

'What a beautiful picture,' Flora enthused. 'You were such a lovely child. And this is?' She pointed to the girl sitting sedately beside Phoebe on the studio's leather bench.

'My sister,' Phoebe said briefly.

'I hadn't realised you had a sister.' She excused herself another lie.

'I don't. Not any longer. She died.'

'I am so sorry.' And Flora was. She'd known, of course, that Cicely Mason was dead but Phoebe's voice, the slight catch, the waver as she'd said the words, brought home the immensity of the girl's loss.

'I am sorry,' she repeated. 'Did you live with her before you came to Abbeymead?'

'My sister was married, so no. She lived in Knightsbridge, in a big house, for what good it did her.'

'And your brother-in-law—'

'Leonard Mason is a horrible man, Miss Steele. I've no wish to speak of him.'

'What a wretched situation!'

Phoebe's lips had compressed into a hard, thin line. 'My sister had a miserable marriage, as many women do.'

Flora felt a strange shock of recognition. Phoebe Tallant had dared to utter words she so often thought herself, but never said. Since the end of the war, women had been pushed back into domesticity, losing the freedoms they'd gained during that dreadful conflict. That their interests, their work, their whole lives, were too often subordinated to male priorities, Flora knew well enough, but Phoebe Tallant's blunt assessment had stung her.

It articulated, she supposed, a deep-seated fear that had never truly gone away, haunting her since the moment she'd learned how her parents had died. It was the fear of losing control, of handing her life and her future into someone else's care. Aunt Violet had told her little of the accident, only that her parents' car had met with very bad weather and ploughed off the road into an iron-barred gate. The questions, the fears, she'd had as a child were still with her. Why had her parents been travelling without her? Had she been abandoned? How fast had her father been driving? Had the two of them quarrelled? And how much had it been her mother's decision to venture into a storm?

Flora pulled herself together. She was here for a purpose. 'Mr Mason was unkind? That's even sadder.'

Phoebe didn't answer directly, but in an angry burst that shattered the cold façade she'd hitherto adopted, she said bitingly, 'I hate the man. He made Cissie deeply unhappy. It was because of him that she died.'

'I don't understand. How could that be?' She'd been surprised by the girl's vehemence.

'My sister was never at peace. Never. The day she died, she was confused, upset. She lost concentration and drove her car off the road.'

That was one way of describing it, Flora thought. Aloud she said, 'That is truly terrible,' and meant it. 'I presume you never see your brother-in-law these days?'

'Why do you ask?'

'Only that Mr Mason is still your family, maybe your only family now, and he was in Abbeymead a short while ago. I believe I saw him at Hugo Rafferty's funeral – the day I met you near the church.'

The girl's mouth settled into a stubborn line. Whether she

was reluctant to think about the man in question or simply didn't want to talk, Flora couldn't guess.

There was a long silence until Phoebe's shoulders lost some of their tension. 'Mason knew where I was living,' she conceded. 'Cissie would have told him, and he sent a message to meet him by the church before the funeral began.'

'So, you did speak to him?'

The girl shook her head. 'I went there but, in the end, I couldn't face talking to him. That's when I saw you.'

'I was surprised to see Mr Mason in the church, but then I learned that Hugo Rafferty had once worked for him. It wasn't that surprising he attended the funeral, after all. Did you know Mr Rafferty?'

'Should I have?'

'You might have met him – he worked at Mason's department store.'

'I've never had anything to do with the shop.'

'You didn't meet him at the vicarage after Miss Lancaster died?' she hazarded. 'When he was playing at being a curate?'

'Goodness, why would I do that? My godmother had no religious faith. I've arranged a civil ceremony for her.'

'But you did call at the vicarage?' Flora pursued.

'I called to see Miss Dunmore,' she said sharply. 'My godmother's passion for still life is one I don't share. If I was to stay in Abbeymead, I knew I couldn't live with so many paintings I disliked and wondered if the vicar or his housekeeper might know where I could donate them. A library or a nursing home perhaps.'

She paused for a moment. 'I've already told the policeman who called exactly the same thing.' The words were said with asperity. 'I can't understand why everyone wants to know what I knew of this disgraceful man.'

It was news to Flora that the police net had spread further than Stephen Henshall. The inspector had seemed unwilling to entertain any other suspect, yet he must have sent his men out to discover who in the village had had dealings with Rafferty.

'Which policeman did you speak to?' she asked. It probably didn't matter, but it just might.

'I can't remember his name. Norton? Norland?'

'Norris. Sergeant Norris.'

'That's him. I've no idea why he called here. It looked very much as though he'd come on a fishing expedition. Much the same as you today.'

After what had been an abrasive encounter, Flora felt in need of sugar. Phoebe Tallant was a beautiful and intelligent young woman and much the same age as her. In theory, she could have been a good friend or at least a pleasant acquaintance. But whenever Flora had spoken to the girl, she'd found her unremittingly hostile, sharp and almost spiteful in her manner. Granted, she'd called at the house uninvited and asked possibly unwelcome questions, but with a killer running free in Abbeymead, surely Phoebe would want to do whatever she could to help, particularly if she were serious about making the village her home.

Flora had used most of her lunch hour for the visit but reckoned she had just enough time to call at the Nook before opening for the afternoon. An iced bun sounded a perfect snack. Sweeping down Fern Hill at breakneck speed, her woollen hat dangerously insecure, she drifted to a halt outside the café's glazed door.

Inside, she was met by the gentle hum of conversation and the warm smell of fresh rolls and vegetable soup. For a Monday, a surprising number of the blue ginghamed tables were occupied and she could see Ivy, Alice Jenner's one-time kitchen maid, speeding from customer to customer as though strapped to a pair of roller skates. Kate was at the counter, pencil in hand,

and talking to Evelyn Barnes of all people. Evelyn rarely wandered into village territory, preferring to stay home at Pelham Lodge with her two fierce dogs or spend hours hammering a small white ball across the Lexington Club fairway. But here she was and, by the sound of it, ordering a considerable tally of food.

The woman turned as she heard the jangle of the doorbell. 'Good morning, Miss Steele,' she said without much enthusiasm. 'Or perhaps I should say good afternoon.'

'Good afternoon, Mrs Barnes,' Flora returned, expressing much the same level of enjoyment. 'No golf today?'

'Back playing up, you know how it is.' Flora didn't but smiled somewhat inanely. 'I thought I'd use the time to plan,' Evelyn went on. 'We're having a party on Saturday and my friend Kate here has agreed to do the honours.'

'A party sounds fun.'

'It won't be, but at least we can say goodbye to Stephen Henshall.'

'A farewell party then?'

'Exactly and thank God for that. I told Harry I've had enough of the police knocking on our door, first over the death of that little tart, Polly Dakers, and now Henshall involved in the Lord knows what. The police obviously think he's guilty.'

'Is he?' she asked, still with the same inane smile.

'I haven't a clue, my dear, and even less interest. I'll give him a good send-off and that will be it. Now, Mrs Mitchell, where were we? I think we should add a little elegance – crab patties, stuffed eggs, that kind of thing – and we'll definitely need something meaty. Something for the men.'

'Cocktail sausages?' Kate sounded hopeful.

'Yes... but... anything else you can think of?'

'I could ask Alice to cook a tray of her individual beef pies.'

'That would be splendid. I suppose we must have some

salad stuff as well and, of course, bread. Do I need to order from the bakery or will you?'

'Leave it to me, Mrs Barnes. I'll make up the entire order and ensure everything arrives on time. If it's convenient, I'll deliver to Pelham Lodge around four o'clock on Saturday.'

'You're a treasure! You can't imagine how much I'm longing to get this party over and done with, wave Stephen from the door and let the village return to normal. No more policemen knocking on doors. No more stupid questions. No more murder, for that matter.' She shuddered rather too theatrically for Flora's liking.

'Did you know the dead man, Mrs Barnes?' she asked. 'Hugo Rafferty?'

'The con artist, you mean.' When she saw Kate's pained face, the woman said testily, 'Well, he was a con artist, wasn't he? Conned the church – and how on earth did he persuade Hopkirk he was genuine – and conned Henshall.'

'I'd heard that Mr Henshall was in some trouble, but you think it was Rafferty who was responsible?' Flora pretended ignorance.

'Defrauded him good and proper. Landed him in one very large mess.'

'I don't know how true it is...' Flora said confidingly, 'but I heard in the village that Rafferty was dismissed from his last post. Apparently, he worked in a large department store called Mason's. That could have been for fraud, too.'

'I wouldn't waste too much sympathy there. Len Mason is as big a crook as Rafferty. I never liked Harry doing business with him. Dismissing one of his managers was the pot calling the kettle black, if you ask me.'

'Even so, fraud is a serious crime and I'm not surprised Mr Rafferty had to go.'

'It was either that or women,' Evelyn said laconically. '*Mr*

Rafferty liked the ladies a little too much. Maybe it wasn't fraud. Maybe the female staff complained once too often.'

It fitted with what Flora already knew. If Cicely Mason had been looking for a lover, Rafferty would have been more than willing to comply.

When the café door had shut behind Evelyn, Flora walked round the counter and gave Kate a hug. 'Well done! You've quite an order on your hands, you and Alice.' She glanced down at the sheet of paper Kate had been writing on. 'It looks as though you already had a long list before I arrived!'

'There'll be a lot of cooking to get through and some of it can't be done until the last minute.' There was a concerned look in her friend's eyes. 'I'm afraid we'll have to cancel our usual Friday this week. Do you mind, Flora?'

'Don't be silly, of course I don't. It's brilliant for your business.'

Kate gave a reluctant nod. 'It is and I couldn't say no. The Nook is doing well – Dad would be so pleased, he always wanted to see the tearoom fly – but outside catering brings in much more profit.'

'Particularly if Evelyn Barnes is doing the ordering.'

They both gave a shout of laughter, causing Kate's customers to look up from their cottage pies.

22

By five o'clock Flora's stomach was rumbling. One iced bun, no matter how tasty, was not sufficient to last her the rest of the day. She would close a little early, she decided, and bring supper forward – trading on Monday was traditionally slow – and had just begun the cashing up when Stephen Henshall walked through the door.

Her eyes widened in surprise. His name had been bouncing around her mind ever since meeting Evelyn Barnes at the café, but he was still the last person she expected to see in the All's Well.

'Were you about to close?' he asked, removing his hat and smoothing flat the stiff bristles of his hair. He was smartly dressed, she noticed, a suit and tie beneath the dark overcoat, as though he had a business meeting to attend.

'I was thinking of it, but you're very welcome to browse.'

'I won't keep you long.' He fiddled with the hat in his hand. 'Actually... I've not come for a book.' There was a pause. 'I've come to apologise.' Flora was surprised for a second time. Did that explain the formal attire?

'I wasn't at my best when we met yesterday,' he went on, his voice half-lost as he stared hard at the floor. 'I'm sorry for my rudeness.'

'Apology accepted and thank you.' Feeling she should offer something in return, Flora added, 'I shouldn't have thrown all those questions at you.'

'They were fair enough, I reckon. Abbeymead is your village and bad things seem to be happening here. As a stranger, I'm bound to arouse suspicion – it's natural that people wonder why I've been hanging around the hotel so long. Though, not for much longer. I've been summarily retired.'

'In what way?' It was best, Flora thought, to pretend ignorance.

He gave a jerky smile. 'I've been dismissed, if you can be dismissed from something that was purely voluntary. Miss Jenner no longer wants me at the Priory.'

Flora felt a sudden sympathy for him, then remembered that he might have been driving the car that could have swept Jack from her life for ever. It was an outside possibility, true, but a possibility nevertheless.

'That seems a shame,' she said cautiously, 'after the help you've given Mr Lister.'

'Not enough, it seems, to outpace the rumours. To be frank, I was very angry with Miss Jenner – to be spoken to in that fashion – and I'm afraid you were the beneficiary. I met you after a heated conversation with her and I rather took it out on you.'

'I can understand why you did. I wonder, though, if Miss Jenner has acted a little hastily.' She would play devil's advocate, she decided. 'There are always rumours in a village.'

'These weren't just any rumours. I have to admit Miss Jenner was right in fearing they could lead to adverse publicity for the Priory at a time when the hotel is just getting back on its feet. The stories have spread widely, found their way into the newspapers, which I suppose they were bound to. You don't get stung for that much money without people getting to hear about it.'

'Mr Barnes mentioned some problem,' she murmured.

'You could put it like that. I'm facing bankruptcy, Miss Steele, through no fault of my own.'

'Hugo Rafferty's doing, I imagine?' When he looked taken aback, she said, 'There's been a flurry of rumours about him, too. Nothing escapes notice in a village, I'm afraid.'

'He was a complete scoundrel.' Henshall banged his hat against his knee, as though metaphorically beating the man. 'When I told you that I went to his funeral to make sure he'd truly left this world, it was the truth. He has ruined my life. A life that was successful and reasonably happy until I became involved with him.'

'I hope very much the ruin won't be permanent.'

He gave small lift of his shoulders. 'It's hard to say. I have a sympathetic bank and seem to be making headway in that direction, but it will be an uphill struggle. Come to think of it, it's as well Miss Jenner gave me my cards. I'll have more than enough work in saving my own business.' The smile did not quite reach his eyes.

'You'll want to return to London soon, I imagine.'

'This coming Sunday, to be precise. I talked it over with Harry and his missus the other night and it's agreed. I'm here a few more days – Evelyn's keen to hold a farewell event. Any excuse, eh? But after that, I'm on the train to the Big Smoke. It's why I wanted to call in and clear the air. I don't suppose we'll meet again.'

'I appreciate the gesture, Mr Henshall. It's gracious of you. And sensible. It's always good to defuse bad feelings before you move on. Was that what you were doing with Mr Vaisey? Offering him an apology?'

Henshall stared at her.

'Shortly after we parted yesterday, I saw you talking

together. I knew you were upset and wondered if you'd quarrelled with the landlord as well.'

'No, nothing like that.' He fidgeted with the fine wool scarf
around his neck, then rammed his hat back on his head. 'A
quick enquiry about the beer, that's all.'

Flora was silenced for a moment. 'Beer?' she asked,
mystified.

'I like a brand they sell at the Cross Keys. The beer is one of
the better memories I'll take from Abbeymead! I was asking
Vaisey where I could get it in London or, if not, could he order
me some and have it sent on.'

'Gosh, that must have required some discussion.' When he
didn't rise to the bait, she said, 'Let's hope you're successful in
buying the beer, and successful in whatever the future holds for
you.'

'Thanks.' He sounded grateful, whether for her good wishes
or the fact that she hadn't pursued his conversation with Daniel
Vaisey, Flora couldn't decide.

'While you *are* here,' she added, 'why not have a wander
around the shop. I cater for most tastes, and you might just find
a book for your journey to London.'

Henshall hadn't been long, disappearing into the depths of the
All's Well and reappearing some minutes later. He'd left
without buying but Flora hadn't minded. She'd been glad to
'clear the air' as he'd said, and even gladder to lock the bookshop
door and ride Betty home for an early supper.

Something about Henshall's visit had disturbed her. She
couldn't put her finger on it, other than the awkward excuse of
the beer, but it was enough to make her restless. Once the
dishes were done, she tuned in the wireless, but there was little
to interest her, then picked up the latest Agatha Christie – the
book she'd been wanting to read ever since it arrived in the shop

last month – but *Dead Man's Folly* didn't hold her attention and was soon laid aside. She was finding it impossible to concentrate.

At seven o'clock, she put on her coat and hat, tugged on winter boots, took the torch from the kitchen drawer and walked along Greenway Lane to Overlay House. She could easily have telephoned Jack. It was wonderful to be able to lift the receiver and hear his voice. After months of refusing even to consider a phone in the house, he'd finally buckled, but then spent even more months languishing on the Post Office waiting list. A telephone call, though, wasn't right this evening. She needed to see him face-to-face, not least because she wanted to be certain that he was definitely on the mend. He wouldn't have been honest at a distance.

When Jack came to the door, she could see even in the dim light of the hall that he was looking a good deal better. There was a faint colour to his cheeks.

'This is unexpected,' he said, leading the way into the sitting room where he'd been doing a crossword puzzle, the newspaper slung haphazardly over the sofa and a pencil lying on the floor. The flames of a wood fire licked their way up the chimney.

'And cosy,' she said. 'I wanted to see you. How are you feeling?'

'Better, much better. The pain in my ribs has eased and my head has stopped playing the 1812 Overture. You really shouldn't have come out on such a cold night.' He bent to kiss her, then fingered her cheek. 'And it is mighty cold. Your skin is icy.'

'I'm fine. Even finer now I know you're truly feeling better.'

'Come over to the fire and get warm. What you need is a glass of something. Brandy, I think.'

'Tea will do. I can't drink brandy.'

'Why not? It's medicinal.' He went over to the teak sideboard that stood against the far wall and fetched two glasses and half a bottle of cognac. 'A mere thimbleful,' he said, pouring a good inch into each glass.

They sat side by side on the sofa, Flora pulling a face as she took an initial sip. Slowly, though, she began to relax, feeling a spiral of warmth uncoil itself through her body.

'Stephen Henshall is leaving the village,' she said, after a second or third sip. 'Evelyn Barnes is holding a farewell party for him on Saturday, and the next day he'll be on the train back to London.'

'His decision?' Jack asked lazily.

'Not entirely. Sally told him his work at the Priory was finished and it was evident that Evelyn – I met her at the Nook this lunchtime ordering food for the party – wanted him gone from Pelham Lodge.'

'Poor old Henshall, a man without friends.'

'You're right. Brandy is just what I needed!' She put the glass of amber liquid back on the coffee table. 'I ended up feeling quite sorry for him. He came to the shop this evening as I was closing, to say he was leaving. And to apologise for the way he spoke to me the other day.'

'Did you think him genuine?'

'I don't see why not. He needn't have come near the All's Well, but he went out of his way to call and say he was sorry. And wore his best suit and tie to do it.'

'He must be genuine then! Only teasing, but we shouldn't forget he's Ridley's number one suspect, though at the moment it seems the Henshall enquiry isn't going too well.' Jack lay back in his seat and studied his brandy. 'Alan telephoned me a few hours ago. Apparently, the police have managed to dig up a photograph of Gareth Beaumont and are going door-to-door asking if anyone in the village has seen the man. Ridley was clear he was only going to do that if he reached an impasse, so... but it's not going down too well in the village. When Mr Preece delivered my lamb chops this afternoon, he seemed most offended at being questioned.'

'They asked the butcher?'

'They're asking everyone, though I got the impression they're not having much luck. Preece said the constable who spoke to him was very downbeat, thinking it a waste of his time.'

'If they're asking the entire village about Beaumont, it's an extraordinary about-face on the inspector's part.' Flora stretched her stockinged legs towards the leaping flames and took another sip from her glass.

'I agree, but whether it will produce anything tangible is another matter. According to Preece's policeman, all they've managed to unearth so far is the landlord at the Cross Keys *thinking* he might have seen the chap. That seems highly unlikely, given what we know of the man we met in Whitbury. I can't see Gareth Beaumont going within a mile of any pub.'

'Yet he's back on the inspector's list of suspects,' she mused. 'I'll be very surprised if the police find anyone who recognises him. If Beaumont *was* in the village prior to the day I bumped into him and planned to send a note to his cousin to meet him at the bell tower, he would have taken the greatest care not to be seen. At this time of the year, it's dark by four o'clock in the afternoon and that wouldn't have been difficult.'

Jack leaned over, delving awkwardly into the nearby wood basket for another log to throw on the fire. 'This whole idea of an earlier visit worries me. It means that after committing murder, Beaumont returned here, to the scene of his crime. To gloat, we decided, but that always sounded far-fetched and still does. Another?' He pointed to the brandy bottle.

She smiled a trifle hazily. 'Definitely not. But is it that far-fetched? By all accounts Rafferty was a scoundrel and hurt countless people. Gloating over his death isn't pleasant but it is a natural reaction. Mason came to the funeral pretending to be a concerned employer, while I'm certain he was there to make sure the man had truly gone. Stephen Henshall the same. So why not allow Beaumont his victory tour of the village?'

'Fair enough but if, as you suspect, the police don't find anyone in the village who can identify him – except you, days after the murder – they'll be forced to drop him as a suspect.'

'And we'll be back to Henshall or Mason,' she said, her languorous mood fast disappearing. 'Jack, I must go. I have a shop to open in the morning.'

He got to his feet, and she saw the suppressed wince as he straightened up. 'I'll walk you back to the cottage.'

'You'll do no such thing.' She reached up to stroke back the flop of hair that never lay flat. 'Go to bed and rest – but leave the brandy in the sideboard!'

23

Jack felt well enough when he woke in the morning to stroll into the village and tackle some shopping. He certainly needed to. Occasional deliveries from the dairyman and the butcher, along with Charlie's help in harvesting sprouts, cabbage and carrots from his own vegetable patch, had kept him going. There had been treats, too – Alice's liver and bacon casserole and Flora cooking a massive shepherd's pie that had taken several days to eat. But he couldn't continue to depend on his friends.

There was also the matter of the package. It had arrived in the post just as he'd stumbled downstairs for breakfast and, rescuing it from the doormat, he'd weighed it in his hands. It felt interestingly heavy. His newspaper colleague, it seemed, had come up trumps, but he would leave opening the large brown envelope until Flora was beside him. It was news they needed to share and a female perspective on what had clearly been an emotional tragedy would be invaluable. After a visit to the grocer's and another to the bakery, he'd call in at the All's Well and hope to find her free to talk.

Two slices of toast and a cup of tea later, he locked the front door of Overlay House and was turning to walk down the flagged path when he became aware of a figure at the garden gate. Alan Ridley. And looking rather too bright and shiny, Jack considered, for this time in the morning.

'Off out?' the inspector asked, raising his trilby in greeting. The answer was self-evident and Jack merely smiled. 'I'll walk with you into the village,' Ridley went on, 'and we can talk as we go. I'm on my way to the Cross Keys, but thought I'd call on you first.'

'A bit early for a beer and a ploughman's, isn't it?'

Jack closed the gate behind him and fell into step with the inspector, the crunch of frost sounding beneath their feet as they began the walk along the lane that led to the high street.

'No such luck. It's purely business today. I need to talk to the landlord. One of my men reported back that this chap Vaisey might have seen Gareth Beaumont lurking around the village days before the curate died. It sounded pretty flimsy to me, but we've so little to go on that every small lead is worth following up.'

'Couldn't you have asked one of your team to go back to the pub and check? It would have saved you a journey.'

The inspector shook his head. 'I wanted to question him myself, get the measure of the man, as it were. And it meant I could catch up with you at the same time.'

'Are you thinking Vaisey is an unreliable witness?'

'Not precisely, but you know what it's like once you start asking questions. Everyone likes to think they've something important to say, even though they haven't. I wanted to talk to the bloke properly, judge how likely it was that he'd imagined the sighting.'

'I don't know the landlord well, but he's always struck me as pretty level-headed.' Jack paused for a moment, thinking how best to dig more deeply. 'I'd heard you'd begun to ask around about Beaumont and was surprised. I thought you'd ruled him out as a suspect.'

'I thought I had, too. And anyone else who Rafferty knew from years past.' The inspector's breath puffed a cloud of white into the cold air. 'I had Sergeant Norris question every individual at that funeral, but no joy.'

'Did your sergeant speak to Mason? He was Rafferty's employer.'

'Mason? The department store chap? Yes, Norris talked to him, along with the rest of the mourners. If I remember rightly, Mason was at some conference in Northamptonshire at the time Rafferty was murdered. Cast-iron alibi, like the rest of them. But there is one bright spot.'

'Really?'

'We've been working flat-out on Henshall, but nothing of interest has come up – at least, not yet – so in an idle moment, I decided to look through Hugo Rafferty's papers. Miss Dunmore, bless her, handed them over as soon as the curate died. I must have mentioned it. A bit of a treasure, that lady. One of my team had already gone through them, but he'd done it fairly rapidly, and I had a hunch they might repay a slower trawl. And I was right and duly rewarded. I found a letter that's thrown a whole different light on events.'

Jack congratulated himself. It was exactly the kind of information he'd hoped to garner on this walk but, before he could ask any of the questions pressing for an answer, he found himself forced to a stop. His breathing had become laboured, the bitter air slicing through his ulster and lacerating a chest already damaged. Evidently, he hadn't recovered as completely as he'd thought.

'Sorry for being a slow coach,' he apologised hoarsely. 'The letter was from Beaumont?'

The inspector nodded. 'The very man. The missive makes clear that Gareth Beaumont knew of his cousin's charade before the man died, even though when my colleagues in Dorset spoke to him, he pretended not to have done. In the letter, he accuses

Rafferty of appalling dishonesty and gross disrespect for a dead man. That would be his brother, Lyle. And then threatens that if Rafferty doesn't come clean, admit the charade and give himself up to the authorities, he, Gareth, will come after him.'

'Phew! That's certainly a find.' Jack was forced to pause his steps again. 'Do you think you could slow down a bit, Alan?'

'Not as fit as in your army days, eh?'

'Afraid not. Must be age catching up with me.'

He was determined to say nothing about the attack he'd suffered in London, and the possible involvement of Len Mason. Beaumont's letter appeared damning, but Jack was unconvinced of his guilt, and even less convinced of Stephen Henshall's. To his mind, the Mason connection had far more going for it despite the alibi, but he knew instinctively that Ridley wouldn't be interested. It was better that he and Flora investigate for themselves and, only then, tell the inspector what they'd found. Over time, it had become clear that the easiest way to convince Alan Ridley was to show him proof. Otherwise, they might as well find a wall to bang their heads against.

'Do you want to come with me to the pub?' Ridley asked. 'Sit in on the interview? You could be useful. You know almost as much as I do about this investigation and you're a good judge of character.'

Jack pulled a face. 'My judgement of Vaisey's character is likely to be biased. I'd be unduly influenced by how much better catering at the Cross Keys has become since he took over.'

The inspector laughed and gave him a playful jab in the ribs. Jack couldn't prevent a gasp of pain.

'Sorry, old chap. You all right?'

'Fine,' Jack muttered, a tight smile stretching his lips. 'You caught me at an awkward angle, that's all.'

'Sorry about that,' Ridley apologised again. 'But come anyway. I reckon you'd be an asset when I talk to Vaisey. If he really did see Beaumont in the village prior to Rafferty's death, coupled with that letter, it could be the breakthrough we need.'

Jack nodded. It could be, he supposed but, somehow, he didn't believe it.

'The question is,' the inspector went on, 'did he see him? He's identified Beaumont from a photograph taken a good five years ago. Plenty of room for mistakes. Then there's the possibility that Vaisey is a bit of a fantasist. Did he say he saw Gareth Beaumont because it makes him sound good when he's talking to drinkers at the bar? Makes him special – the only person in the village to have seen a possible murderer.'

'From what I've seen of Daniel, I would say the man is completely down-to-earth. The way he's turned the pub around is testimony to how practical he is. But I'm happy enough to tag along, if you think I can help. I need to do a small detour first, though. I've something to leave at the All's Well with Flora.' He waved the wodge of brown paper in the air.

'Always happy to walk into a bookshop. I love books, though I get precious little time to read 'em.'

Opening the All's Well's front door, Jack paused on the threshold, but made no move to go further. There was a sudden tingling in his limbs and the pain in his chest grew sharper. Something was wrong. He knew it. He checked his watch. Still early, which might explain the absence of customers, but there was a silence filling the shop that felt alien. A silence that shouldn't have been there.

He walked slowly towards Flora's desk and spied her shopping bag sitting beneath and a small stack of letters and various account books scattered across the top. Piled against the front display table were two large cardboard boxes, the name of a warehouse in bold print on their exterior. New books, waiting to be unpacked.

Ridley had followed in his footsteps and turned to him now, his expression uncertain. 'Is she here, do you think?'

'She must be. The door's open, her bag is here. I'll just check...'

Jack darted into the kitchenette and saw Flora's red wool coat and woollen hat and gloves hanging from one of the pegs.

'She's definitely here,' he confirmed, walking back into the bookshop. Agitated, he furrowed a hand through his hair. 'I don't like this, Alan. It's not like Flora. I'm going to look round the shop.'

His mouth felt dry as he began to wind a path through the angled bookcases, the inspector close behind. The All's Well's building was old – parts of it from the fifteenth century, he'd been told – and its walls twisted and turned in dizzying fashion, often ending in a dead end. Jack had almost reached the final bend when he stumbled over a heap of books scattered across the parquet floor. In a second, he saw the bookcase they'd come from. Not where it should be, but tumbled flat, the whole of its contents spewed wide.

'This looks bad.' Alan Ridley had caught him up. 'Very bad. Where's the girl, do you think?'

Jack pushed the scattering of books to one side and jumped over the fallen bookcase, narrowly missing a stockinged foot. He stared rigidly downwards, his heart pumping wildly. Then, with a frantic effort, thrust aside more of the books to reveal a corduroy skirt and a pair of legs.

'Flora!'

He felt the beads of sweat stand out on his forehead. Flora's slender figure was splayed flat, her arms outstretched, her face turned to one side and almost buried in one of the rugs that made the bookshop a cosy haven.

In a trice, he was down on his knees. 'Flora,' he said softly. 'Flora, are you all right?' What he meant was are you alive, but he dared not voice the question.

'Here, let me.' The inspector joined him on the floor and

placed his fingers against Flora's throat. Turning to look at Jack's anguished face, he nodded. 'She's alive, at least.'

He reached for a limp hand and began patting it gently, while at the same time urging her to come awake. There was no response.

Jack crouched lower, his ribs feeling as though they would cut a hole in his side, and, cradling her face in his hands, he kissed her gently on the forehead. Flora stirred slightly and, with Ridley's continued pressure on her hand, slowly came back to life. Her eyes, when she opened them, were dazed.

'Can you move anything?' Jack said.

There was the smallest shake of her head.

'Does anything feel broken?' he asked a trifle desperately.

She tried to lift her head, but it was evidently too painful because she dropped back onto the rug.

'We need to get her sitting up,' the inspector said authoritatively. 'Jack, you tuck a hand under one arm while I take the other. When I give the signal, we both lift.'

Moving very slowly in case there were broken bones, they managed to manoeuvre Flora into a sitting position and prop her against the nearest upright bookcase.

The inspector straightened up, but Jack stayed where he was, kneeling beside her, terrified that every vestige of colour had drained from Flora's face. For minutes, they stayed immobile until she whispered, 'I'm OK, Jack.' There was a long pause. 'It's just that everything hurts right now.'

'I'm not surprised.' The inspector bent down again. 'You've been knocked sideways. I reckon you were lucky not to end up underneath that brute.' He pointed to the tumbled heap of heavy wood that lay to one side of them.

'I felt it move,' she said hesitantly. She was grappling with her memory, Jack could see. 'I was reshelving a book and felt the bookcase move. I think I took a step to one side, I don't know why... instinct perhaps... and then there were books being hurled around and some of them hit me hard and then I don't remember much else.'

'That step to one side probably saved your life.' Ridley sounded sombre. He glanced up at the wall where the bookcase had stood and frowned heavily. 'Those are massive shelves. The fittings would have to be immensely strong.'

'Aunt Violet made certain of that.' Flora had revived a little. 'I remember as a child watching workmen put them up. It took them an age.'

The inspector peered at the wall, reaching up with his hand to feel the holes where the fixings had once been. 'Has anything been changed since that time?' he asked.

'Michael Worthington added extra fittings to one of them several years ago.' Flora closed her eyes, seeming too exhausted to keep speaking, but then gathered what small amount of strength she had left, to say, 'We had a leak in the ceiling and my aunt suspected the original fittings might have rusted and weren't safe any longer. Michael would have made certain the job was properly done.'

Jack nodded agreement. 'He's the most trustworthy of men,' he said to the inspector.

Ridley bent down again, this time to examine the back of the fallen bookcase. 'I'm sure he is,' he said grimly. 'These fittings have been deliberately tampered with. Look, Jack.' He pointed to what was left hanging on the wall and then what was left on the bookcase.

Jack fumbled in his coat pocket for a pair of tortoiseshell glasses. 'You're right,' he said. 'They've been sliced through.' He felt his scalp prickling.

'Exactly so. With some kind of bolt cutters, it looks. They wouldn't have needed to be that big to sever the steel.'

'But—' Flora began.

Jack shook his head at her, and she said no more.

'You were saying?' The inspector's eyebrows rose.

'I don't know what I'm saying,' she said quickly. 'My head is thumping and I ache from the bottom of my feet up.'

'You need to be home,' Jack decided. 'And I'm taking you. I'm sorry, Alan, but I won't be making it to the Cross Keys after all.'

Ridley looked uncertain. 'I do need to talk to Vaisey before the pub opens and he gets too busy, but...' Jack could see the inspector being pulled in two directions. 'I also want to find out what's been going on here.'

'You will, I'm sure,' Jack soothed, accompanying him to the shop door. If Alan Ridley didn't find out, he certainly would.

'But about Miss Steele...' the inspector began.

'I'll look after her, you can be sure. But let me know what the landlord says, won't you?' Jack gave him a farewell wave as he shut the door.

When he returned to Flora, still slumped uncomfortably against a bookcase, her first words were, 'I can't shut the shop.'

'You can and you will. You're going home. The only question is how. Shall I walk back to Overlay and fetch the car?'

'I'll shut for a few hours,' she conceded. 'I have aspirin at home and when it's done its trick, I can use Betty to get back.'

'That's ridiculous. You can't cycle. And while I think of it, I should really be taking you to a doctor, not home.'

'No doctor,' she said firmly. 'If I can't cycle, I'll walk and leave Betty in her shelter.'

Jack felt considerable doubt that she would manage even to stand, let alone walk. Putting his arm around her, he helped her to her feet, Flora gasping with the effort. For a moment, they looked at each other, then burst into laughter, holding their sides because they hurt so much.

'We are the most ridiculous pair of crocks,' she said.

'We are,' he agreed. 'But a pair of crocks that are still alive. And I don't think that was the plan.'

24

Once Jack had retrieved her coat and hat from the kitchenette, he took her arm and walked her to the All's Well's door, turning the shop notice to Closed.

'Here.' Flora fumbled in her handbag. 'I don't even think I've the strength to turn the key.'

She'd meant it as a joke but, on the slow and painful walk to her cottage along the length of Greenway Lane, it proved a sad reality. The tumble she'd taken, the mass of bruising – her legs already covered in dark angry splotches, and goodness knows what lay beneath her clothes – had quite literally crushed her, so much so that every step required a bitten lip and immense determination.

The grandmother clock was striking ten as Jack opened the cottage door and helped her into the house. Still holding her by the arm, he led her into the sitting room and somehow lowered her into one of the fireside chairs. She was grateful for his gentleness.

'Best keep your coat on for now,' he said. 'You need to keep warm.'

The air in the cottage, tinged with damp, was almost colder

than the lane outside and, despite her woollen overcoat, Flora had begun to shiver.

He pointed to the grate, already laid with paper and kindling. 'Thanks to your phenomenal efficiency, I'll get the fire going in a tick.'

Picking up the tongs, he burrowed into the brass coal bucket and proceeded to add a layer of coal. She frowned as he produced a box of matches from his pocket.

'Are you smoking again?' she asked, her voice slightly stronger.

'You're an invalid. Your job is to get well, not ask awkward questions.' He bent down and set a match to the crumpled paper.

'I'm not the only invalid. What about you? Your accident was far worse.'

'Fully recovered,' he claimed, though Flora doubted it. 'It's you we need to nurture. I'll make some tea.'

'Tea? How disappointing! Don't say you've come without the brandy?'

'Afraid so. The best I can offer is tea but hot and sweet – and biscuits, if you have any.'

'There's a packet of digestives in the top cupboard,' she called out faintly as he disappeared towards the kitchen.

By the time Jack returned with a tray of tea and biscuits, and a bottle of aspirin, the fire had well and truly caught, and the crackle of twigs filled the room, the warm scent of apple wood leaving Flora drowsy and contented.

With some difficulty, he manoeuvred her out of her coat, then took the seat opposite. His expression was stern when he asked, 'So, who was it? Any idea at all?'

'Maybe,' she replied cautiously.

'So, who?'

'When I came round – I suppose it was from a faint – I had the time to think a little. Before I blacked out again.'

'I thought you might have.' His eyes lit with amusement.

'The only person it could have been is Stephen Henshall.'

Jack raised his eyebrows. 'Really? When I talked to Ridley on our way to the village, he seems to have abandoned Henshall as his chief suspect, mainly because he's been unable to find anything to implicate the man. It's Gareth Beaumont who appears flavour of the day.'

'It wasn't Beaumont.' Flora was adamant. 'You know I told you that Henshall came into the shop yesterday?'

He nodded.

'I thought it a generous gesture, calling on me to apologise for his discourtesy, but it's plain now that it was for a quite different reason.' She took a slow sip of her tea and looked through the far window onto a bleak winter garden. 'It's as you've always said, I'm too trusting.'

'Are you sure it was him? If he simply came into apologise, how could he have tampered with the bookcase?'

'Easy enough. While I was cashing up, he walked round the shop looking at books. I actually invited him to browse!'

Jack studied the rag rug at his feet. 'OK, but it still doesn't make a lot of sense. Why make a special trip to apologise for his behaviour and then decide he'd try to kill you?'

'The apology was probably a front. He wasn't sorry at all but was out to punish me for the questions I asked. More to the point, out to stop me from asking more.'

'It's possible.' Jack balanced his half-empty cup on the wooden fender. 'And possible that he could have been carrying an instrument of some kind in his overcoat pocket. It would take only a few seconds to cut through those fixings. One slice and it would be done. If you were busy cashing up at the front of the shop, you'd be unlikely to hear a thing. Can you think of anyone else who might have smuggled a bolt cutter into the bookshop in recent days?'

She took her time. 'No one,' she said at last. 'There have

been a fair number of villagers in and out, Alice and Kate have both called – oh, and Sally for a few minutes – but no one else. There's no sign of a break-in so it has to have been someone coming into the shop. Henshall is our only suspect, Jack, but...'

'But what?'

'There is one aspect that doesn't fit. He couldn't be sure it would be me going to that bookcase. And he couldn't be sure either that I'd be reshelving a heavy enough book to destabilise it.'

'All the books tumbled to the floor were very substantial. He could have deliberately avoided a bookcase that only carried paperbacks.'

'I suppose, but it doesn't mean he'd get me. A customer might have beaten me to it, and they'd be the one seriously injured or killed.'

'If Henshall *is* our villain and he's desperate to prevent you nosing further into his affairs, he wouldn't care who he targeted. He'd just hope it was you and, if you think about it, that's the most likely. He chose shelving at the very end of the shop – how many customers penetrate that far? How many want to buy a reference book? Customers from the village normally know what they want, don't they, or they buy from the front display table, or ask for your recommendation. Very few walk right through the shop. And any stranger would think twice before tackling that maze of shelves, if they were simply browsing. They could get lost quite easily.'

'They do,' she said, trying to smile through a racking pain that had started up in her back. A particularly heavy ency-clopaedia had hit her mid-spine.

'He'd have good odds then,' Jack summarised, 'that it was you he'd incapacitate, maybe not today but on a day not too far distant.'

She leant forward, then wincing, straightened up again. 'Henshall is leaving Abbeymead on Sunday, isn't he? Evelyn

Barnes is throwing a farewell party the evening before. He may have hoped I'd come to grief once he was far from the village.'

'Could be.' Jack tapped a teaspoon against his saucer, while he thought. 'It's beginning to look as though Ridley called this one correctly from the start. You questioned Henshall and he was evasive or he simply lied, but the encounter unnerved him, so to stop you questioning further, he needed to get you out of his life. Injure you seriously – or kill you. The fact that he called at the shop yesterday has to be significant. He's never been to the All's Well before?'

Flora shook her head.

'An apology gave him the perfect excuse to call and, if you hadn't invited him to look round the shop, he could have suggested it himself. I think we should tell Ridley what's happened. It might encourage him to put Beaumont to one side and go back to digging for crucial evidence against Henshall.'

'It could be good timing. The inspector seemed keen to discover how that bookcase came to fall.' She sat back in her chair, trying to relieve the pressure on her back. 'But there's still the attack on you to explain. Is it possible that Henshall followed you to London? I know you convinced yourself it was Mason behind the attack, but...'

'I don't see how Henshall could have known I was going to London or where I was going when I got there. It doesn't add up, Flora.'

His foot tapped a tattoo on the rug. 'It doesn't have to have been the same person, though, does it?' he said at last. 'You were probably hurt because you asked too many questions. I was hurt because I did the same. We could have different adversaries, with quite different reasons for preventing us from probing into their affairs.'

'If that's so, it makes things even harder. We've been unable to track down one killer, let alone find two.'

She shifted uncomfortably again, trying now to ease the

throb in both arms and legs, a throb that was becoming stronger every minute despite the aspirin. A hot bath, she thought. That should do the trick.

Jack collected up their cups and stood looking down at her. 'If we leave aside the attack in London, Henshall is definitely our front runner. Mason no longer looks such a great idea, I have to admit. Apparently, he was nowhere near Abbeymead the day the curate died. He has witnesses to prove he was at a conference in Northamptonshire, or so Ridley told me.'

'Mason might not have been in Abbeymead himself, but he could have sent one of his men to kill Rafferty. In the same way, he could have sent one of them to run you down.'

'There's been nothing to suggest any of his henchmen have ever been in the village. If they had, I reckon they'd have been spotted pretty quickly. Stephen Henshall, on the other hand, has been living at Pelham Lodge for several weeks and we know he had as much of a grievance against Rafferty.'

'More than a grievance,' she said. 'He told me that Hugo Rafferty had ruined his life.'

'Pretty damning,' was Jack's only comment. 'But no more talk for now. You need to be in bed.'

'I thought I'd have a bath,' she began, her voice fading despite her best efforts.

'Later, Flora. Much later. Come on, I'll help you upstairs, though I don't think I can manage your clothes.'

Flora put on a shocked face. 'I should think not! Whatever are you suggesting, Mr Carrington!' Her fingers traced a line down his cheek as he bent to help her from the chair and, in response, he kissed her gently on the lips.

'We'll crack this,' he said. 'Together.'

～

Once he saw Flora comfortably tucked into bed, watching from the doorway as she fell asleep – she had stayed fully dressed after all – Jack took the empty cups into the kitchen, washing and drying them while his mind was busy elsewhere. Flora's words had sent a hare racing. The villain had to have been someone who came into the shop, she'd said. But did it? Could her attacker have got to that bookcase in any other way? He'd go back to the All's Well, he decided, and poke around while she slept. Then come back later and try his hand at cooking her lunch. Poached eggs. He was good at those.

Within ten minutes, he was in the high street again and, ignoring the All's Well's front door, walked around to the court-yard at the rear of the building. Betty was safe in her shelter where Flora had parked her earlier that morning. If he could remember how to ride a bike, he'd take her with him when he left for the cottage.

Turning his mind to the job in hand, he walked over to the only window at the back of the shop. It had been the one smashed all those months ago when he'd first met Flora. Shattered in that instance by an intruder looking for a clue to buried treasure. He smiled to himself, recalling the adventure that had followed their discovery of a man's very dead body. It felt now as though they'd been part of a fairy tale. This current investigation was very different, imbued with a resentment that was impossible to ignore. An extreme bitterness, some kind of payback. It tasted sour.

Jack looked at the window closely. It appeared intact, lacking any visible sign of damage. Yet when he ran a finger along the ledge and up one side of the wood frame, flakes of white paint came away in his hand. Fumbling in his coat pocket, he brought out his glasses again. He needed a better look. Sure enough, there was a dent in the wood exactly opposite the case-ment handle. Another intruder, but this time one who hadn't advertised their presence. He or she had slid something very fine down the side of the window frame and triggered the latch. From that point, it would have taken only seconds to unhook the handle and pull open the window.

He stood motionless, plunged into thought. He was certain that after that break-in at the All's Well, Michael Worthington had been asked to fix a window lock. Had Flora opened the window during the summer months and, when closing it, forgotten to engage the lock? More than likely – it had been a stifling September. It didn't necessarily follow, of course, that the tampering of the bookcase was connected with the damage to the window frame, but it was a good guess that it was.

Which meant... that it didn't have to have been a visitor to the shop who'd plotted to injure Flora. It didn't have to be Stephen Henshall. Turning this over in his mind, Jack walked back into the high street to begin at last on the shopping he'd meant to do hours earlier. Henshall had a motive – a very strong one – and he'd had the opportunity to tamper with the bookcase when he'd called at the shop.

Even so, the field was once again wide open.

25

Jack's package had been left on a display table at the front of the All's Well. He had been keen to share its contents but in his panic over Flora, and still concerned for her safety, had forgotten it had even arrived. It wasn't until two days later that Flora discovered its existence. She had limped along Greenway Lane on her way to the bookshop, deciding that riding Betty would be too painful, the bruising now at its most tender, and the large envelope was the first thing she saw as she opened the door.

It was lying sideways, half on and half off the low table. An object out of place. Flora didn't like things out of place and tutting to herself, she picked it up and, without thinking, was about to deposit it in the bin behind her desk when she caught sight of the subscription. The package was addressed to Jack and – she squinted at the postmark – it had been sent from London. Realising what it must contain, she turned the envelope from side to side, front to back. Should she open it? It was certainly tempting, but she couldn't. It was clear Jack had wanted them to explore his colleague's research together.

Shrugging off her coat, she picked up the telephone and he answered on the second ring.

'That was quick,' she said, surprised.

'I was in the hall, on my way out. How are you feeling?'

'Not amazing but getting there. I'm at the shop. I might manage a few hours today, catching up with the paperwork, but I'll probably close early.'

'Good. You're sounding sensible for once.'

She let the comment float. 'Jack, you left a brown paper package here. I think it might be *the* package?'

'Damn. I'd forgotten it. In fact, it's gone out of my mind completely. I suppose we already know the most important fact – that Phoebe Tallant's sister was Mason's wife.'

'Are you saying it's not worth opening?' she asked dubiously.

'No, not that. Sadler will have done his research – the packet felt quite hefty. But maybe leave it until we can both read whatever he's come up with.'

'How about Saturday afternoon? I'll be closed from lunchtime.'

There was a moment's silence. 'That might be difficult. I've promised to help Alice and Kate with the party food.'

'For Pelham Lodge?' Flora was surprised, having heard nothing more about the farewell party, but then she'd been squirrelled away in bed for the last two days.

'In case you're worried, I'm not doing the cooking,' he joked. 'My role is to fetch and carry. Apparently, Tony Farraday has dared to leave the Priory kitchen for a few days! He's away visiting family and has taken his van with him, so I offered the Austin's services. It looks as though there'll be a ton of food to transport, far too much for Alice and Kate to carry up Fern Hill.'

'That's good of you.' There was a pause before she said,

'Really, I should be helping, too.' She heard the irritation in her voice. Her new-found frailty was unwelcome and taking its toll.

'You're to put up your feet and rest. There'll be more than enough of us on Saturday to do the job. Charlie has been roped in to help. I think Kate has promised him a chocolate cake all to himself! How about Sunday? We could meet on Sunday. I could come to the cottage but after lunch. I don't want you cooking.'

Flora felt relieved to be spared the chore, then felt guilty she felt relieved. 'Perfect,' she said aloud. 'If you're very good, you can help me with my Christmas decorations – after we've sifted through whatever Mr Sadler's sent.'

He groaned. 'You're not making those wretched paper chains, are you?'

'Not this year. But I do have a cardboard Rudolph I need to put together.'

His second groan was interrupted by the clang of the shop doorbell. 'I have to go, Jack,' she said quickly. 'Alice has just walked in.'

Replacing the receiver, she slipped from her chair to give her friend a big hug. Alice stood back, holding her at arm's length, better to survey her.

'Now, how are you, my love? Still bad, I'll be bound.'

'Not too wonderful,' Flora admitted, 'but better with each day. The hot baths have helped most.'

Her friend nodded sagely. 'Epsom salts, that's the thing. You can't beat it for aches and pains.' She glared deep into the shop, as though the shelving was personally responsible for Flora's plight. 'Now you're back, I hope you're getting Michael to check every single bookcase.'

Flora nodded. 'He's coming round tomorrow.'

She would say nothing to contradict Alice's belief that it had been a freak accident. If her friend knew it had been delib-erate, Flora would be taken to task for once more getting involved in something she shouldn't. There would be constant warnings, too, that on no account must she carry on with whatever foolish thing she was doing.

It was time to change the conversation. 'That was Jack on the phone. He tells me he's helping to take the party food to Pelham Lodge on Saturday.'

'He is that, and very grateful we are, too. My sous-chef only decides he has to go home to see his ma right when we need his van. He knew all about the party – he's been cookin' for it – and you'd think he could have chosen a more convenient time. I said as much to Kate, but she won't hear a word against him.'

'How is the... friendship... going?'

Alice spread her hands, seeming not to know how to answer. 'They seem close enough, the pair of 'em, but I'm not sure Kate is ready for anythin' too serious.'

'Has she said so?'

Over the last few months, Flora had been concerned for Kate, worrying she might be rushing into trouble. Very little time had elapsed since their friend had lost her husband. Bernie Mitchell had been a ne'er-do-well and a totally unsatisfactory man, but Kate's faith in him had never wavered.

'She doesn't talk about it much,' Alice said. 'Mind, you,' she added shrewdly, 'she doesn't talk much about that wretched husband either. Not any more. After he'd gone, it was all Bernie this and Bernie that, but I don't remember hearin' his name for an age now.'

It was a good sign, Flora thought, but it couldn't be why Alice had called at a time when she would normally be elbow-deep in pastry making.

'Can I sell you a book?' she asked, light-heartedly. 'There's a new cookery tome out, *The Cornish Kitchen*. You've used a lot of Jessie's recipes and I thought you might like it. It came in last week.'

'Maybe when I get paid next. My purse is lookin' a bit sad

right now – I had that Michael distemper the sittin' room and it's cost a fair bit. Oh...' Alice had remembered something crucial. 'What do you think?'

It was the phrase that usually presaged the latest piece of gossip circulating the village, and Flora waited to hear.

'I went to the post office yesterday,' Alice began. 'Just to check I still had somethin' in the account, but Dilys decided to close early. Just like her, I thought. She was lockin' the door when I arrived and refused point-blank to unlock it, even though it was five minutes short of closin' time. She'd got her knickers in a right old twist.'

Flora grinned. 'Come and sit down and tell me.' After several minutes of standing, her back had begun to ache badly. Taking Alice by the hand, she led her to the window seat. 'What's upset our treasure of a postmistress?'

'Apparently, some policeman came callin' as Dilys was cashin' up and made her late for her supper. That's what she said. She didn't seem that late to me, but most indignant, she was. You know what she's like.'

'Did she tell you what the police wanted?'

'Same as they've wanted with everyone. They've been flashin' this photograph round the village. Some man they're chasin', though I dunno why.'

Flora nodded. 'Jack told me the inspector had asked his team to circulate a photograph.'

Alice's wiry grey curls bobbed in unison. 'It was one of that inspector's men,' she agreed. 'Seems like he'd been to the post office before, but it was Dilys's day off and he spoke to Maggie Unwin instead. She's helpin' out there, did you know, until Dr Hanson gets back? And that's another thing, we've to go all the way to Steyning now to see a doctor. It's ridiculous.'

'Had Maggie seen the man in the photograph?' She was keen to keep Alice on track.

'No, she hadn't, and told the constable or detective or whatever he was that he'd have to call again when Dilys was back.'

'And the detective showed Dilys the photograph?'

'That's right. Seems that the man they're after's not from round here. They showed his picture to me, but I didn't know him from Adam.'

'I believe it's a photograph of Gareth Beaumont. He's Hugo Rafferty's cousin.'

'Really? Why are they chasin' him?'

Flora ducked the question, saying instead, 'Did Dilys recognise the picture?'

'Amazin'! She did. She must be the only one in the village.'

Not the only one, Flora thought to herself.

'Very effusive over him, Dilys was. He gave her a present for helpin' him, apparently. I dunno what that was about either.'

Flora knew that, too.

Beaumont had been the one! The man who had called at the post office searching for Phoebe Tallant. She did a quick calculation. He couldn't have called there on the day of the murder – the dates didn't add up – but how many times had he been to the village? How many visits to make himself familiar with the area? It was looking likely now that he *had* been in Abbeymead the day of the killing. And more than ever likely that he'd sent a note to Rafferty to meet him at the bell tower that evening.

'I'll be off then.'

Her friend's voice startled Flora back into the present. 'Sorry, Alice. I was daydreaming. Look, I know I'm not much use at the moment, but if there's anything I can help with...'

'Not a thing, my love. I'll be a bit frantic for the next few days, so I thought I'd call in now, make sure you were all right.'

'I am and thank you. And good luck on Saturday. I'm sure the party will go brilliantly, but if it doesn't it won't be the fault of the food!'

'I'll let you know.' Her friend's mouth stretched into a wide smile. 'You never know, if the party's a success, Evelyn might be feeling particularly generous. Then I'll be back for that cookery book.'

When Alice had gone, Flora settled back on the window seat, too fatigued to dust the shelves and tidy her stock as she would normally do. Her friend had brought with her new information and she was glad of the time to think through its extraordinary nature. Dilys had recognised the photograph of Gareth Beaumont. He had been the one who'd given the postmistress the pretty felt brooch Flora had praised, given it for the help he'd had in finding Phoebe Tallant. But why had Beaumont been searching for Phoebe? What on earth was the connection between them, if there was one?

Could it be a complete red herring and have nothing to do with Rafferty or Mason or, indeed, with Stephen Henshall? Jack had told her of the damage to the bookshop window and she'd had to concede that her attacker might not, after all, have been Stephen, though her heart told her otherwise. It was a furious puzzle that sent her mind spinning, until she realised how pointless such speculation was. Best not to get trapped in it. Best to concentrate on the one clear case they had – against Stephen Henshall.

26

Jack had never been to Pelham Lodge though he'd heard plenty of talk in the village. Abbeymead seemed in awe of its palatial size and huge grounds but was not above mocking its claim to be a lodge. As soon as he turned the Austin into the long, gravel drive, he saw there was nothing remotely lodge-like about the sprawling building ahead. It was three storeys high, sporting incongruous Dutch gables, and on one side had seemingly been extended to include another entire wing. An architectural mess, though evidently a very expensive one.

His acquaintance with Evelyn Barnes was minimal and what he knew of her Jack did not particularly like, but as an apprentice gardener he had to admire the hand that had designed and nurtured the extensive grounds. The lawns on either side of the driveway were pristine, heavily manicured even during these winter months. Flowering shrubs – daphne, viburnum, winter honeysuckle, he felt proud he could recognise at least some – had taken the place of summer planting, with every weed banished from sight.

As he brought the car to a halt at the rear of the building,

Alice bustled out of what he took to be the kitchen door, a relieved expression on her face.

'Did you think I'd let you down?' His smile took any sting out of the question.

'Course I didn't.' She was already heaving the boot open. 'But there's so much food – why did the silly woman want to order so much?'

'I can't answer that. But I can tell you that Kate is bringing the last of the goodies, along with herself. Flora has lent her the bike and she's using Betty's wicker tray for three very large cakes.'

Alice nodded. 'Katie won't be far behind, I'm sure. We'll get this lot inside and I can start laying it out. They've got a maid, believe it or not, but she's next to useless.'

'How many guests have you catered for?'

'You'd think it was an army, wouldn't you, but there's no more than six in there.' She jerked a thumb towards the house. 'And with the Barnes and that Henshall, a grand total of nine people.'

He pulled a face. 'Over catered?'

'Just a tad,' she said, laughing. 'But who cares? Me and Katie have made a decent profit.'

The kitchen, when he walked through the rear door, laden with a tray of savoury nibbles and one of sweetmeats, was as large as he'd expected. A great, hollow space that echoed to his footsteps.

'Hello, Mr C,' a young voice piped up. 'Good here, in't it?'

'Charlie Teague. I might have known. And already into the chocolate cake!'

'He's been a great help.' Alice defended him. 'If you'd take those through to the sitting room, Jack, I'll bring serving plates and spoons.'

'I can bring some, too,' Charlie offered.

'Not with those hands, you can't. I don't want to be paying cleaners to get chocolate off Mrs Barnes' moquette.'

Unloading his trays onto the buffet table, Jack thought the small gathering appeared subdued. A woman dressed in maid's uniform, a plate of appetisers in each hand, drifted between the several people who stood awkwardly around the room. Her languid expression suggested complete indifference to both guests and appetisers alike. On the pretext of organising the trays he'd carried in, Jack looked around the group.

There were several women he didn't recognise talking to Evelyn, their voices staccato as though trying to compensate for the torpid air in the room. Her fellow golfers from the Lexington, he reckoned. Two of the men, holding court with Harry Barnes, were also unknown to him. He put them down as Harry's one-time business associates. As for the residents of Abbeymead, there appeared to be only Mr Preece and his wife.

Jack went up to them, surprised to find the village butcher a guest. 'How's the party going?' he asked.

'What do you think?' Preece sounded glum. 'Had to come, though. Can't let the bell-ringers down.'

'Ah!' The butcher's presence became clearer. As a very new member, Harry was struggling to be accepted into the group and an invitation to Pelham Lodge might help. 'What of your fellow bell-ringers?'

'Dilys was invited but couldn't leave her dad. The girl who keeps an eye on him for her was off to the cinema tonight. She won't be sorry to have missed it – 'cept she's missed the food, too.'

Out of the corner of his eye, Jack saw Stephen Henshall sitting alone in a chair placed tight against the opposite wall. He had a glass in his hand and wore a brooding expression.

'The food looks excellent,' he replied, bringing his attention back to Mr Preece.

'Bound to. Alice and Kate cooked it,' the butcher said simply. 'About the only thing worth coming for.'

'Hush,' his wife warned him. 'Mrs Barnes will hear.'

Preece looked as though he was about to retort when Harry, breaking away from the men he'd been talking to, came over to speak to them.

'Make sure you eat plenty,' Harry boomed at the Preeces, nodding to the groaning table behind them. 'And nice to see you, Mr Carrington.' Despite the greeting, Harry sounded dubious and there was a challenge in his eyes.

'I'm not gate-crashing,' Jack said, amused by the man's evident assumption. 'I'm transport for this evening.'

Harry looked relieved. 'That's OK. My wife... she gets a bit twitchy about strangers in the house. Not that you're precisely a stranger.' Harry was tangling himself into knots. 'But you must stay. Make yourself at home.'

If there was something he would never feel at Pelham Lodge, Jack thought, it was at home. Smiling, he excused himself. 'Better get back to the kitchen. Alice still needs some help.'

When he returned with the next tranche of food, the groups had dissolved and reordered themselves. The golf club ladies were talking to the businessmen, Evelyn was holding forth to Mrs Preece and Mr Preece had taken refuge in another glass of some decidedly expensive wine.

Harry was talking to Stephen Henshall who'd emerged from his chair to collect food from the buffet. Taking his time to unload the two trays Alice had passed him, Jack strained to listen.

'I've had to give the police my address in London,' Henshall was saying. 'Bloody cheek. I can't seem to shake the buggers off.'

'It doesn't mean anything, Steve,' Harry said mildly. 'The police always ask for an address in case they need to contact you. Just go along with it.'

'It means something to me.' His friend was aggrieved. 'I need to be shot of them. I'm having to borrow God knows how much money and while the police are on my doorstep, what chance do I have?'

'It's just an admin thing.' Harry was still soothing. 'There's no serious reason they'd want to keep tabs on you, is there? I've given them my address and they haven't bothered me since the interview I had with their sergeant.'

Henshall gave an irritated flick of his hand. 'They're looking for someone to blame for that wretched man's death and I reckon they're hoping to pin it on me.'

'That's ridiculous! We were both there, at the bell tower, but are they trying to pin it on me? Of course not. You're letting your imagination run amok.'

'They can't dig up a motive for you,' his friend pointed out. 'Whereas I'm in trouble. Severe trouble – and Rafferty's to blame. That's some motive, isn't it?'

It was, Jack acknowledged silently.

'Well, yes, but it's no more of a motive than others will have. Think how many people that chap must have harmed. He was a dab hand at scams. He'd have harmed me if I hadn't already retired! I know you didn't like Rafferty—'

'Like him? I hated his guts. Still do, even though he's dead. But I didn't kill him, Harry. You believe me, don't you?'

'You know I do.' To Jack's ear, the confirmation sounded less than fulsome. 'You did go ahead of me that night, though, didn't you? You didn't see anything, I suppose?'

'No, I didn't.' Henshall smacked a spoon into a dish of mayonnaise. 'And I'd be glad if you keep that little nugget to yourself.'

At that moment, Alice brought in the main dessert, an enormous baked Alaska. 'There's a cup of tea in the kitchen,' she whispered to Jack.

Unobtrusively, he moved away. His eavesdropping had

been worth the potential embarrassment. He and Flora had speculated before on whether Stephen Henshall could have arrived at the bell tower separately from his host and now, it seemed, it was confirmed that he had. Henshall had gone ahead. Far enough ahead to climb the stairs to the tower gallery and push the curate to his death before the bell-ringers arrived?

In the kitchen, he found Kate was already busy washing up. Charlie, his mouth still smeared in chocolate, was drying alongside her. She turned as she heard him walk in.

'Thank you for taking so much of the food, Jack. Betty's tray was perfect for the cakes, but not much more.'

'How did the ride go?'

'Fern Hill was a bit tough,' she admitted, 'but we made it together. It would have been even tougher without your car.'

'Have you heard from Tony?' The mention of a car reminded him to enquire of Kate's special friend.

Her face lit from within. 'A letter came this morning. His mother is a lot better. She's had a bout of flu and been really poorly. It's why he felt he had to go home as soon as he could. But he'll be back shortly.'

She stacked the clean plates to one side. 'I'm not sure where these go. Alice must have found them in one of the cupboards, but I've no idea which one. There are so many.'

'It's a large house,' was all he said.

'Not as large as Beaumont Park! Tony told me all about it in his letter. He called there, once he knew his mum was on the mend. He's still got friends working on the estate.'

'I remember him talking about the park.' This was where Jack's interest lay. 'How did he find the place?'

'Not good, it seems. There's been a real kerfuffle in the house. The police have called several times. They've even conducted a search, would you believe? The Beaumonts are pretty starched up and were absolutely furious, particularly when the inspector took away their son's papers. That's the eldest son,' she said in explanation.

'Gareth Beaumont?'

'That's him. There was some kind of letter linking the man to Abbeymead. I can't believe it, but that's what Tony said. And they've had this Gareth into the police station for questioning. Tony's mum cleans for Hugo Rafferty's mother – she still lives on the estate – and she says that Ellen Rafferty is convinced that Gareth Beaumont is responsible for her son's death. There was a lot of talk about the chap, his mum said, even before Rafferty died.'

Jack was intrigued. 'What kind of talk?'

Kate paused, her hands deep in washing-up water. 'It seems that Gareth runs the place now his father is bedridden and he's always in his office or tramping round the grounds. Day and night. A real stickler for things being done properly. But then he changed, kept disappearing for days on end. No one knew what he was doing or where he was going. It gave rise to a lot of gossip.'

'Mysterious.'

'Isn't it? And the letter the police found. Who on earth could be writing to him from Abbeymead?'

'Does Tony's mum have a theory?'

'No, but Mrs Rafferty does. She reckons it was her son who wrote to Beaumont, asking him for help.'

'Help for what?' Jack was mystified.

Kate hung up the tea towel Charlie had left dangling from the draining board. 'He was pretending to be a curate, wasn't he? Maybe he started pretending, who knows why, but then realised what an awful thing he'd done and wanted to stop.'

'So, he writes to the brother of the man he was impersonating?'

'Why not? If he was truly sorry for what he'd done. He could have asked for forgiveness, as well as help. The Beaumonts are a very religious family, so Tony says, and perhaps Gareth would have felt it a duty to come to his rescue.'

Or a duty to kill him, Jack thought silently, washing up his empty teacup. He didn't dispute what Kate had told him, but somehow the image he'd built of Hugo Rafferty was not of someone who would willingly have sought help, least of all from a man who, by report, had always disliked him intensely. That was one kite that wouldn't fly.

27

Jack dropped Kate and Alice at their respective homes and was tempted then to call on Flora, but it was late, and he decided the news could wait until tomorrow. She would be pleased at what he had to tell her, certain to pounce on the fact that, for a short time that fatal evening, Stephen Henshall had not been with his friend. Hensall's confession was the golden nugget of what had been a fairly dismal party. Almost, it sealed his crime for Jack. He wondered if Alan Ridley was aware of it. Probably not, given that Henshall had sworn Harry to secrecy.

As for Beaumont Park, Tony's letter was interesting but, when Jack thought more of it, what had he really learned? That people other than themselves believed Gareth Beaumont might be a killer. In any case, Mrs Rafferty would be prejudiced. She would naturally want to blame someone for her son's death, and if the elder brother had always been hostile to Hugo it made him a good fit. Once the police had shown interest in the man and suspicions had been raised, it wouldn't be too much of a stretch for Ellen Rafferty to assume without any proof that Gareth was a murderer.

The party had been dull, Jack reflected, but as far as Evelyn Barnes was concerned, she had done her duty and given Henshall a decent send-off. A send-off with which Henshall was far from happy. He was returning not to the successful business he loved, but to the demeaning prospect of trying to raise enough capital to save his life's work. And all because of Hugo Rafferty. The man had motive in spades! It had been opportunity missing: they'd believed Henshall to have been in Harry's company throughout. But not so, it seemed. There was a lot to talk over with Flora.

It was in the small hours that he woke to the clanging of bells. At first, struggling from a heavy sleep, he thought it must be the bell of St Saviour's that was tolling. Another death? Was he walking through a nightmare and Rafferty was to be killed all over again? It took him several minutes to realise the sound was very different – loud and harsh, stripping peace from the night. The clang of a fire engine!

Stumbling to the window, he pulled back the curtains. Far along the lane, he caught a glimpse of a flashing amber light, then darkness. Another clang of bells sounded in the distance. Another crew? His eyes travelled upwards. A dirty cloud of red bloomed on the horizon, like blood seeping into a starlit sky. Wherever those engines were rushing, it was to a massive conflagration.

An unexplained dread took hold of him. For several minutes, he stood motionless, staring out of the window. He was teetering on the brink of doing something foolish. And then he'd done it, grabbing the clothes he'd thrown off last night and dressing in seconds. On his way out, he snatched a torch from the kitchen drawer and car keys from the table.

It was easy enough to follow in the firemen's wake, the blaze burning up the sky helping Jack plot his direction. He was in the high street now and heading for Fern Hill. In that instant, he knew. It was Pelham Lodge, almost certainly. Reduced to ashes? Maybe.

Leaving the Austin parked on the lane beyond the Lodge's grandiose gates, themselves bulldozed aside by the fire crew, Jack took his torch in hand and half walked, half ran, up the gravelled drive. The sting of smoke was almost immediate, a cloud of acrid grey hanging ominously in the air. In seconds, his nostrils were smarting and his breath felt choked. From somewhere to his right came the sound of frantic barking. The Lodge's two ferocious brutes had not been in evidence at the party, locked away, he imagined, to keep the guests safe. The animals sounded panicked, and he could only hope that someone had set them free.

He felt the heat before he saw the fireball the house had become. A great tower of flame that reached to the top floor and was even now extending sideways to take in the additional wing. The growl of a vehicle behind him had him jump onto the grass verge. A flash of red, a spiral of amber light, and a third engine joined its two colleagues.

He switched off his torch. In the glare of the crews' emergency lighting, its beam was pointless. Two huddled figures, husband and wife with blankets draped around their shoulders, cowered in the lee of one of the engines. Another woman stood close by, the gaunt figure of the live-in maid, illuminated in the harsh stare of the lights. She was being pulled this way and that by two large dogs, straining hard at their leashes, eyes bulging, and clearly terrified.

A fireman passed close by, and Jack caught his attention. 'Everyone safe?' he asked.

The man's grave expression was just discernible beneath the all-encompassing helmet. He shook his head, raising a begrimed glove in some kind of recognition.

'Sorry, no. One poor chap – couldn't get to him in time.'

Who else but Stephen Henshall, unless one of the other guests had decided to stay the night? Stephen Henshall, their chief suspect.

Jack walked over to the Barnes couple, still huddled close to the leading engine. 'I'm so sorry,' he said, feeling how inadequate it sounded. 'I heard the bells, saw the sky...' He was making a mull of it, but what else was there to say?

'My beautiful house.' There were actual tears in Evelyn's eyes. That must be the first time ever, Jack thought.

'Steve,' Harry Barnes croaked. 'He was asleep on the top floor.'

'He's—'

'Dead,' Evelyn said abruptly.

'We've lost Stephen,' Harry confirmed, his head lowered.

'I'm so sorry,' Jack repeated. 'You must have been asleep, all of you, when the fire caught. How did you escape?'

'The dogs woke us,' Harry muttered. 'It was so cold last night that I kept them indoors. That was lucky – for them and for us. They came into the bedroom, barking their heads off, and we got out fast.'

'But not Mr Henshall?'

'I called up to him – he was on the top floor. I thought I heard him call back. I expected he'd be down the back stairs in a trice and we'd see him on the driveway.' Harry's head dropped even lower. 'He couldn't have heard me.'

'You here, Jack? That is a surprise!'

He turned at the voice. A police car had quietly pulled up at the scene and Alan Ridley was at his elbow.

'I heard the bells,' he began to explain again, 'and wondered if there was anything I could do to help. But what a hideous accident.'

The inspector had no time to reply before they were interrupted by a giant of a man, clad entirely in black, his helmet bouncing shards of light from its glossy surface. The officer in charge, Jack presumed.

'Inspector Ridley,' the man said in greeting. 'Glad you got here. Looks like we're going to need the police. Can we have a word?'

Ridley nodded and moved slightly away, while Jack edged inches in the same direction.

'I'm not happy, Inspector,' the chief was saying. 'One of my men found what was left of an oil lamp on the top floor. What was it doing there? Why would you need an oil lamp when you've got electricity?'

'For decoration?' Ridley suggested.

The giant shook his head. 'It's been used. There was still oil dripping out of the base.'

'And you're thinking?'

'It needs a proper investigation, that's all I'm saying. How many houses today – houses like this, leastways – use oil lamps?'

'Care to give me your assessment? Off the record.'

The officer adjusted his helmet. 'If that lamp were lit, then toppled, the fire would have caught immediately. There was carpet up there and, beneath the carpet, wooden floorboards. The spread would have been rapid. Add the underlay to that – it probably contains asbestos, a lot of them do – and you've got fumes that are lethal. The bloke sleeping on that floor didn't have a chance. We found him on the landing, near the back stairs. He'd evidently woken and tried to escape, but the fumes must have got him before the flames.'

'Have you brought the body down yet?'

'We've got him round the corner until the ambulance arrives. No need to distress these good folk.' He waved a hand at husband and wife, sheltering just feet away. 'He's not a pretty sight. Poor bloke must have been staying the night, seems they had some kind of party here.'

Stephen Henshall had been staying at Pelham Lodge for more than one night, but what else had he been doing? Jack wondered. Now, they would never know for sure. One thing *was* certain. If the man were the villain they'd been seeking, he had received summary justice.

28

It had been past three o'clock before Jack crawled wearily into bed and fell into an immediate and deep sleep. Precisely four hours later, a loud banging on his front door woke him with a start. Bleary-eyed, he fumbled for his spectacles and peered at the travelling clock he still used. Half past seven on a Sunday morning. Who on earth would create such a clamour? He really didn't need to ask.

Almost falling over his feet, he somehow got to the front door and was brushed past by an excited Flora. 'Were you still asleep?'

'Have a guess.' He hugged his dressing gown more tightly.

'I'd guess, yes. But you won't want to sleep when I tell you the news.'

'Won't I?' He staggered into the kitchen and reached for the kettle, managing in the process to knock several cups to the floor.

'Sit down,' she commanded. 'I'll make the tea.'

'Coffee,' he contradicted. 'It has to be coffee.'

'OK. But listen, I've so much to tell you.'

'I know what you've come to say.' He held his head between his hands. It had begun to ache.

'How can you?' She lit the gas and turned round. 'You can't know.' She was trying to sound certain, but a note of caution had crept in.

'Well, my annoying sleuth, that's where you're wrong. I went to the fire.'

'You what!' She dropped the jar of coffee on the draining board. The bang made Jack hold his head harder, but in fits and starts he briefly related the night's events.

Flora looked at him sadly, spooning the coffee into the cup so liberally he reckoned he'd be unlikely to sleep for days. 'How could you do that, Jack?'

'Quite easily. I climbed out of bed, put some clothes on and—'

'You know what I mean. How could you have gone and left me behind?'

'You're not seriously suggesting I should have come to your cottage, knocked you up at midnight and waited for you to dress – still a painful experience, I'd guess.'

'It can be,' she conceded. 'But why not?'

'For one thing, because you're supposed to be getting as much rest as you can.'

'Oh, that. I've decided to forget my bruises. I'm fine.'

'I'm beginning to see that,' he said feelingly. 'Is the coffee ready yet?'

'I'll make any number of cups for you as long as you give me a blow-by-blow account of what happened last night.'

He'd drained the first cup, the ends of his hair bristling, before he told her everything that had happened, from the party and its guests to the moment the ambulance had drawn up and removed Henshall's burnt body to the morgue.

Flora was looking perturbed. 'If the fire chief is right and the fire *is* suspicious, someone tried to kill Henshall.'

'And succeeded. They could, of course, have been after Evelyn or Harry.'

'But you don't think so?'

He shook his head.

'Neither do I. The arson was directed at Henshall. So, it must follow, mustn't it, that he can't be our villain? He didn't murder Rafferty, he didn't run you down, and he didn't try to kill me.'

'Maybe not, but I can't be absolutely sure. It's still possible he could be responsible for one of those attacks, or more than one. I've suggested before there could be two different people involved in this case.'

Flora gave a decided shake of her head. 'I'm certain it's just the one person. Put it down to one of my famous hunches. He or she is a double murderer. Whoever killed Rafferty tried to kill you in London and me in Abbeymead and has now made away with Henshall. But we still don't know why. Another cup?'

'Please.'

'Will the fire service investigate the blaze?' she asked, reaching for the coffee jar again.

'They'll file a report, I guess, and then it will be up to Ridley to decide what to do with it.'

'It couldn't have been an accident, I suppose?'

'The fire chief thought it unlikely.'

'Not an accident,' she said thoughtfully, 'but there is another possibility. Could it have been started deliberately to claim the insurance – and Henshall was just unlucky?'

'You think the Barneses are so hard up they'd destroy their home for the insurance money which, if there's an investigation that proves the fire was arson, would make sure they wouldn't get a penny? What they would get, though, is a long prison sentence.'

'It was only a thought,' Flora said, sounding peeved. 'I'm really quite annoyed that Henshall has been killed.'

'I imagine he must be, too.'

'It leaves us with no one to pursue and he was such a good suspect.'

'Not true, Flora. It leaves us with Gareth Beaumont and with Mason, still.'

'Pff.'

'Not so much of the pff. According to Kate, who had it from Tony – he's been at Beaumont Park recently – the police have raided the place, if you can call it a raid. They've taken away papers belonging to Gareth Beaumont, which is why they've been hawking his photograph around Abbeymead.'

Flora's slender figure became alert. 'I know about the photograph. Mr Vaisey *thought* he knew the man, but Alice tells me that Dilys definitely recognised him. Beaumont was the man who called at the post office looking for Phoebe Tallant. Which means we can place him in Abbeymead before I first saw him here and before Rafferty was murdered. So, yes, you're right, the case against him is building, but it's not enough. Henshall was a much better bet.'

Jack nodded vaguely. 'There is something else...' His mind was drowsy and the thought kept escaping. 'That's it!' He thumped down his coffee cup. 'We've still not looked at that package – the one my colleague sent. I knew we should have got on and opened it. His research might just add the pieces that we need for this jigsaw. You haven't brought it with you, by any chance?'

She shook her head. 'Sorry, it's at home.'

'Let me get shaved and dressed and we'll go back to your cottage and do a grand opening. See what Sadler has come up with. You can cook me a splendid Sunday breakfast, too.'

'I might, but only after you've put Rudolph together.'

Flora was hopping with anticipation. She had wanted to tear open that brown paper ever since she'd brought the packet back from the shop. Each time she'd looked at it lying innocuously on her kitchen table, she'd itched to take her hands to it. Somehow, she'd managed to subdue the temptation but now, waiting for Jack to munch through two bowls of cornflakes, a soft-boiled egg, followed by toast and more coffee, she was on edge.

'I might just have another egg,' he said, as he drained his second cup. 'Or maybe some bacon. Only teasing,' he added. She must have looked ready to explode, she thought. 'I'm as keen as you to see what's in the magic bundle.'

'Let's hope it *is* magic.' Picking up the package, Flora offered it to him.

'Go on,' he urged. 'You've waited too long already.'

Wanting no further encouragement, she slit the brown paper open and pulled out a sheaf of papers. They seemed to be copies of various photographs, all dated, and taken over the last year or so. Pushing aside Jack's empty plate, she spread the first on the table. It was a terrible image of a smashed car and a crumbling brick wall. A second photograph had been taken from a distance and the mangled car, bearing a broken body, appeared small and insignificant against an expansive landscape.

Jack stared down at them. 'That settles the accident theory,' he said. 'Look at the road she was travelling along. Straight as a die. Unless the car had a mechanical malfunction, which doesn't appear to be the case, there's no way Mrs Mason could have veered off that road. She had to have turned the car directly into the wall. You can see, the wall is at the bottom of a hill, so maximum impact. The spot was deliberately chosen. She definitely committed suicide.'

'How very sad.' Flora sat for a while looking at the

photographs. 'The question is why. Was it because of Mason? That this was the only way she could free herself from her husband?'

'Divorce might have been easier. What do the others show?'

There were a number of pictures of the couple's wedding. It had evidently been widely reported.

'It was a lavish affair,' she remarked. 'There seems to have been at least a hundred guests. There's Mason and Cicely in this one. The happy couple. He looks so old in comparison and she is beautiful.'

'A true beauty queen.'

Flora nodded, holding the picture to what light there was on a grey December morning. In the background, she made out a disconsolate-looking Phoebe. Picking up a second photograph, she opened her eyes wide.

'Look, Jack,' she said, handing it to him. 'Look who else was there.' It was Hugo Rafferty at the edge of a group of men. He was smiling.

'Rafferty went to the wedding!'

'Went to the wedding and charmed Mrs Mason maybe? Here's one that must have been taken at the reception. A sit-down meal for a hundred. It must have cost a fortune. Cicely looks nervous, doesn't she?'

'Wondering what she's done, perhaps.'

'And this one' – she shuffled the last sheet from the packet – 'was taken at the dance that followed. Just look at the size of the band. It must have been the wedding of the year.'

Jack took the last photograph from her and nodded. It was of couples dancing and both of them stared at it for a moment. Then Flora gasped. Almost out of the camera's eye, there was Rafferty. He'd taken to the floor and was dancing with Cicely, holding her as close to his chest as was possible.

'Look at her face,' she said. 'Look at her eyes. Warm and

dreamy. The camera has just caught her. Cicely is loving this dance. And she's only just been married – to another man!'

'An affair? Is that what the suicide is about? She had an affair with Rafferty and he let her down.'

'It would fit with what we know of him.'

'And Phoebe was there at the wedding,' he went on. 'Watching her sister, maybe, realising what might be about to happen. No wonder she looks so miserable.' The jigsaw shifted to one side, the pieces sliding out of place and rearranging themselves. 'Is that the connection?'

Flora frowned. 'What do you mean?'

'I never got to say earlier but, amid the papers the police took away from Beaumont Park, there was a letter postmarked Abbeymead. No one, except the police, is aware of its contents, but what if it was Phoebe Tallant who wrote that letter?'

'You're suggesting that Phoebe wrote to Gareth Beaumont?'

'I'm allowed the occasional wild speculation, too! We know that Beaumont came to the village prior to Rafferty's death looking for Miss Tallant. Supposedly, to offer her a job.'

Flora gave a fierce shake of her head.

'Exactly. That has to be a nonsense. But what if Phoebe had written to ask him to meet her?'

'He didn't have her address,' Flora said practically. 'If she'd asked him to meet her, would she really have forgotten to tell him where she lived? If he'd had the address, Beaumont wouldn't have needed to go the post office to ask for directions. He wouldn't have needed to buy that brooch.'

'That piece of jewellery really annoys you, doesn't it?'

'It's beautiful and totally wasted on Dilys. She has no taste.'

'She hasn't, but that's neither here nor there. I disagree about the letter. I think it could have been from Phoebe. It might not have asked Beaumont to meet her specifically. It could have been some kind of anonymous warning and, even if there was no address, he might have felt compelled to seek out the writer.'

'What kind of warning?'

'That his cousin was up to no good. If her sister was having an affair with Rafferty, and Phoebe knew or guessed it, she could have contacted Gareth Beaumont, as Rafferty's nearest relation, in an attempt to end it. She might even have told him that Rafferty was impersonating his brother. That would have put a stop to the charade *and* removed Rafferty from the scene.'

'If so, it would mean that Phoebe recognised the curate for who he really was.'

'Why not? They were both at the wedding. Like I say, she could have been watching Cicely at the reception, suspected that Rafferty was out to seduce her sister. Then he turns up in Abbeymead saying he's Lyle Beaumont.'

'The wedding was huge and we don't know for certain that Phoebe even saw him there. There's no photograph showing Phoebe and Rafferty in the same frame.'

'OK. I think she must have seen him.' Jack sounded stubborn. 'But say she didn't, say he was lost in the crowd, he worked at Mason's, didn't he? And Phoebe could have met him there.'

'She said she never went near the store.'

'I don't necessarily believe her. She's Mason's sister-in-law, after all.'

'She hates Mason. She wouldn't care if he was being cuckolded.'

'But she'd care for Cicely. Don't forget we've been told Mason is a dangerous man. Phoebe might have been trying to save her sister from disaster.'

Flora drummed her fingertips on the table. 'We're at odds, Jack, but doesn't it depend on when that letter was written? Was it before or after her sister's death? If it was before, maybe it did work as you suggest, a warning to Beaumont that his cousin was having an illicit affair. An attempt to get Rafferty out of her sister's life.'

'And if it was after,' Jack continued, thinking it through as he spoke, 'it was a warning to Beaumont that his cousin was masquerading as his brother and designed to pay Rafferty back for whatever Phoebe believed he'd done to her sister. With that knowledge, Gareth Beaumont could have preferred charges and Rafferty face prison.'

'Or it might not be from Phoebe at all. We need to know what's in that letter.' She stood up slowly, clearing the table and filling the washing-up bowl with their breakfast china. 'But' – she turned from the sink to face Jack – 'what we do know is that the letter brought Beaumont to Abbeymead on several occasions. Why not on the night Rafferty was killed?'

It was possible, he acknowledged silently but, to his mind, improbable. Despite the evidence the man could have been in Abbeymead on the crucial night, Jack couldn't see Gareth Beaumont as a killer. The man was a hard, cold individual, but he was also a man who claimed to live his life by the Bible. And there was a commandment in that book, wasn't there, that prohibited murder?

Flora had fallen silent, too, the only sound in the kitchen the slooshing of cups and plates through the soapy water.

Shaking her hands free of the foam at last, she said, 'You know, if you could pump Ridley for more information, if he has a date for the letter, we might actually begin to make headway.'

'I've to ask more sneaky questions?' He gave a deep sigh. 'And all because I went to a party.'

'All because you did,' she agreed, throwing him a tea towel. 'Now, where did I put Rudolph's bits and pieces?'

29

Monday was never the best day for a funeral and this Monday was proving particularly miserable. From the moment Flora looked out of her bedroom window to see rain smashing into the brick path below, the depressed spirits she'd woken with sank a little lower. But despite the weather, she needed to get moving. The funeral wouldn't wait, and Jack would be at her door very soon, having promised to drive Alice and herself to the crematorium at Chiltington.

I didn't know Miss Lancaster, he'd said. *I don't think I even said hello to her. It would feel odd going to her funeral, but I'll drive you both there and wait in the car until the service is over.*

After a sparse breakfast, Flora took up position at her sitting room window and within minutes saw the red Austin come to a halt in the lane. The rain was still falling in torrents and, before Jack could practise his gallantry and leap from the car with an umbrella, she grabbed her own from the hall and hurried out of the cottage and down the front path. In the stiff wind that had begun to blow, the umbrella proved useless and she ended clambering into the passenger seat breathless and crumpled, her raincoat soaked and her copper waves corkscrewing wildly.

Jack grinned at her. 'I like it,' he said, pointing to the halo of mad hair.

'Say no more! Just go.'

In another five minutes, they had collected a similarly wet Alice and were driving out of Abbeymead on their way to Oakleaves Crematorium.

'It's clearin' a bit,' Alice said hopefully from the back seat, after they'd been travelling a while.

Flora peered through the windscreen. The sky above seemed to her more lowering than ever and the wet ribbon of road that lay ahead badly flooded. Rain-washed Downs and empty, dank fields offered little more cheer. As the miles rolled by, the hills were left behind, their smooth curves becoming ever fainter, and thickly wooded country-side took their place. Fat goblets of water hammered against the car roof as they drove beneath an avenue of bare branches.

Flora peered again. It might just be clearing a little and perhaps they'd be lucky to make the service without a second drenching. Not that it would matter to her hair, which had dried at the oddest angles. She hoped that Phoebe wouldn't be offended.

'How much further is this bloomin' place?' Alice asked.

'Not much,' Jack reassured her. 'As far as I could make out from the map I borrowed at the post office, Oakleaves is a few miles outside Chiltington village.'

'Don't say Dilys let you consult a map without buying it?' Flora pulled a face.

'Only because she wanted directions as well! She was still grumbling about the funeral not being at St Saviour's.'

'Shouldn't we have given her a lift?' was Flora's immediate thought.

'I offered but she said that Daniel Vaisey was driving her, along with Elsie.' Had Elsie Flowers, her most avid crime reader, known Miss Lancaster well, Flora wondered, or did she simply enjoy funerals?

'Vaisey?'

'His way of contributing to village life, I think, having made a good profit from us all. I doubt he'll be at the funeral itself.'

In that Jack was wrong. As they pulled into the car park beyond the large painted sign that announced Oakleaves Crematorium, Flora spotted the landlord guiding the two women towards the building's entrance.

'Heathen, that's what it is,' Alice muttered, glaring through the car window.

The crematorium was a squat box of dark red brick, hugging a taller V-shaped section to its middle. On either side, a double row of narrow oblong windows was topped by a flat roof which in no way disguised the tall chimney behind. Some effort had been made to soften the building's appearance with a large circular flower bed at the front entrance, but its concrete surrounds remained empty apart from one or two unhappy shrubs.

It wasn't exactly heathen, Flora thought, but it was certainly depressing. What had led Phoebe Tallant to choose such a place? Miss Lancaster had never been exactly lively but, surely, she deserved a warmer farewell than this.

Leaving Jack in the car, she took Alice's arm and together they walked the few yards to the door. The interior appeared slightly less depressing, but judgment was relative. Two lines of wooden chairs had been set out in mathematically straight lines on a shining marble floor, with a wide aisle left between. A velvet-covered platform at the far end of the room stared back at them. For the coffin, she realised, and, hanging above, a single wooden cross, the only decoration to relieve the stark whiteness of the walls.

The congregation was as small as Flora had expected. Several of the villagers she recognised by sight, women much the same age as Miss Lancaster – had they been her close friends? It felt strange imagining that austere lady gossiping over the teacups, but perhaps she had. Alice made straight for a seat at the back and Flora followed her. Elsie and Dilys were two rows ahead, she noticed, Daniel Vaisey sitting between them. On the other side of the central aisle, Phoebe Tallant sat alone, wearing a bright blue coat and a rather fetching hat in paler blue.

'Look at that Phoebe,' Alice whispered. 'If that hat and coat isn't heathen, I don't know what is!'

The service itself was short, two hymns, several prayers, a five-minute eulogy from a priest no one knew, and curtains that Flora hadn't noticed before closing around the coffin. She could feel Alice stiffen beside her as the heavy material swished together. Flora felt the tension, too. The whole event had been utterly soulless.

'How was the service?' Jack asked, as they climbed into the car less than half an hour later.

'Heathen,' Alice said for the third time.

'Phoebe looked sad.' Flora reached up to fiddle with her hair, still trying to disentangle the mess of waves.

'Not that sad that she couldn't wear something decent.' Alice was unforgiving.

'Perhaps Miss Lancaster asked her to wear something bright?' Flora suggested. 'She was in blue,' she explained to Jack.

'Bright blue.' Alice's lips tightened. 'And that hat!' There was a pause before she burst out again. 'Sad? She should have been sad, sending her godmother off in that shabby way. The funeral should have been at St Saviour's. That would have been fittin' *and* we'd have had a full church.'

'Who attended?' Jack asked.

'Hardly anyone from the village,' Flora started to say when there was a tap on the passenger window.

'What did you think of that then?' It was Elsie, her short stature almost squashed by the large black turban covering her head and most of her face.

'Not a lot,' Alice answered for Flora.

'Nor me neither. Ruby Lancaster must be turning in her grave 'cept she can't turn. Not in that.' She looked across at the chimney, soon to be smoking.

'I see Mr Vaisey drove you,' Flora said, intrigued by the publican's appearance at the funeral. He could hardly have said a good morning to Miss Lancaster, let alone known her well.

'He's a decent man, I'll say that for him, even though he was a soldier.' Elsie swatted at the turban that had slipped further down her face. 'I'm not one for the pub but he heard I wanted to pay my respects and offered to bring me. And when I asked about Dilys – I knew she'd have a problem – he said the more the merrier.'

'That was good of him,' Flora agreed.

''Specially when it was such a let-down. Two hymns, that's all. No chance to sing out. And no food afterwards, either, like we were promised. I call it shameful. And when that girl has been left everythin' by her godmother!'

A toot of Vaisey's horn had Elsie abandon her complaints and hurry over to the waiting car, while Jack started the Austin.

The journey to Abbeymead was accomplished in silence, Flora deep in thought and Jack, she recognised, too diplomatic to say anything that might cause further upset. Alice had been unusually ruffled by the morning's events, but Flora was at a loss to come up with any kind of diversion, her mind fixed on how much she was looking forward to taking off her funeral garb and turning the key in the All's Well's door.

She managed to open the shop around eleven o'clock and by lunchtime was feeling pleased with her progress. Despite opening late, she'd found sufficient energy to complete her routine Monday chores, grab a cheese roll from the Nook – Kate had wanted to hear about the funeral, and she'd promised to regale her later – and begin on some serious book-keeping.

She had totalled her first column when Inspector Ridley walked through the door. To say she was surprised was an understatement. As far as she was aware, he'd only ever called at the bookshop once – the time he'd been with Jack, bent on a rescue mission. To Flora, it always felt that the inspector treated her ownership of the All's Well as a kind of hobby to be indulged, rather than as the precarious means by which she earned a living.

'Good afternoon, Miss Steele.' He raised his trilby in greeting.

She returned his greeting but with half her mind occupied with why exactly he was here. Had Jack contacted him from Overlay House on his return from the funeral? It was only reluctantly that he'd agreed to ask the inspector about the letter Gareth Beaumont had received, and it seemed unlikely he would have done it this quickly. Even more unlikely that the inspector would have told him much.

Ridley was looking fixedly at her, a quizzical expression on his face. 'I called in, Miss Steele, hoping you might order a book I'm after.'

'Yes, of course.' She found it difficult not to sound surprised; it was the last thing she'd expected.

'I seem to be spending a fair amount of time in Abbeymead these days,' he offered in explanation. 'Not much chance, you see, of getting to a bookshop in Brighton.'

'The town has plenty of them.'

'It does.' He smiled benignly, and Flora felt sure a book order was not his prime objective in paying this visit.

'Let me have a note of the book and I'll put an order in straight away.'

He shuffled in his pocket, bringing out a dog-eared slip of paper. There was certainly a book title written there and an author's name, but still...

'I imagine it's Pelham Lodge that's taking up your time,' she said cautiously.

He shook his head. 'Not much point spending time there. The place is devastated.'

'It was a dreadful accident.'

'I don't think you believe that, Miss Steele.'

'Do you, Inspector?'

He smiled again. 'The jury's out. The fire service report is inconclusive. They suggest the possibility of arson, but won't commit to it, and our own investigation has turned up nothing that might settle the matter.'

'If the fire *was* deliberately started, was it to kill Stephen Henshall?' Flora abandoned any attempt to appear indifferent.

'It's looking that way. Pity the chap's dead. He was our chief suspect.'

'And ours. For once, we agree!'

'Any reason in particular you settled on him as the guilty party?' Ridley asked casually. Was this why the inspector was here, to discover how far she and Jack had progressed? Not far, was the answer.

'It seemed to me, to us, that he had the strongest motive.'

The inspector nodded.

'And there's the fact that he arrived at the bell tower before anyone else. He would have had the time to kill Hugo Rafferty – just.'

Ridley's eyes became sharply alert. 'What was that you said?'

Harry Barnes had evidently not divulged to the police that he'd walked from Pelham Lodge that night alone. Was this the kind of tidbit the inspector had come for?

'Stephen Henshall went ahead to the bell tower,' she

confirmed. 'Mr Barnes followed him down to the village, but Henshall was alone at the church for at least a few minutes, until the bell-ringers arrived.'

'Thank you, Miss Steele. I knew this visit would be worthwhile. Anything else I should know?'

She put her head on one side, considering. 'Only that for a while I was convinced Henshall had been the one to tamper with the bookcase.'

Ridley frowned. 'What a mess that was! You were lucky to survive, you know. How are you now?'

'Better.' She wouldn't admit that her bruises still kept her awake at night.

'We should have investigated the incident,' he confessed. 'But to be honest, I don't have the men. Not with a murder case on my shoulders. A double murder now.'

'It would have been a waste of your time, in any case. Jack came back to the shop that day to check on the rear window. He had a hunch, and he was proved right. Someone had jemmied it open. They probably wore gloves, so no fingerprints, and just about anyone could have done it. Including Gareth Beaumont,' she threw out.

Ridley said nothing for a moment. 'It's possible,' he agreed at last.

'He's the man you're chasing now?' she asked boldly.

'He's the one option we're left with,' he admitted. 'Pursuing him should lead us somewhere, though where I'm not sure.'

'If *he* doesn't, the letter should. The one he received from Abbeymead.'

'You know about that?' The inspector sounded annoyed. He looked annoyed.

'Word gets around.'

'It certainly does in this place,' he grumbled.

'Can you tell me about the letter?' It was worth a try, Flora thought.

'Seeing as you and that writer bloke of yours seem one step ahead, I don't see why not, though there's not much to tell. We've no idea when the letter was written – there's no date. And no address either. And it's guesswork who sent it.'

The missing date was a blow. It could have provided a definite motive for Gareth Beaumont, evidence of a strong reason to kill. Jack had a theory and she rather thought he was right, but for the moment Flora decided to say nothing. That way she might learn more. She would certainly avoid looking foolish if Jack's stab in the dark was way out of line.

'Are you at liberty to tell me what the letter said?'

Ridley gave a small shrug. 'There were only a few lines. "Rafferty's impersonating your brother. He's killed my sister. What are you going to do about it?" It wasn't exactly forthcoming.'

Flora's eyes opened wide. Seemingly, those words meant little to Ridley, but they blazed a trail for her.

'I mean, whose sister are we talking about?' the inspector went on. 'From what I've learned of Rafferty, before he decided to play curate, his life was pretty... loose... not to put too fine a point on it. It would take an army of coppers to question every one of the women he was involved with and I've barely a handful.'

If the inspector's team had questioned Phoebe Tallant further, her connection to Rafferty would have been revealed. But why would they have done that? The girl hadn't been at the bell tower when Rafferty died, hadn't been at the funeral when he'd been buried, and appeared to have no interest in any of the mourners. It was only Jack's ill-fated journey to London that had unearthed Phoebe's relationship to Mason's wife. Not so ill-fated, after all, it turned out.

The missing date they needed was there in the letter, implied if not stated. Phoebe had written *after* Cicely had died. Written not only to warn Beaumont that his cousin was masquerading as Lyle, but also to stir him to revenge. Revenge for his brother's early demise and revenge for her sister's terrible end.

'The letter will give you a lead, I guess.' Her heart was thumping a little too hard, but she forced her mouth to smile.

'Maybe. It's pinning the blighter down,' he said heavily. 'The letter gives us a motive of sorts and we know Beaumont came to the village on more than one occasion. We'll need to go back to him, hammer him again until we know just what he was doing here. At the moment, we've nothing concrete. Nothing to prove he was in Abbeymead on the night in question.'

He rammed the trilby back on his head. 'Thanks for putting in the order. And you'll pass on anything that comes your way, I hope? Jack, too?'

'Of course,' she assured him.

30

It seemed to Flora that Inspector Ridley had made little progress in finding Rafferty's killer. The pursuit of his prime suspect, Stephen Henshall, had come to nothing. The man's motive had been clear, his opportunity to kill a possibility but, if Stephen had been guilty, he was now beyond justice. He hadn't been, though, had he? If the fire had been arson – and how could it not – it would mean that someone had set out to murder the murderer. Which didn't make a lot of sense.

Ridley's concentration was now on Beaumont and Flora thought he was probably right. Knowing what she did about Cicely Mason, the letter the police had found appeared to damn him. Even so, she wasn't completely convinced. Leonard Mason hadn't entirely disappeared from her mind. His name had been absent from their conversation and Flora had wondered while the inspector was talking whether she should throw Mason into the mix.

In the end, she'd decided not. The inspector would know of Mrs Mason's death, police searches into the mourners at Rafferty's funeral would have turned up the story of the supposed accident, but there was nothing to suggest that Len Mason was anything more than a grieving widower. He'd turned up unexpectedly at Rafferty's funeral, true, but Hugo had been his employee for a number of years. It was explanation enough. Unless Phoebe had talked to the police, spilled out her hatred of Mason and the wretched marriage her sister had made, there was nothing of which the police could suspect him.

He was also the wealthy owner of a prestigious department store and Ridley would be circumspect in any questioning he did. Asking a man whose wife had suffered a tragic accident whether he thought she had committed suicide because she'd been abandoned by her lover was not likely to endear the questioner. And accusing a man of some influence of seeking revenge for her death was not something even the boldest policeman was likely to do.

Jack seemed certain that in some way Mason was involved but, if he was, it would have been at a distance. Charlie had seen him in Abbeymead after Rafferty had died, the boy tumbled into a ditch by Mason's chauffeur-driven saloon. And she and Jack had seen him at Rafferty's funeral. But if he were responsible for the curate's death, it would have been by ordering one of his henchmen to do the deed. Mason himself would be too noticeable if he'd come to Abbeymead bent on murder, apart from the fact that he was supposed to have a cast-iron alibi.

Unless... had he come to the village that night in some kind of disguise? Ditched the chauffeur, ditched the homburg and dark tailoring. Adopted the local dress of corduroys and ancient overcoat. Then sent that note – also disguised – and waited for Rafferty at the bell tower. It could have happened. But why then did Henshall have to die a month later?

There was nothing concrete about this case, as Ridley had said. Possibilities beckoned from the shadows, but they were only possibilities. It was frustrating in the extreme and Flora wished she didn't care. When Sally's future was threatened at the Priory, she'd felt impelled to help. When their Cornish landlord had been brutally murdered, she'd wanted justice for him. For Polly Dakers, too. And when the All's Well had begun to fail because a murderer was at large, determination and a burning anger had led Flora to the truth. But this time? Did she care about Hugo Rafferty? She'd barely known the curate and from what she'd learned since, the man was hardly an estimable human being. Did she care about Stephen Henshall, the second victim? A little, perhaps, but that was all. She should give up this investigation and tell Jack to do the same. Concentrate on making her bookshop the best in Sussex and encourage Jack to write his best novel ever.

But... she didn't like to be beaten. And it was a big 'but'.

Two days later, a typewritten note arrived through the All's Well's letter box. It was waiting for Flora when she walked through the white-painted front door. The note was two lines long, typewritten and unsigned, and gave little away. If she really wanted to get to the bottom of this case, the note suggested, she could. The writer had information they were willing to divulge, but only in person. If she was interested, she should come to the churchyard at noon today.

Flora read the slip of paper several times before deciding it was a joke. She almost telephoned Jack to share it, but then thought he might be annoyed to have his work interrupted for a triviality. Leaving the note on her desk, she began the morning's cleaning routine, though a steady flow of customers soon had her lay her duster aside. Christmas was almost here and trade was correspondingly busy. In addition, it was Wednesday and early closing, a day when Abbeymead inhabitants often realised on waking that they had only a few hours to purchase the book they'd been meaning to buy all month.

As the shop bell ushered one of her customers, Miss

Bancroft, into the street, a satisfying bag of books in the school-teacher's basket, Flora went back to her desk and once more turned the note over. The meeting time had been well chosen, she reflected. Whoever had sent those lines must know that today she closed at one o'clock and guessed rightly that she might be willing to close an hour before time, but no earlier. Who was this prankster? If she went to the churchyard, would someone jump out at her with a bucket of water or a bag of flour? It was that kind of childish message.

Halfway through the morning, the telephone rang.

'I've had this note,' Jack said. 'It sounds a bit bonkers but—'

'Asking you to meet in the churchyard?'

'Yes, you, too?'

'It's a joke, Jack. Someone who knows we're amateur sleuths and fancies playing a trick on us. I wondered if it could be Charlie.'

'Charlie?! Why would he do a thing like that?'

'The boys in his class have been messing about for weeks and, with Christmas holidays so close, there's not much work being done. When Charlie came in for his delivery round on Friday, he told me they'd even started some kind of competition. Vying with each other on how best to trick people.'

She could hear Jack thinking. 'I suppose it could be Charlie. If it is, I've a good mind to go to the churchyard and teach the rascal a lesson. Why don't you meet me there? We could have fun.'

'I have a shop to run,' she protested, 'and you have a book to edit. Fun isn't going to do either.'

'OK, but I could do with a walk. I'm at a sticky point and walking helps me think it through.'

'If you must...'

Replacing the receiver, she stared out of the bookshop's latticed window, watching for long minutes as the queue outside the bakery gradually diminished. Could it be Charlie?

Or something more sinister? She frowned. It was a joke, surely, but she felt sufficiently concerned to pick the phone up again and dial Alan Ridley's number – Jack had given it to her months ago. She felt stupid ringing him, but the more she thought about the note and those two uncompromising lines, the more uneasy she'd become. The fact that both she and Jack had received exactly the same instruction had unnerved her.

She was lucky. The inspector answered immediately, and she briefly told him of the message they'd both received.

'I believe it's a trick,' she said, 'and nothing with which you need get involved, but you did say to tell you of any developments. We think the writer is probably a boy we know, or one of his school friends, playing what they think is a joke on us.'

Flora had flushed to the roots of her hair as she'd been speaking. It was embarrassing to call a policeman, an inspector at that, merely to pass on a likely joke. Humiliating or not, she felt better for telling him.

Ridley's response surprised her. Shocked her, in fact. 'I don't think you should go,' he said.

'But—'

'I know... it's a boy's trick. But what if it isn't? I'm in the village this morning, seeing the vicar again. Let me do the meeting and if that young urchin is behind it, I'll give him a cuff for you.'

'He's a good lad. He won't have meant harm. I wonder... can I be there, too?'

There was a long pause, before the inspector said, 'If you really must – I suppose I might scare the boy if I'm on my own. But make sure you wait for me at the lych gate.'

'And Jack? I think he'll be there, too.'

'I'll phone him now and tell him to stay home!'

. . .

Flora locked the All's Well's door at five minutes to twelve. Alan Ridley hadn't wanted her to go to the churchyard, it was clear, but if this was Charlie being silly, she wanted to make sure the inspector didn't frighten him too much. And if it wasn't... why was a policeman – and not just a policeman but a detective inspector – so interested in a young boy's misdemeanour? If nothing else, it had made Flora sure she should be there.

Approaching St Saviour's, the churchyard looked deserted. A fitful wind was blowing and the few autumn leaves that remained were giving themselves up to an occasional swirl, landing in heaps around the gravestones. At least it was no longer raining. Or snowing. Even though it was very cold, they'd been lucky so far. Perhaps Christmas would be wearing white.

Hunched against the icy breeze, she stood beneath the lychgate roof and waited. There was still a minute to go to midday. She tried to remember if Charlie had a watch, but now she thought about it, he'd probably arrived earlier and found a hiding place. Stamping her feet in a pointless attempt to keep warm, Flora was itching to walk into the churchyard and winkle him out. But she waited. Five minutes passed, then another five. The inspector appeared not to have kept his promise. She would give him a few more minutes and then go looking.

A faint cry reached her ears. It came from behind the church, from the oblong of ground where the graveyard stretched almost to the border with Fern Hill. She strained her ears to listen again, so hard they hurt. For a second, the wind brought with it only muffled sounds. Then another definite cry. That sent Flora racing towards the noise, running up the brick path that circled the church, before jumping soft tussocks of grass and zigzagging a path through old lichen-covered gravestones.

Once clear of the church's grey stone bulk, she saw through

narrowed eyes a figure, its arm raised high in the air and with what looked to be a gravedigger's shovel clasped in both hands. Another figure, a man crouching, had launched himself at the attacker, the shovel swaying dangerously above their heads. Still running, a last burst of energy brought her to within a few yards of the fight. Jack! It was Jack. What was he doing here after Ridley's call?

His adversary had thrown the shovel to one side – he had lost the room to manoeuvre – and was now raining punches on Jack with his bare fists, at the same time kicking him with what seemed to be army boots. Didn't army boots have steel caps? she thought frantically. The attacker's solid muscle, the power of his punch, was too strong and Jack was gradually losing the fight, gradually being beaten to the ground.

Flora launched herself forward, making a grab for the man's legs. Startled, he spun around, his face contorted in a snarl, ready to land a fist on her. For the first time, she saw his face. The face of the killer they'd sought. Daniel Vaisey! For a moment, he appeared to hesitate from wielding the blow and, taking her chance, Flora grabbed her aunt's hat pin, still nestled in the pocket of her coat, and drove it fiercely into his leg. He gave a howl of rage, let go of Jack and instead grabbed her by the hair, and—

The thud of footsteps sounded from behind. Ridley and two of his men were racing towards them. Flora was let go, her already bruised body thudding to the ground, while Vaisey attempted to run. But the police were too quick. In an instant, the handcuffs were on, and the landlord dragged out of the churchyard to the waiting police car. The inspector helped her to her feet, then turned to aid Jack.

'I told you to wait,' Ridley said, shaking his head at Flora.

'But you didn't come.'

'Held up,' he said briefly. 'A farmer's cart broken down on

the Brighton road. But you, Jack – pity you'd left home before I phoned.'

'It was,' Jack agreed, his breath coming short. Then he was beside Flora, his arms around her and hugging her tight. 'How are you, wild woman?'

'Hurting, and my head could definitely feel better,' she said, sounding a trifle wobbly. 'I thought I was being scalped. But how about you?' She stroked his cheek.

'Could be better,' he admitted. 'I've probably got bruises to match yours.'

'We didn't do too well on our sleuthing, did we? Vaisey! I had no idea, although...'

'You had a hunch!'

They both laughed aloud, leaving Alan Ridley to shake his head. 'I don't know what there is to laugh about. You could both have been killed.'

'But we weren't,' they chanted in chorus.

31

On the Saturday before Christmas, Flora closed the All's Well for the holiday and, since it was a few days before the bank would reopen, tucked away what had been bumper takings at the back of the safe. The till had been ringing from nine that morning until closing time: books, bookmarks, calendars – she'd stocked them this Christmas to the annoyance of Dilys – and various other literary knick-knacks, had been walking out of the door all day, destined to sit under some lucky person's Christmas tree. Flora was exhausted but happy.

Packing her basket for home, she hid Jack's present beneath a thick, woollen scarf. After rejecting a dozen other gift ideas, she'd chosen to have a special bookmark made for him, red-tasselled with his name inscribed in gold on the soft black leather. She hoped he would think it a worthy present. Smiling to herself, she locked the bookshop door, remembering how tempted she'd been to use Jack's real name, Jolyon, but at the last minute had managed to resist the impulse.

Collecting Betty from the rear courtyard, she set off for Overlay House. It seemed the inspector wanted to talk to them both and Jack had promised drinks and a special treat. It had been mortifying how completely they'd been blindsided by Vaisey, a first failure that sat uncomfortably with them. In their defence, the man had given little away. After Rafferty's funeral, Mason's chauffeur had told Jack he was driving his boss to the local pub, but how suspicious was that? Neither of them had thought twice of the casual comment. Then there'd been the time she'd seen Vaisey talking intently to Stephen Henshall. She'd questioned the conversation but gone nowhere with it. There'd been the sense of something odd at Miss Lancaster's funeral, too. Why had Vaisey been there? Elsie mentioning Daniel had been a soldier. None of it, though, added up to much.

The inspector was already in Jack's sitting room when she arrived and raised his glass to her as she walked through the door.

'Still no snow,' Jack mourned, taking her coat. 'But perishing, nevertheless.'

'Not here, though. It's wonderfully warm.' She made for the deep glow of the fire, catching sight in the mantelpiece mirror of two bright pink cheeks. It had been an invigorating ride.

When Jack returned from hanging her coat on the hall stand, he plumped down on the saggy sofa, looking weary and in pain. He must still be hurting from Vaisey's savage attack, she thought.

'The fire's a triumph,' Alan Ridley announced, 'and so are these.' He'd been helping himself from a large dish in the centre of the coffee table and held up for inspection what looked like a square of toast.

'Caviar,' their host explained. 'From Arthur.'

'Knowing you has been an education, Jack.' Her hazel eyes were alight with fun. 'First champagne, now caviar!'

'You might not like it,' he warned. 'Not everyone does.'

That didn't appear to include the inspector who'd cleared at least half the dish before he took up his glass of whisky once more and seemed ready to tell them why he'd called.

'Daniel Vaisey was a bit of a shock,' he began. 'I never figured him for one minute.'

'Nor did we,' Flora said. 'But I should have known it had something to do with Phoebe Tallant. Am I right?' She took a bite of the toast and decided that caviar was something she could take or leave. She much preferred the champagne.

'You are. What made you think it?'

'For one thing, Vaisey was at Miss Lancaster's cremation – and there was no obvious reason for him to be there. I don't know him well, but he didn't seem the kind of person who'd go out of his way to offer lifts to the funeral of someone he hardly knew. Unless there was an enticement. And Phoebe was the only attraction I could see.'

'She was also the girl I saw at the bar in the Cross Keys,' Jack put in, 'looking very much at home there. She evidently knew Vaisey well.'

'You didn't tell me that,' Flora said, reaching for another square of caviar. It was beginning to taste better.

'It hardly seemed important.'

'And I didn't tell you about Vaisey talking to Stephen Henshall in a way that looked odd. When I questioned him, Stephen said he was placing an order with the landlord for beer. I didn't believe him, but I didn't follow it up, and I still don't know what the conversation was about.'

'That's been the problem.' Jack stretched his legs and yawned. 'The hints have always been there, but not strong enough. Separately, they came to nothing. Together they built a picture.'

'So, what is the picture, Inspector? Hugo Rafferty was killed because he harmed Phoebe's sister?'

'Got it in one. This bloke Rafferty was not a nice man. A charmer, though, so we've learnt. He charmed Cicely Mason all right.'

'Did her husband know of her affair?'

'We interviewed Mr Mason recently. He didn't give us much, but he knew all right. And he knew who to blame for her death.'

'Yet he didn't take any action.' Given Mason's reputation, Flora thought it strange.

'He was about to, I reckon, when Vaisey did it for him.'

Flora finished her toast before she said, 'When Mason came to Abbeymead a few days after Rafferty died – the day Charlie was knocked off his bike – was he here to confirm the murder had happened?'

'More than likely,' Ridley answered her, 'though we'll probably never know.'

'And when his chauffeur mentioned he was driving his boss to the pub after the funeral,' Jack put in, 'it must have been to congratulate Vaisey on a job well done. That never occurred to me.'

'It was Miss Tallant who persuaded the landlord to kill Hugo Rafferty,' the inspector said seriously. 'They all had grudges against the man – Beaumont and Mason as well as Phoebe Tallant – but she was the one who took action. Vaisey is an ex-soldier and still pretty fit. Tipping Rafferty over the gallery wall would have been child's play.'

'What I don't understand,' Flora said, 'is why he decided to lure Rafferty to the bell tower on the evening the bell-ringers had their practice. He couldn't have chosen a worse time.'

'Dilys said it wasn't their regular evening, didn't she?' Jack reminded her.

'That's right,' Ridley continued. 'It wasn't. Vaisey thought he'd have a clear run, but suddenly there were bell-ringers appearing from all over the place. And a few minutes before them, Stephen Henshall was at the door. As you told me, Miss Steele, he went ahead of his friend. Harry Barnes confirmed it – after we'd twisted his arm sufficiently.'

'And Henshall saw Vaisey?'

'Saw him but only later recognised him. When he did, it gave him a lever. I imagine that was the reason for the conversation you saw. Henshall decided on a little blackmail, in case he couldn't raise the money he needed. On the evening of the murder, he'd seen Vaisey leave the bell tower. There'd been just enough light to know him again when Harry Barnes took his friend for a drink at the pub. My guess would be that Vaisey was refusing to pay when you saw them talking. We've no evidence to suggest he passed any money over. He might have taken it out of the Cross Keys' till, of course, but Henshall needed far more than petty cash to see him right. Rafferty left him thousands in debt.'

'Stephen should have been grateful to Vaisey for getting rid of a man he hated,' Flora remarked.

'I'm sure he was, but the chance to recoup some money was too tempting.'

'And Mason?' Jack pursued. 'He was at the funeral to make sure Rafferty had gone but also to see Phoebe. Flora spoke to her outside the church.'

Alan Ridley gave a small sigh and finished his whisky. 'Mason won't admit to anything, but Miss Tallant has been helpful. Hoping for a lighter sentence, I imagine. We have her under arrest, as well.'

Flora shuffled forward in her seat. 'She told me her brother-in-law had asked to meet her, but that she'd chickened out and gone away without speaking to him.'

'She lied.' The inspector's expression was bland. 'She seems to be a frequent liar. Mason made the funeral an excuse to return to Abbeymead – it was an old employee of his being buried, so why wouldn't he be there? – but it was Miss Tallant he wanted to see. Wanted to make sure, I think, that nothing to do with the murder could incriminate him. When she met him outside the church, it was to tell him quite simply that she'd done his dirty work for him and never wanted to see him again.'

'Did she tell Gareth Beaumont much the same, that she'd done his dirty work for him?' Jack asked.

'That's why she wrote the letter, wasn't it?' Flora said excitedly, taking a large gulp of the whisky and soda Jack had mixed for her. She spluttered. 'That's what those words meant,' she said hoarsely.

Jack smiled at her, his grey eyes laughing. 'Try sipping, Flora.'

The inspector nodded in a fatherly manner. 'Whisky isn't a ladies' drink,' he warned. Flora took another sip, this time making sure there was no splutter.

'It was why Beaumont came to the village looking for Miss Tallant,' Ridley confirmed. 'She'd issued a challenge, albeit an anonymous one, and he responded. He wanted his revenge, too. But, by the time he found Miss Tallant, she had already persuaded our friend Vaisey to be the assassin. She sent Beaumont back to his estate with a pat on the head, telling him not to worry himself, all would be sorted.'

Flora's forehead creased. 'How did Beaumont find her? The envelope must have had an Abbeymead postmark, and I know he asked Dilys for Phoebe's address. But how would he know it *was* Phoebe Tallant he needed to speak to?'

'Ah, that's where gossip works so well.' Ridley almost rubbed his hands. 'There'd been gossip on the estate about Rafferty, I imagine for years, but then it got known that some poor woman had come to a dreadful end because of him. If Beaumont heard the rumour, I reckon he'd have ignored it. Far too lordly to listen to gossip. Until he got that letter. Then he must have put two and two together. He asked around – we got that from the servants at Beaumont Park – and once he had a name for the woman who'd died, finding her sister wasn't too difficult.'

'With his high moral scruples, he must have been relieved he wasn't being asked to soil his hands,' she remarked. 'And Phoebe and Daniel Vaisey – they were definitely a couple?' To Flora, it seemed the most unlikely of pairings.

'Hard to say. I'm not sure Miss Tallant cares for anyone very much. But Vaisey, he's head over heels for the girl. Trying to protect her, telling us she had nothing to do with any plan, though of course he disputes there was a plan.'

'Did she ask him to murder Henshall, too?'

'We still can't be sure that it was murder but, no, she doesn't seem to have been involved. That was a little private enterprise on Vaisey's part. Also, I suspect the break-in at the All's Well was his own idea. You were asking too many questions, Miss Steele, and needed to be stopped.'

Flora looked deflated for a moment. 'I was sure it was Stephen Henshall, although... I couldn't see how he could have attacked Jack in London.'

Ridley looked surprised. 'What's this?'

'I was run down by a car near my father's home,' Jack confessed. 'I should have told you, but we couldn't be certain... it was difficult to see how anyone from Abbeymead could have been involved.'

'Is it still difficult?' Flora asked.

He shook his head. 'Not now I've had the time to work out what happened. Once I knew Vaisey was our villain, I realised he'd been the one in the car. I was at the pub with you, Alan. Do you remember? And Vaisey was serving your meal – you were having omelette and chips – and I mentioned I wanted to go to London and follow up on Mason. The landlord was still in earshot at the time and the mention of Mason must have rung alarm bells. If I was allowed to start digging around in Mason's affairs, it would inevitably lead me to his wife and her suicide, which at the time we knew nothing about. And from there it would be a small stretch to Rafferty's affair with Cicely Mason, and who might want to take revenge for her death.'

'How did he manage it, though?'

'I've thought about that, too. I caught the bus to Worthing station from outside the Cross Keys that morning—the car had begun to make an odd clanking sound and I didn't want to risk driving. I was wearing a smart overcoat and carrying a briefcase, so where else would I be going but London? Vaisey has a van and must have tailed the bus to make sure I got off at the station —his deputy was left in charge of the pub, I guess. He caught the same train to London, then followed me from Victoria. After the Old Vestry Hall, I went to Knightsbridge and Mason's house and from there to his department store. That must have been enough to decide Vaisey that I was too dangerous to live. Somehow, he got hold of a car and mowed me down.'

'Must have stolen it,' the inspector muttered. 'Ex-army, Royal Engineers, he'd know how to do it. He was dotting every "i", wasn't he?'

'Trying to. Sorry, we interrupted. You were talking about the fire at Pelham Lodge.'

'Only that we've traced the oil lamp the fire chief reckons was the source of the fire. It came from a warehouse that supplies the Cross Keys with the same model. But that's as far as we've got.'

'It might be enough.' Jack poured the inspector another whisky. 'How did Vaisey do it, do you think? He wasn't at the party.'

'He wasn't invited, true.' The inspector stroked his newly grown moustache. 'Easy enough, though, to walk through an open rear door and hide out until the guests had gone home. He was lucky, or maybe he chose party night deliberately. The dogs were locked up in one of the bedrooms and not on the roam as they usually were. They're brutes, by all accounts. If they'd been loose, he'd not have escaped with his life.'

'He won't anyway,' Jack pointed out.

'No,' the inspector said sadly. 'Waste of a good publican.'

32

Jack had allowed himself to be persuaded into singing carols. Until he'd emerged from the cloistered life he'd led at Overlay House, he had never visited St Saviour's and, since then, his church attendance had consisted entirely of funerals. A carol service made a pleasant change. He was still feeling battered from the pummelling Vaisey had given him but grateful he hadn't suffered more. Grateful, too, that Flora had stayed unhurt. Thank the Lord for hat pins.

The Christmas Eve service took place late in the afternoon, late enough for winter dark to have fallen and for the tall tree erected every year outside the church to shine its lights far into the high street. They were halfway through the hymn sheet when he realised how much he was enjoying the singing. It reminded him of carols from his childhood, sung for the most part in the boarding school he'd hated, but Christmas there had been the best time of the year, as it probably was in every school.

He'd called at the Teagues' house this morning with presents for both Charlie and his mother, feeling slightly guilty that both he and Flora had assumed the boy might be responsible for the dangerous notes they'd received. On enquiry, Mrs Teague was clear they had nothing like a typewriter in the house which, of course, he should have guessed. She seemed to find the suggestion hilarious. For Flora, he'd bought a beautifully stitched blouse he'd seen in a Steyning craft shop a month or so ago. He wasn't sure about it. Not the blouse, she would look wonderful wearing it – a deep green silk with delicate cream embroidery. It was the whole business of giving such a personal present. Was it too personal? He'd already ditched the idea of the perfume he'd bought at Mason's for that very reason. The village had settled to the idea, strange though it was, that the reclusive writer in their midst had found himself a girlfriend, none other than that most independent young woman, Flora Steele. It had provided endless food for gossip, he knew. His girlfriend, but how deep did their feelings go? He wanted much more from her, he was quite sure of that. But he wasn't sure of Flora, and too apprehensive to put it to the touch. Maybe the blouse would present him with the answer.

'Shall we go on to the vicarage for mince pies?' she asked after the service, tucking her arm in his.

'Why not? I've eaten a ton already. A few more won't hurt.'

At the door, they were greeted by the vicar, now recovered from the chest infection that had plagued him for weeks. A crowd of parishioners was spilling out of his sitting room into the hall and beyond and Amy Dunmore, her bun slightly askew, was trying valiantly to offer a mince pie and a glass of mulled wine to anyone who looked to have a hand free.

'How lovely you've come,' she said, catching sight of them hovering in the hallway. Beyond her steamed-up glasses, Miss Dunmore's eyes were shining.

'She enjoys Christmas,' Jack said in Flora's ear.

'Who doesn't? Look, there's Alice and Kate, by the window.' Wriggling a path through the mass of people, she'd soon reached her friends, with Jack in her wake.

'Let's find another seat where it's warm,' were Alice's first words to them. 'I'm fair shrammed here. These big houses are so blessed draughty. I thought my place was bad enough, but this one takes the biscuit.'

Kate threw her a warning glance as Miss Dunmore passed by with yet another plate of sweetmeats.

'Mulled wine should do the trick.' Jack reached out to take two glasses from Miss Dunmore's tray.

At that moment, the housekeeper was jolted from behind and the wine from one of the glasses slopped over Flora's woollen skirt. 'Oh, I'm so sorry.' Amy Dunmore looked help-lessly around, hoping, it seemed, for a drying cloth to mate-rialise.

'Don't worry,' Flora reassured her. 'It's unlikely to stain and I've a handkerchief to mop with.'

Bending down to her handbag, she accidentally flicked the clasp open, and a thin, blue airmail sheet fluttered to the floor. Alice rescued the letter and handed it back.

'Who's been writing to you from abroad, then?' she asked, a coy look on her face.

'Aha! A mystery communication. Who is it?' Jack teased.

'Richard,' she said and flushed. 'Richard Frant.'

'Not that Richard,' Kate put in. 'The one that...'

'Yes, the one that got away,' she said lightly. 'He's in Paris apparently. He managed to make it to the city, all the way from Dieppe. What a hero!'

Jack waited until the group's attention was diverted by the arrival of the postmistress and her father, before he braved a question.

'Why is he writing now, so long after... after...'

'After he walked out on me? He has news,' she said crisply.

Jack waited.

'He spent a weekend with friends recently, in a village in Provence.' He could hear the reluctance in her voice. She hadn't wanted to speak of it. 'They took a walk around and Richard looked in at the church. Strolled through the graveyard. He's written to say that he saw what he was sure were my parents' graves.'

He frowned. 'They're buried in Highgate, aren't they?'

'They are. Richard is mistaken.'

Flora wanted the matter closed, he could see, but while Alice and Kate were chattering to Dilys and her father, he took the chance to say, 'I couldn't find them in Highgate, you know.'

Flora stared at him. 'What do you mean?'

'When I was in London this summer, I had some time on my hands,' he said awkwardly, remembering that he'd made a deliberate choice to stay away from Abbeymead, and from Flora. 'I took a saunter around Highgate Cemetery – it's a brilliant place to walk – and looked for your parents' graves while I was there. But I couldn't find them.'

Flora looked decidedly upset and he wished he hadn't told her.

'Why were you... poking... around? It's my family's business.'

'It was just something to do in an idle moment, that's all. I was in the vicinity and I know you'd never visited your parents' graves. I thought that maybe I could tell you their exact location. Highgate is a huge cemetery,' he finished somewhat limply.

'I know where they are.' He noticed how pale her face had become.

'Really?' Jack glanced at the letter, nestled in her open handbag.

She snapped the bag closed. 'Richard is mistaken,' she repeated, 'and so are you.'

~

Walking back to the cottage together, Flora took hold of his hand. She felt bad that she'd been so cross. Jack had meant no harm, he'd thought he was helping, but it was a subject that still, after so many years, she found painful. Her parents' deaths were one mystery she'd learned not to probe.

'I'm sorry,' she said, as they reached her cottage door.

'I'm sorry, too.' He put his arms around her and hugged her close. 'I barged in where I wasn't wanted.'

'You were trying to help. The thing is,' she said with difficulty, 'I've never really known what happened to them. Never really knew my parents. Just the bare facts – their names, their ages, what my father did for a living. But about them as people, about their life together, nothing. I don't even know what happened to the family home – after the accident. My father had inherited it from his father, but then what?'

'I've always thought that strange,' he confessed. 'It didn't pass to you?'

'No, and not to Violet either. I've no idea whether the house was sold and, if it was, where the money went.' Flora took the keys from her handbag and unlocked the front door. 'It was a legacy from her godfather that allowed my aunt to buy the bookshop and this cottage.'

'It's certainly a mystery, and one I'm guessing you'd rather leave alone?'

'If you don't mind,' she said gratefully. 'Do you fancy a cup of tea? I need a tumbler after all that mulled wine.'

'Tea sounds good,' he said, following her in. 'And we need to talk – Christmas lunch? Have you thought any more about it?'

'No worries. It's organised. I have a large chicken in the larder, vegetables in the garden, and you can bring something to drink. Perhaps not the whisky, though!'

'We're eating on our own?'

'Do you mind?' She peeled off her coat and hung it on the coat stand.

'Not one bit.' He bent down and kissed her firmly on the lips.

'I should perhaps mention we'll be off later to the Nook, for the next round. Kate and Tony and Alice will be there to wish us Happy Christmas and cut the cake – or cakes,' she said ominously.

He groaned. 'Do we have to?'

'They're our friends. Yes, we have to.'

'Don't we get any time on our own? Time together when we're not actually eating.'

'We do,' she said serenely. 'You can stay over, if you like.'

He stared at her. 'Really?'

'I believe the couch is quite comfortable,' she murmured, walking into the kitchen.

'Right,' he said, swallowing his disappointment. Then he saw she was smiling.

A LETTER FROM MERRYN

Dear Reader,

I want to say a huge thank you for choosing to read *Murder at St Saviour's*. If you enjoyed the book and want to keep up to date with all my latest releases, just sign up at the following link. Your email address will never be shared, and you can unsubscribe at any time.

www.bookouture.com/merryn-allingham

The 1950s is a fascinating period to write about, outwardly conformist but beneath the surface there's rebellion brewing, even in the very south of England! It's a beautiful part of the world and I hope Flora's and Jack's exploits have entertained you. If so, you can follow their fortunes in the next Flora Steele Mystery or discover their earlier adventures, beginning with *The Bookshop Murder*.

If you enjoyed *Murder at St Saviour's*, I would love a short review. Getting feedback from readers is amazing and it helps new readers to discover one of my books for the first time. And do get in touch on my Facebook page, through Twitter, Goodreads or my website – I love to chat.

Thank you for reading,

Merryn x

KEEP IN TOUCH WITH MERRYN

www.merrynallingham.com

 facebook.com/MerrynWrites

twitter.com/merrynwrites